CHANCEY PRESENTS

CHANCEY PRESENTS

8

KAY DEW SHOSTAK

August South
PUBLISHING

CHANCEY PRESENTS
Copyright © 2019 by Kay Dew Shostak.
All rights reserved.

ISBN: 978-0-9991064-8-8

Library of Congress Control Number: 2019952773

SOUTHERN FICTION: Women's Fiction / Southern Fiction / Railroad / Bed & Breakfast / Mountains / Georgia / Family/ Small Town

Text Layout and Cover Design by Roseanna White Designs
Cover Images from www.Shutterstock.com

Author photo by Susan Eason with www.EasonGallery.com

Published by August South Publishing. You may contact the publisher at:
AugustSouthPublisher@gmail.com

Dedicated to Cas, Liddy, Tucker, and Tate -
This book wouldn't be possible without you four.
You've taught me how very special it is to be a grandma.
Thank you for being the best grandkids, ever!

CHARACTER LIST

Jackson and Carolina Jessup – Moved to Chancey one year ago. Operate Crossings, a bed-and-breakfast for railfans in their home. They have three children: Will, 22, a recent college grad; Savannah, 16; Bryan, 13. Jackson works for the railroad and is out of town often. Carolina also runs the bookstore side of Blooming Books.

Jackson's family – Mother Etta lives at the beach in South Carolina. Father Hank is married to Shelby and lives in Kentucky. Two brothers, Emerson and Colt. Emerson is the oldest, and he and his wife have three daughters and live in Virginia. Colt is the youngest, is single, and lives in their hometown in Kentucky.

Carolina's family – Parents Goldie and Jack live in Tennessee. Carolina is an only child. Missus and FM Bedwell – Lifelong residents of Chancey.

Peter Bedwell, 45 - lives two doors down from his parents. Owns Peter's Bistro on the square.

Anna Jessup, 19 - Missus' granddaughter. Her mother was given up for adoption and died when Anna was 16. Anna found Missus and came to Chancey. Married Will Jessup when she got pregnant. They are currently separated.

Laney and Shaw Conner – Both from Chancey. Shaw owns an automotive dealership. Laney partners with Carolina in the B&B. They have three children: twins Angie and Jenna, 17; Cayden, 4 months.

Susan and Griffin Lyles – Susan is sister to Laney and manages the Lake Park. Griffin recently got a big job with the electric company and moved his family to the well-to-do community on the mountain of Laurel Cove. They have three children: Leslie, 19; Susie Mae, 15; Grant, 13. Laney and Susan's mother is Gladys Troutman.

Gertie Samson – She has one child: Patty, 28, married to Andy Taylor. Gertie was raised in Chancey and returned after her daughter, Patty, settled there. She owns a lot of property in town. She lives in the house she, Patty, and Andy run their businesses out of.

Ruby Harden – Owns and runs Ruby's Café on the town square. Lifelong Chancey resident.

Libby Stone – Works with Ruby at the café and is married to Bill Stone. Daughter

Cathy Stone Cross – Libby and Bill's daughter is married to Stephen Cross, a teacher at the high school. They have a young son, Forrest. Cathy sells lingerie through at-home parties. Her previous role as a high school cheerleader still has a profound impact on her life.

Kendrick family – Moved to town for father Kyle to open new Dollar Store where he hired Anna Jessup as assistant manager and then began an affair with her. Currently he lives with Anna. Wife Kimmy and their four children live in Chancey. Kyle's daughter, Zoe, from a previous marriage lives with Kimmy and cares for the younger three children.

Shannon Chilton – Operates florist part of Blooming Books. Lifelong Chancey resident. She's 30 and in a relationship with Peter Bedwell.

Bonnie Cuneo – Works in Blooming Books. Retired teacher who lives in Laurel Cove.

Hello.

This is Phoenix. I know. The last person you thought you'd be hearing from here. This won't take long, though I felt I needed to come clear up some things.

First, I wasn't actually a stripper. Not exactly, but if you've ever seen those Vegas shows, well, I might as well have been. So, when all that came out in that crazy paper, Taking Chances in Chancey, by that girl—Susie Mae or something else extremely Southern—I wanted to try and explain myself to everyone.

Then I read the paper and realized my secrets weren't all that interesting compared to everything else in there. Especially since all the people here actually know each other, or thought they knew each other. I hated for Colt to find out that way, but he said everybody back in Kentucky had told him I was worse than a stripper so he was okay with it all. Actually, I've found he's pretty much okay most the time, which actually kind of gets on my nerves.

Also, I think having all those movie people in town for a month made everything crazy seem more normal. Especially when it was found out that Mr. Herbert Fisk, famous for playing a stable, sweet grandpa, was playing around with more than a couple of ladies in town. I'm not sure Missus has fully recovered from that whole thing. Some say she's more upset about her son Peter's proposal to Shannon being turned down in public, but the way Mr. Fisk got her to wear that gold gown with the jewels for the wrap party? She's got to be still smarting over that. (Fisk has also got to still be smarting over that slap she gave him!)

Colt and I had left the wrap party by the time everything happened, but we heard about it plenty over Thanksgiving up in Kentucky. Someone else is going to have to tell you about Colt's daddy's wedding to that Shelby. I was there, but I just don't feel it's my place to share that kind of family stuff.

Speaking of family stuff, Anna is bigger than ever and Will is getting more nervous by the day. So is Carolina, but whether it's over her first grandbaby or Savannah's desire to be an actress on a movie set out of town, I'm not sure. One thing I am sure of is that the whole town is nervous about Laney wanting to be mayor. I don't know what to think about that except that I think it'd be fun to watch.

Like I said at the beginning, I know you didn't expect me to be writing something like this. I bet you also didn't expect me to stick around in Chancey for long either, did you? Well, I am and I have. Colt has already made noise about moving back to Kentucky. I think that week up there made him homesick. But if he goes, he'll be going alone.

I think Chancey and I are a perfect fit.

I have big plans.

Phoenix

XOXO

Chapter 1

"Let's go see it."

Closing the lid on the washer, I look over my shoulder at my daughter and ask, "When?"

"Now." She hangs up one of her polo shirts on a plastic hanger, then lays it in the basket of laundry she was supposed to be folding. "It won't take a minute. Besides, aren't we pretty much through here?"

Our basement is empty. Well, not exactly empty. There's the laundry, some furniture, Savannah and me, but it feels really empty. Will is no longer living in our basement while he finishes his second degree. The first one at the University of Georgia was good enough to get him into law school, but not good enough to get him a teaching position in Georgia. This second degree should have him teaching by next fall. The basement was not only home for him, but also recently for his wife, Anna, who is expecting their daughter in the next couple of weeks. So, now that they've moved out, you can see why I say it feels empty.

Instead of waiting for my answer, Savannah is already heading up the stairs with the laundry basket on her hip. While I've been thinking and looking around, she's been moving on. "You know you're dying to see it!" she shouts as she nears the top. "Come on."

The washer and dryer are both doing their thing, and folding clothes is not exactly something that has to be done right this minute. Besides, I want to see my son's new house. We've been gone the past week, and before that they were really tight-lipped about its address. All last week, up in Kentucky at my father-in-law's wedding, they said they didn't have any pictures, and well, to be honest, there was too much other drama to even wonder about it. Lord, wait until you hear about that wedding.

I grab a handful of dry shirts on hangers and follow Savannah's path upstairs, shouting, "Should we warn them we're coming?"

The stairwell door opens. Will stands there grinning. "Warn who?"

"Oh. You're here." Weaving around him, I hang the shirts on the doorjamb between the kitchen and dining room.

My oldest motions to the laundry basket sitting on the kitchen table behind him. "Found out our washer isn't exactly hooked up yet, so we need to use yours."

"Where's Anna?"

"Home resting. I told her I'd come take care of laundry from the trip. Savannah said you want to go see the house?"

"We do, but we don't want to disturb Anna. It was a long week for her."

Will lifts the basket and laughs. "Long week for everyone. I'll make a deal with you. I was going to put a load in and then go pick up a couple things from the grocery store." He digs a piece of paper out of his jean pocket. "How 'bout I give you my list and you can shop, then take it to our house and check on Anna? I've been promising Bryan I'd come play some video games. He's here, right?"

Savannah answers for me as she sails into the kitchen, takes the list from his hand, and says, "Sure." Then she adds, "Come on, Mom. The tree lighting is at six, so we've got to get this done quick."

"Okay," I say as Bryan, my youngest, strolls into the kitchen. I grab his arm to get his attention. "Tell your dad we're going to the store then taking some groceries to Anna. We'll be back in time to go to the lighting."

He grunts as freshman boys do, but in a striking show of courtesy, he adds a clear nod of his head. He's grown several inches since the summer, and football has added a heft to his frame that his brother never had. When Bryan appeared at the front of the small Kentucky church as his grandfather's best man, I didn't realize who he was for a minute. He looked like a man.

With a sly look he says to his big brother, "So you say your wife made you come do laundry? You probably don't even remember how to play a video game anymore!" With a guffaw he lopes down the stairs. His big brother follows.

Looks like a man, but acts like a boy.

Savannah and I share an eye roll. "Ignore him," she says. "Will'll set him straight. Face it, Mom. High school boys are jerks. Even the ones you're related to."

This time the eye roll is all mine. Savannah's time on a movie set this fall has grown her weary of everything small town and provincial. She's completely bought into her delusion of maturity and worldliness. It didn't help that she spent so much time with her cousins from Virginia. Jackson's brother and his wife obviously accepted their infant daughters straight from the hands of the gods on Mount Olympus and deigned to share them with the rest of us mortals. Immediately, the coastal teenage beauties recognized Savannah as coming from her own holy mountain and welcomed her into their presence. The four were insufferable.

Until the Virginia goddesses were mean to Anna.

It was a scene from end times—lightning bolts, celestial hair flips, and supernatural glacial freezing. But I can't talk about that right now... the chariot is leaving!

"It's still not coming up on your phone?" I ask Savannah again.

She quit answering me a bit ago. The shady, deserted road we're driving back and forth on is Rainy Road, the one Will told us their house is on. We no longer have cell service although we're only ten minutes out of Chancey. After the store, I'd decided to drive so Savannah could navigate.

"It should be right here," she says. "Stop and let me get out. Maybe I can see something." The road is blacktopped but just barely. It feels like there are more ruts in the pavement than good patches. I pull over, but don't let the tires leave the road as the dirt and gravel there looks even less stable. Savannah leaves her car door open and leans to the side. I crank up the heater, as she's letting the afternoon chill into the car.

After really cold weather at the end of November, we're having a warm spell, but here in the shadows, it's chilly. Plus, neither she nor I wore a coat. I know, I know. What if we get stuck? What if we have to walk? What if we fall off the side of this road and have to climb out? Why do I never think of those things *before* I leave wearing only a long-sleeved T-shirt?

Savannah jumps back into her seat shivering. Her T-shirt isn't even long-sleeved. "Believe it or not, there is actually a road right there to the right. It goes down the side of the hill at an angle. I think that might be it." She looks at me, not at all convinced. "There's a car down there and a house, I think."

I ease the wheels forward and can see what she's talking about. A mud-and-gravel road, which could be a driveway, is sloping and angling along the side of the road. I pull onto it, and the van heads down. Then we straighten as the gravel road levels out before heading into the woods. We only go a short way before we see a house, a very little house with Anna's car sitting out front.

Parked, Savannah and I look around. It's a tiny cabin in the woods, a real log cabin with a porch and a fireplace. We get out and go around to the back of the van to get the groceries. As we walk up to the front steps, I'm charmed. Anna said it was adorable, and she's right. Somewhere I hear a creek running, and the woods are alive with birds and breezes.

Anna opens the front door as we step onto the porch. "Hi. Where's Will?"

"He's at our house doing the laundry. We picked up the groceries. Didn't he call and tell you?"

We all wait looking at each other. Anna is blocking the door, but she suddenly realizes that and steps back. "Oh. Sorry. Come in. No, I didn't know. Uh, cell phones don't work so good out here."

"But your new house is charming!" I say, stepping across the threshold.

With a one-arm hug for her sister-in-law, Savannah exclaims, "It's like a cute little movie set! We got some extra grocery things for y'all. I can't wait to see the inside." The chattering is just not like her, but it covers for me because I'm inside and am speechless. It's one room. A one-room cabin.

"Oh!" Savannah says behind me. "Oh, so cute!"

Anna clears her throat and then moves to the kitchen table. I guess it's also the bedroom table, the dining room table, and the living room table. "You can just put the groceries here. And, yeah, this is it." She's biting her lip and looks like she's ready to cry.

I give her a hug. "Oh, honey. It's as adorable on the inside as it is on the outside. How cozy!"

The furniture from our basement fits perfectly. Matter of fact, it may be too much for the space. The loveseat and chair are set in one corner with the television only three feet in front of them on an end table. The bed is in another corner, and at the bottom of it is the dresser, its back serving as the footboard. In the other corner is what looks like a closet? Or… oh. "Is this the bathroom here?" I reach for the wooden door and pray that they have indoor plumbing.

"Yes," Anna says. "Check out the old-fashioned tub."

There's a sink without a counter and an old-fashioned tub with legs. I recognize our old towels from the basement bathroom stacked on a cardboard box; another cardboard box holds their toiletry items. "It's adorable."

Savannah is right behind me, and I push her so I can get out of the closet bathroom. I hug Anna again. "It looks so clean! Just charming."

"Yeah, the lady we're renting from loves it and takes good care of it. She and her husband used it as their mountain getaway, but he's sick now so she put it up for rent. She came up here last week and made sure it was move-in ready for us. Do you really like it? We know it's awful small, but…" She shrugs.

"But what else do you need?" I say, giving her another pat on the back. I frown at my daughter who looks like she has a list right on the tip of her tongue of what else is needed.

Savannah turns away from me with a shoulder roll and a side stretching of her neck and steps to the table. "Y'all coming to the tree lighting?" she asks as she begins emptying the grocery bags onto the table.

"Probably not." Anna goes to the kitchen table and gently sits down. "We're actually kind of nervous about finding our driveway in the dark."

Savannah says, "I bet. We almost never found it in the daylight."

Keeping my voice merry, I say, "We'll get some reflectors for you to put along the edges." Looking out the windows, I can't help but think about how absolutely dark it must be out here at night. There's nothing but woods in every direction. "So, how is it spending the nights out here?" I laugh, but not because I find anything funny.

"Good. We like how private it is. It's like camping, Will says."

"I hate camping," Savannah growls.

"You don't hate camping," I say. "Quit acting like such a princess."

Anna smiles and shakes her head. "Well, I never got to go camping, so I'm enjoying this. It's very romantic."

I dare my daughter to say anything with a look. "Where are you going to put the baby?"

Anna lets out a long breath. "She'll be in the cradle, so we figure we'll just see where it works best." She stands up and stretches her back. "Thanks for bringing the groceries. We're having tacos tonight."

"One of Will's favorites. He'll be happy. We better get going. Can't be late for the tree lighting." I collect all the plastic grocery bags and put them into one. "This place is just adorable."

Savannah walks around the room once more. "You're not scared out here by yourself?"

Anna turns from the cabinet she was putting things away in and leans back on the counter. "No. Don't know why 'cause I kind of thought I would be, but I'm not."

"Good. That's really good." My smile feels a little fake at this point, so we probably should leave. "Well, enjoy your tacos."

We dash to the car, because, well, it's getting cold and there's the no-coat thing. I start the car while I stretch my mouth, which aches from being held in a fake smile for so long.

Savannah chuckles as we head up the steep grade to get to the so-called road.

"What's so funny?" I ask.

She lifts an eyebrow at me. "Don't you mean what's so charming? And adorable?"

I sigh and dismiss her with a shake of my head.

Setting her feet against the dashboard, she reaches for the

radio. "I wanna be here when Missus sees it. Have you ever seen such a tiny place? How can they live there?"

"It's the size of a loft apartment. I'm sure a lot of actresses in New York live in smaller places than that. Have you thought about that?"

At the top of the hill the van climbs up onto the road. Luckily it's a straight shot in both directions, so there's no fear of another car racing up on us unseen.

Christmas music is playing on the all-Christmas station, and we listen for a moment. We are back to the main road past the high school before long. Out from underneath the thick tree canopy, everything lightens. I sing along with Bing for a minute and then smile.

Savannah cocks her head at me, skepticism all over her face. "Soooo, you're actually happy about that place?"

"Sure. It's charming and adorable." I smile sweetly at her then sing louder.

Of course I'm lying, but it is what it is.

Lying will have to do for now.

Chapter 2

"What do you mean you can't turn off the lights?" Missus demands into the microphone, from her position in front of the big, dark Christmas tree. She has on a blue coat I know she specifically bought for this event. And all the other Christmas events. We might've created a monster with our Missus Blue Christmas decorating scheme. Bowing to Mr. Fisk's urban sophistication, she'd shed her ever-present gloves. Apparently, his unveiling as a cheat and charlatan set her values back to their rightful place. Now, she's back to wearing gloves, not only for warmth but also for decorum, and they are the same blue as her coat. Matching her gloves, and everything else, her blue suede boots were specially made and rushed here for tonight. However, despite all that blue, right now her face is red. Very red. Or could that be a reflection from the bonfire?

As we witnessed as newcomers last year, all the lights in the town are turned off in anticipation of the slow tree lighting. The bonfire should die down to embers, and in that darkness the mountain stars have center stage for a few glorious moments. Except…

"Unplug them! Cut the wires! Set the whole truck on fire for all I care. Turn *off* those lights, Laney Conner!" Missus' chin and right arm are pointed toward the street. Parked sideways and taking up three primo parking spots near the gazebo is

Shaw Conner's truck. In the back is a huge, wooden sign that reads "Laney Troutman Conner for Mayor." Bright lights frame the sign—not just a string or two of Christmas lights, but big bulbs that you still see even when you close your eyes.

Beside Missus at the tree is our current mayor, Jed Taylor. His large, round face is naturally red, but even with the dying fire glow Jed is looking kind of pale. I don't think he's ever had a competitor in the mayor's race, at least not one like he has now.

Laney strolls over toward Missus and the tree and Jed. She's wearing a Kelly green coat with a big fur collar. Her short, dark hair doesn't have the impact her beauty pageant hair had, but it bounces on top of the fur collar and frames her big, false-lashed eyes. She pushes open her coat and places her hands on her hips. She has on a black sweater and black pants. I think we all automatically expected cleavage the way she opened her coat, but there is none on display. Maybe she really is trying to tone down her old version of a Southern belle. All the same, her sweet Southern tang is back but good. "Missus and Mr. Mayor, I'd *love* to turn those lights off, but I can't." She shrugs and widens her eyes. "We had a dickens of a time getting them on in the first place. Just go on with the tree lighting and put them right on out of your mind."

Laney smiles then shifts to better see the tree, completely ignoring the meltdown happening at the microphone. Jed finally sits down, and I'm glad to see his normal red coloring returning. Missus leaves the stage, head high, purse hanging from her forearm—did I mention it's blue?— and eyes staring straight ahead. As she gets closer to Laney's truck the crowd shifts to see what she's doing. At the sidewalk she reaches into her purse and pulls something out of it, but then I lose sight of her. The people in that area, especially the men, surge forward, shouting, "No!"

"What's happening?" Savannah asks, stepping on my foot.

"If you can't see, you know I can't. Where's your daddy?" I ask as I push in the same direction as Missus.

Sparks. Gasps. Darkness.

Then the crowd parts for her to walk back to her perch, pocketknife in hand, which we can see as she walks near the dying fire. Laney marches up to her, checks that the knife is closed—just because she's a former beauty queen doesn't mean she's stupid—then shouts, "You cut the wires? You ruined my sign?!" She shakes a warning finger at Missus' back. "You just wait until I'm the mayor!"

Again at the microphone Missus purrs, which she can do because, you know, the microphone, "You'll be mayor over my dead body." Jed, who'd stood back up, moves closer to her, smiles, and waves. Missus gives him a bit of side-eye and adds, "I've always thought being mayor was in my blood."

There's no spark this time, at least not of the electrical-wires-shorting-out variety, but there are lots of gasps.

Jed takes a step back, his mouth falling open. Missus turns around and looks at him and the council members standing behind her. "Calm down, Jed. You know I *probably* wouldn't run against you. Now where is the kid who's supposed to push this button? Let's get this done."

The boy is pushed forward, a painted cardboard box with a fake button put into his hands. He pushes it several times before the plug behind the tree is finally connected and the tree lit. There are a few oohs and ahhs, but it feels anti-climactic.

Hm. Wonder why?

As the rest of the lights in town slowly come back on, Jackson wanders over to help rekindle the bonfire. Last Christmas Missus brought it to everyone's attention that Chancey's celebrations were a tad skimpy, so this year we've added some events to the tree lighting. Her hastily called meeting led to several committees being formed—of course. One is called something like Children's Activities or Kids Events or Parents

Without Enough To Do, something like that. But anyway, we're having a s'more station. Couldn't do it before the lighting because the children have to look good for their pictures with Santa. We were allowed to keep Santa and Mrs. Claus and their little house, but we also had to offer a picture with a reindeer for those not adhering to the Santa way of things. *You* probably knew reindeer are expensive to rent this time of year, but I never thought about it before this past week. So we have one of Murray Glidden's cows in a Santa hat, which folks seems to think should be handing out Chick-fil-A sandwiches.

Athena Markum is the young woman in charge of the s'mores and the new kids committee. She and her husband are part of about a dozen young couples that have moved to Chancey in recent years. They mostly work from home and want a rural life for their families with access to Atlanta. They don't live up in the well-to-do community of Laurel Cove but in a new development out past the schools, toward the interstate. It's a planned community with a park, eco-friendly green homes (no, they are not all colored green despite what you read in the *Chancey Vedette* letters to the editor), and everything is close together with sidewalks everywhere. Their children are young, and the families always kept to themselves, at least until the big Christmas meeting last year.

At that time, they came ready to change things in Chancey, which they did. Ruby now carries almond milk or whatever they tell her is the latest life-sustaining craze. They have started a mother's morning out program at the Methodist church, and they are helping me start a children's reading time at my store. They had a big falling out with the library, which surprises no one as Ida May is still in charge over there. Bonnie, Shannon, and I are a little apprehensive about kids in the shop, but these moms are pretty hard to say no to. Hence, me looking for a reindeer last week while out of town at the wedding.

Feeling a little crowded, I pull back to look at my daughter hunched up beside me. "Go on over there with the other kids. Why are you sitting here anyway?" I say, with a nudge of my elbow into her side.

She shakes her head as she leans away from me and buries her nose down into the front of her coat. We're seated on a long log bench at the fire across from the s'more action. From inside the collar of her coat, she says, "It's too cold over there."

"Well, you're burning me up sitting so close like that." Of course, in response to not wearing coats earlier, we now have on our heaviest winter coats, gloves, scarves, the whole rigmarole, and I'm suffocating. Plus, there's this whole having my daughter attached to my hip thing that isn't helping matters at all.

She scoots over an inch and shakes her long hair again. "Besides, they're so juvenile."

Laney plops down beside Savannah. "Who is? Missus? I so *very* much agree. Cutting my lights like that. Can you believe it?" Then she takes another look. "Savannah, what are you doing here with your mother? Get up and go play. I need to talk to her."

Savannah swivels her head, mouth dropped open, to look at me. "Go play?"

I laugh and give her a push up. "Yeah, go play. Go talk to your friends."

She gets up in a huff. We watch her stalk off in the direction of the teenagers, but then she slows and heads off toward the Santa Claus house. "What's with her?" Laney asks.

"Missing the spotlight of the movie, I think. Plus, it's that awkward time in every girl's life when they're ready for change but not sure what should actually change or if change is a good idea at all."

Laney nods emphatically. "Preach it, sister! Angie's still not speaking to me or Shaw. On the Savannah front, Jenna says she thinks she's too good for them now. She's really not doing basketball cheerleading?"

"It started while she was doing the movie, but they told her she could join after. She said no at the time, but I wish we'd pushed her to do it. She's hanging around with me, and you know what a pain that is."

"Amen. Nobody's happy when that's happening." We laugh, and Laney points back toward her truck. "So, back to me. Can you believe that witch cut the lights on my truck?"

"Yes. I completely can. Matter of fact, you practically dared her to. Why couldn't Shaw just drive it around for a bit if you couldn't turn them off? I'm actually ticked that you ruined such an incredible moment. I was really looking forward to it."

Laney shrugs. "Yeah, I know. I mighta been fibbing about not being able to turn them off. I thought she'd give me more of a warning before doing something so drastic." She looks around, leans closer and whispers, "She's a little more on edge than usual, don't ya think?"

My nod is emphasized by a long sigh. "She is, and while I understand and sympathize…"

My voice trails off. We're quiet as we watch the children around us making messes with burnt marshmallows and melted chocolate. Laney directs my eye to one little boy, about five years old, across from us. He has on a hooded sweatshirt with the hood halfway back on his head and a swag of hair hanging down his forehead. He's holding his graham cracker, marshmallow, and chocolate sandwich with both chubby little hands. Between bites, he takes turns wiping his hands down his shirt or on his jeans. He's thoroughly enjoying himself, and when he shoves the last, big bite in while saying he wants "some more," we both break out laughing.

"Enjoying yourselves?"

We turn around to see Susan, her arms wrapped up in her movie-star boyfriend's arms. He's as tall as she is, and as thin, so they tend to often look like one body with two heads. Silas stuck around after the movie wrapped and doesn't appear to be going anywhere. Susan's divorce is nowhere near final, but she doesn't appear to care. Still not sure how she's managing that, but if all the evil eyes and wagging tongues don't bother her, who am I to worry about it? Except I do worry. She's not being the normal, rational Susan I know. She's acting more like a teenager than her teenagers and we all know how I feel about teenagers.

Laney gives the by-now-familiar evil eye as she stands up. "I *was* enjoying myself," she says, then marches off, saying from her tower of righteousness, "I better go check on Cayden."

There has been no thaw in the sisters' relationship since their fight in the fall. As a matter of fact, it's more frozen than ever. Susan disentangles herself from her beau. "Can you get us some marshmallows to roast? I want to talk to Carolina for a minute." He leans down for a kiss, not a peck, not an I'll-be-right-back smack, but a genuine, long, deep kiss.

An older boy sitting at the end of the log looks up and says, "Get a room."

Susan breaks off the kiss and looks at the boy. "John Walker!"

Silas chuckles as he ambles off to find marshmallows. John Walker gets up and hurries off, too.

Susan sits down. "Can you believe that awful boy said that?"

With a smirk at her, I ask, "Can you believe no one else did? Y'all are over the top."

She grins and stretches. "Yes. Yes, we are." Then she pulls her arms in and folds them tight across her tweedy blazer, crosses her legs, and turns her whole body towards me. "Okay. Now that that's established, how do I get rid of him?"

CHAPTER 3

Monday mornings find me going through the books collected by Andy Taylor, Patty's husband and a new father-to-be. He's young, but a regular, old-fashioned junkman. He prowls estate sales, junk stores, yard sales, and flea markets, finding things for the shop named after him at the end of Main Street, in a house his mother-in-law owns and lives in. He actually does most of his sales online, but there are some rooms in the house piled high with whatever Kewpie dolls or vintage dress patterns you might want to dig through.

Except books. All the books he brings to me. Well, to us. To Blooming Books, the bookstore and flower shop combination on Main Street, across from the square where the now-lit Christmas tree stands. Well, it's a bright, sunny morning, so I'm not exactly sure if it's lit right this minute, but you know what I mean.

I'm in charge of the bookstore. I used to say I managed it, but Bonnie Cuneo actually does that. She comes down the mountain from Laurel Cove to make most of the decisions, while I play with the books. Shannon Chilton has run the florist shop here for years, and despite some rocky patches, we've actually come to be friends. Mostly we've learned to work well together, with Bonnie holding us together. Andy's mother-in-law, Gertie Samson, owns our building, too, and she's pretty good to work with. All in all, it's a typical small-town endeavor. We do our best to take care of folks and make everyone happy. So far it's working better than anyone, mostly me, ever imagined.

And, I grin as I put the key in the lock, I get to play with books.

Just as I finish logging in some new books on my laptop for Bonnie to categorize later, Andy comes bustling through the front door. "Here's two more bags I picked up at an estate sale last week while y'all were gone. Forgot about them until Gertie practically tripped over them this morning."

"Ugh. I just finished. Do they look any good?"

The happy, young man, a little on the hefty side, grins. "A store owner's work is never done! These won't take long, though. Mostly hardback, so there aren't too many in each bag. They just looked interesting to me. Got the whole bunch for five dollars. Folks can't hardly give hardback books away these days."

"I know. Believe me, I know. But that is too good of a deal to pass up, I agree. Thanks."

He sits the bags on the counter beside me. "You seen Patty this morning?"

"Oh, she's still upstairs?" The young couple lives above our shop. Patty's mother gave them the apartment until they got pregnant and then we've assumed she'll move them into a larger place. Gertie always has a plan. "I haven't heard anything from her. How's she feeling?"

He wrinkles his freckled nose. "Not too good. That's why she's still here. Bad morning sickness. I don't handle people throwing up too good." He shudders and looks back at the stairs on the back wall. With a sniff he finally mumbles, "Guess I'll go check on her."

"Good idea. Have her try eating some crackers before she gets out of bed. Might help."

He nods and slogs back to the stairs and then up them. Poor

Patty. I don't care how much he slogs around, though; I have not one ounce of sympathy for Andy despite how pitiful he tries to look.

I pull out the books and see they are classics in pretty covers. Not leather, but nicely bound. They'd be a great addition to a home. Like my home.

With a quick peek in the second bag, I make an executive decision. There's no need to even log these books in. I'll even pay double what they cost.

I bet I can even get Andy to carry them to my car for me.

Whew, I'm exhausted. Working and shopping all in one morning! Glad I'm headed over to Ruby's when Shannon gets in. I'm not used to this much work!

I'm joking, I'm joking.

Kind of.

"Hey, scooch over," Laney demands, standing at the end of the booth bench where I'm sitting. I slide my eyes from her to Ruby's front door. Susan isn't here yet, but I learned my lesson the last time I tried to secretly get the two sisters together. Ever heard of scorched-earth policy? William Tecumseh Sherman had nothing on the Troutman sisters.

"Laney, I'm meeting someone. So, uh, no." I don't budge and even move my purse from next to the wall to the edge she wants to occupy.

She grins and her eyes light up like—okay, I know it's trite and overused, but 'tis the season—she lights up like a Christmas tree as she exclaims, "I know! Scooch!" She picks up my purse and tucks it under her arm with her designer bag. (No, I can't tell that kind of thing just by looking, but she *only* carries designer bags, so…) She has on a long, black dress with a creamy leather belt. The dress fits her curves and around the mock turtleneck is a beautiful ivory necklace. Very classy, except she's now sitting in the booth, forcing me to move over. That's not classy at all.

"Okay, okay. I'm moving. Susan's wrath is on your head. I tried." Smooshed against the wall I take my purse from her, but there is no room on the bench. We are both healthy-sized women, and her purse is huge.

She leans into me and winks. "I know what's going on."

After the last month of me letting secrets out, I'm working so hard to keep things to myself. "I didn't tell you anything. Wait. What do you think is going on?" The bell on the door chimes and I look up to see Susan striding into Ruby's. "I didn't tell her anything!" I practically shout.

Susan picks up her pace and slides into the other side of the booth like a runner stealing home, her frown leading the way. "For crying out loud, Carolina. What are you doing? I thought you were going to try and keep things quiet after all that gossip around the movie." She shakes her head at me.

"But… I… she…"

Susan sighs, winks at me, then turns her cup upright so it'll be filled with coffee. "I called her. No one on earth is better at breaking up with a man than my sister."

Laney beams, more like a policeman's flashlight glaring into the backseat of a car parked on Lover's Lane than a Christmas tree this time. "I told you I knew, didn't I?"

I do not think Chancey fully appreciated the calm we enjoyed when these two were fighting.

Poor Silas. Poor us.

"Thank the Lord this isn't a boat," Ruby says with a cocked eyebrow as she leans on the end of our table. "That side there is plum overloaded." She puts one knee on Susan's bench. "Here. I'll try and help you stay upright."

And then it's quiet.

Something is off. Susan's looking in our direction. Ruby slowly lifts her head with a funny look to our side of the booth. Like a periscope, I survey the café around me before I finally turn to the right. Oh, I get it. Laney's not saying anything. No comeback. No sass. No putting Ruby in her place. She is pretty much rubbing her lipstick off with all the pressing her lips together she's doing, and I'm not sure how those false eyelashes will hold up with her eyes batting like that. But there are no words.

Ruby takes her knee off the seat then leaves without offering us coffee or muffins.

"Let me guess. More of your new Southern woman running for mayor thing?" I ask as I look around for Libby and a pot of coffee. With some relief, I see her heading our way.

"About time!" Laney bites Libby's head off when she reaches our table. "Oh, sorry, Libby. Thank you. I'm in mighty need of some coffee."

"No worries, sweetie. You'll be back to normal in no time." Libby misses Laney's mouth popping open because she's gone right on talking. "Wasn't that right fun last night? We had a good time with all those kid activities. Forrest ate two full s'mores, fed the reindeer cow a carrot, and made a candy-cane decoration for our tree. I'm sure glad that Athena put all of it together. You'll see, Carolina. Won't be long until your little granddaughter will be enjoying all of it, too. I'll get y'all some muffins. Ruby's trying another healthy one, carrot and something—"

"No!" we all say. Then, with little chuckles, we say stuff to cover up the fact that Ruby's healthy options are inedible.

"Just bring us three regular muffins," I say. "Has she got the Christmas flavors yet?"

"Yep, there's an orange one with dark chocolate bits, a vanilla mint, and one with cinnamon and brown sugar. Then there's a cheese one and a sausage one if you don't want sweet."

We tell her our choices, and she dashes off. Susan grimaces. "How can everything Ruby makes be so delicious, while her healthy muffins taste like cardboard?"

"Worse." Laney picks up her paper napkin. "At least cardboard would stay together in your mouth. Hers are more like this napkin. They fall apart but won't go away. Coats your mouth the rest of the day." She shudders. "But never mind that. Silas. Please tell me why you want to be rid of him?"

"Yes," I chime in. "You didn't look tired of him last night at the bonfire." Even after she asked me how to get rid of him, they were all over each other the rest of the night. Laney and I share a look of agreement, then focus across the table.

"Well, I, uh, I thought I wanted passion. You know, all the feels and excitement and," she whispers, "sex." She pauses to let her blush build and settle. "But it's a little much."

Our side of the booth creaks as Laney and I lean back.

"A little much?" I ask. Laney's still thinking.

Susan swallows and shrugs. "I'm not some kid who wants to just run on hormones and adrenaline. I mean it's fun, but…" She sits up straighter as Libby sits a plate of muffins down along with three small plates.

"Y'all can divvy them up however you please." Placing her hands on her hips, she shakes her head. "Might as well tell you. Cathy and Stephen are separated again." She leans forward and whispers, "If she hadn't lost it, the baby would be due about now, you know."

Laney and I both nod. Before they'd gotten to really celebrate a new baby, Cathy had miscarried. Not many people even knew she'd been pregnant. "I can see how that would make things difficult."

Libby sighs. "Yeah, but I honestly think their main problem is the hullabaloo over that actor Mr. Fisk. Cathy says she never was with him really, but he did send her them roses. That's why we had Forrest last night. Cathy has to make a go of her lingerie business if she's going to be a single mother again. She's not moving back in our house without a job, Bill says." She wipes her hands on her apron. "Anywho, y'all enjoy your muffins. I'll bring more coffee around in a jiffy."

Susan cuts each of the muffins in half. "See? Maybe I should introduce Silas to Cathy. I'm just not made for this living on the edge all the time."

Laney chooses a muffin half, but before it makes it to her mouth she says, "This just beats all, but I actually think I understand what you're saying. It's about maturity. I know I could've had my pick of the crazy, good-lookin' guys, but I knew Shaw was what I wanted for the long haul." She takes a bite, then after a quick chew talks out of the side of her mouth. "Not saying he's not plenty exciting, but there's more. Plus, you're a grown woman, Susan. Silas? Why, he's practically a boy."

"He's not a boy!" Susan says a bit too loudly.

Crumbs blow out of my mouth as I try to stop my friends before they're fighting again. "No! That's not what she meant. Right, Laney?" I do not look to Laney for an answer because I'm sure that is exactly what she meant. "She meant he just doesn't have a grown-up life like you do. Kids, and your mom, and a house."

Laney shrugs and sips her coffee. Susan scowls at her, but takes a breath. "So, how do I get rid of him?"

"You're going to have to quit having sex, you know? That would be the first step." Laney is not ready to make this easy.

Susan's scowl deepens. "For your information he actually left this morning for a commercial shoot. I won't be seeing him until the weekend after next."

"Wait," I interject. "Then what's the problem? Just tell him he can't come back. You're through. It's over."

Laney has been buttering half of a muffin, but she takes time to raise her eyebrows at me, then look at her sister with one lifted eyebrow. "But…"

Susan finishes for her. "But wouldn't that be rude?"

Laney bites into her muffin with a nod of her head.

"Rude? I don't understand." I stare at Susan who's struggling to find the words.

Laney talks again from the side of her full mouth. "And there's the problem with most of Southern womanhood." She takes on a whiny tone as she says, "I don't want them to be mad at me." She rolls her eyes and folds her arms on the table. "Tell her. Tell her I'm right."

Susan smiles at me. "He's been so nice to me. How can I just tell him to go away?"

I lift my coffee cup, but it's empty. Where's Libby?

I'm probably the last person on the planet to be giving advice on not being a wimp, but I dang sure can't do it without more coffee.

CHAPTER 4

"Then who's paying for all this?" Shannon is shouting as I walk back in Blooming Books. I make the assumption—you know what they say about making assumptions?—that she's on the phone. She's not a very gracious person to deal with on the phone. Maybe because she knows the person can't see she's young and short and dressed like a wood nymph—though her time with Peter did do wonders for her wardrobe.

The assumption thing comes true as I let the door close behind me and find her toe to toe with Missus at her worktable. Missus is drawn up tall and wearing another blue ensemble. "You agreed to provide corsages for the parade. Of course, that agreement included you assuming the cost. How much can a half-dead flower and a pin cost, anyway? I'm sure you just pick up a giant roll of ribbon at the Dollar Store." Missus turns to me. "Hello, Carolina. Glad to see you have time to wander around town when we have our first annual Christmas parade kicking off in exactly 143 hours. I'd ask if your duties are complete, but there's only so much disappointment a person can take at one time." She turns away from me, arms folded, eyebrow arched, to look down on the woman she only a few weeks ago was hoping would be her daughter-in-law.

Shannon works her mouth around, and for a minute I'm

afraid she's going to spit at Missus. She wouldn't do that, would she?

I'm not putting anything past these two. "Hey, hey." I step in between them. "What's the problem? I'm sure it's not a big deal."

Then they both turn on me, and I'm really hoping spitting is off the table.

"Oh! Our young women not being treated with dignity and common graciousness is not a big deal?" Missus demands as Shannon spits—verbally, "Forty-five corsages is not a big deal? Have you ever even *made* a corsage?"

"Forty-five?" I try not to gape. "That does seem a bit much."

Missus points at me, lifting her arm so her white-gloved hand is front and center. I guess the white gloves are more of a daytime look. Plus, she knows their power. "And just which of the young ladies would you disregard? The majorettes? The flag carriers? The cheerleaders? Perhaps since your darling Savannah is no longer a cheerleader you think they should be ignored. How selfish of you, Carolina."

"Now, Missus. You know that's not right, but you do have to think about the cost."

She roars, "I do not have to think about the cost! I am too busy thinking about Chancey!"

Shannon and I both take a step back. Missus demands and threatens and insults, but she rarely shrieks. Expecting to see her looking ashamed, I find she's smiling and her chin is lifted to an unattractive tilt. She whirls to face Shannon again. "I will take my business elsewhere," she hisses, and she turns to stalk out the front door.

The bell over the door is still ringing when Shannon whispers, "Forty-five really is a lot."

"It is. I think I'll see where she's going. Maybe calm her down a bit." I look back to see my partner bent over her flower table, her elbows holding her up. "You okay here?"

"Sure." She straightens. "Tell her I'm sorry. I probably over-reacted, you know? I did agree to do the flowers. I can make it work."

"I'll tell her. I'm sure she came in hot. Don't worry."

Outside on the sidewalk I look to see if Missus might be headed to Ruby's. Then I look back to my left and I'm surprised to see her standing just next door. Outside Peter's bistro. I walk over to her.

"Any word from Peter?"

She looks at me, and her anger fights to keep in place on her face; then she lets it go, and her face falls. "No. He left Thanksgiving night and said he'd be in touch. But he hasn't." She looks up hopefully at me. "You?"

"No. Just that text I told you about when he told me to check in on you for a couple days. I hated that we were all the way up in Kentucky." I step closer to her and pat her on the back. She stiffens.

"No sympathy, Carolina. I will not have it." She shrugs away from me. "He just needs some time to heal from the broken heart he suffered at the hands of *that* woman."

"Shannon told me to tell you she's sorry. You know, she's hurting, too."

"She could have a ring on her finger at this very moment. Engaged to the most eligible bachelor in Georgia. Instead she chose to embarrass my son in front of the entire town."

"Peter had a ring? It seemed more impromptu to me."

She waves a hand at me. "None of that matters. She broke his heart and now he's gone, but I *will* place my order and she *will* take it!"

I step in front of her. "Let me. I'll take care of it. I'm sure you have a million other things to do."

"Finally, a correct statement out of your mouth." She opens her purse and pulls out a notebook. She yanks off the top page. "Here you are. Take care of the items on this list. Place the flower order through Shannon or another vendor. I'll leave that up to you."

Then she's gone in a flurry of white gloves and righteous indignation, with her work list now in my hands.

I believe this is pretty much how I ended up spending last week searching North Georgia for a reindeer.

"It's all good," I announce, walking back inside the store. "She said she *so* appreciates you doing the corsages."

"Liar," Shannon retorts. But she's smiling, so it was a good lie. She takes a deep breath as she clips the ties off a bunch of ferns. "Did she say anything about Peter?"

"Just that she hasn't heard from him. I told her I hadn't heard anything since that text he sent saying he was going away for a couple days." I meander back to watch her work. "You hear anything more?"

"Not since he walked out the door that night, after the party and his proposal." She's fluffing pink carnations with her fingers and blowing on them to separate their petals. I never imagined how much there is to flower arranging. She pauses to sniff a flower. "Even when I moved out we still talked. Saw each other at his shop or here. It's really weird not talking to him at all. Guess it's not weird to him, though."

"Guys are different. He's just off licking his wounds. He'll be back, don't you think?"

She looks up at me and gives me a half-smile. "I don't know. It's kind of his pattern to disappear for a while. A week, a day, a couple years."

"Yeah, that's what I've heard. Only living here a little while, I didn't know that about him."

Shannon clears her throat, but her voice is husky. "I did. I just thought he'd changed." She stabs the flower into the bucket of water. "Stupid me."

I push away from the table. "Stop saying that. I know you think it's true, and honestly, maybe it is. Goodness knows I've sure been stupid over a man, but dwelling on it serves no purpose at all. Forgive yourself and move on."

I grab the duster from under the front counter and make my way into the bookshelves. Shannon is a wallower. She likes to wallow in her sorrow, guilt, and anything else negative she can find. I'm a pretty good wallower myself, so I know you can't let it get out of hand.

It's quiet in the store, Shannon working on her side, me working in the shelves. Bonnie is off, so I'm here all day. It's unusual for me to spend a whole day here, though. That was never the idea behind the bookstore. It was a refuge from the B&B, not its own sort of jail.

I never planned to actually sell many books.

Susan's daughter Susie Mae is starting work here this week after school. I decided I'd trust her to help, since she's backed off on the false gossip on her blog. She expanded it from only covering the high school and her following is growing. She begged to work here, and we're giving her a try. She starts tomorrow, so we'll see. I imagine she'll be a big help once Christmas break starts.

Sitting in the window seat I consider pulling books for a new arrangement in the window, but that is Bonnie's forte. She's also the computer guru, so I can't shelve the new books until she logs them in. See what I mean about her being the manager? Okay, I've put it off long enough. I pull the list Missus gave me out of my pants pocket. I might as well get started on it.

Most of it is checking up on people who've already agreed to do something for the parade. Missus believes in babysitting folks. "Hey, Shannon. Okay with you if I go up and talk to Charles at the *Vedette* about the parade?"

"Sure. I've got plenty to do, so I'll hold down the fort. Did you bring your lunch?"

I'm already at the front door as I turn to her. "No. Did you?"

"No." She frowns. "I got too used to the movie food all being here." The made-for-TV movie that filmed here in the fall used the back area of our business for craft services. Part of that deal was we got to eat from it, too.

"I have to check in with the Piggly Wiggly for Missus, so I'll bring back something. Even if it's just peanut butter and crackers."

It's still nice outside, not too cold at all. No need for a coat. I pull open the door to a neighboring building down Main Street. It opens into a small vestibule with doors on both sides and a dark stairwell going up. I jog up the stairs, well, the first three, then I slog up the rest. At the top the glass inset in the door has printed on it "Chancey Vedette, 1893."

Opening it I shout, "Hello."

"Hello, yourself! Come in whoever you are," Charles yells, so I close the door and turn down the hall. There are open doors along the hall, all of them full of furniture and boxes, but none of them where you usually find Charles Spoon, the editor. His office is at the end where there are two desks facing each other.

"Carolina! Good to see you. What can I do for you?"

This room is warm in contrast to the hallway and other spaces. There's a small square heater on the floor, and it's producing heat and noise. Charles shouts over it, so I do, too.

"I'm working on Missus' check list for the parade, and beside your name she has 'banners.'"

"Yep, got those, you know. But have a seat, have a seat." I sit at the desk facing his. It's empty and has been since I first came up a while back checking into some advertising for the store and B&B. I guess he's just always hopeful he'll need staff at some point. But wait...

"Hey, what happened to Kimmy Kendrick? Isn't this her desk?"

"Naw, she works mostly from home, you know. Works from her laptop. Besides, she brings them kids with her, and I can't get anything done. She can type with 'em climbing the walls, but not me, you know. Nope, couldn't take that. I like to maintain a professional office."

I can't help but look around at the piles of papers and boxes of papers, the layers of dust on layers of papers. "Also I'm supposed to ask about coverage of the parade. Missus wants to make sure you'll be there taking pictures."

He nods. "Yup. Kimmy and I both, plus she said she's got a photographer lined up to take group pictures."

"Oh." I study the full list. I even turn over the paper, but I don't see anything about group photos. "She doesn't have group photos on here. I guess that's okay."

Leaning back in his chair he grins at me. "It'll be better than fine is what she told me." He abruptly leans up. "Hey, you heard anything about where Peter Bedwell has gotten off to?"

It seems Peter is on everyone's mind these days. "No, I think he just needed some space." I lean forward. "Have you heard any thoughts on what he'll do with the bistro?"

Charles looks out the window to his left and shakes his head. "No. Sure hate to see another business go belly up. Think that young fella with the food truck would be interested in it?"

"Alex Carrera? Oh, that would be nice. We don't have anywhere to get a decent sandwich. He's on my list to check in about having the food truck here on Saturday. I'll ask him. I mean, it's a shame for it to sit empty." I stand up. "Better get on with my rounds."

"I'll walk you out," Charles says as he also stands up then maneuvers around the desks.

"Why don't you get rid of this desk? At least until you hire someone else."

"What would I go to all that trouble for? It doesn't bother nothing sitting there. Besides, the way this mayoral race is heating up, I may need to hire a political writer." He laughs as he opens his office door.

"Heating up? You don't think Missus will actually run, do you?"

He tilts his head at me and surprises me with his answer. "I sure hope so. 'Bout time we got someone who actually knows what they're doing. Jed's nice and Laney's got a lot of ideas, but sometimes you just need a few more years to know how things get done."

On the landing, I hold onto the railing and look around to see if he's laughing, but all I see as he's closing the door is him staring at me with raised eyebrows.

And then he winks.

Chapter 5

"Yes. I agree, and I'm sure she thought of that." Apparently, this is my day for sitting in tiny, cramped offices thanks to Missus. Maybe it's because I love books, but the smell of old newspapers and dust was preferable to overripe vegetables and bleach and hairspray. I'm doing a lot of nodding while I answer without breathing through my nose.

"I'll try to keep that in mind." Nod. Smile.

"I'll tell her." Nod. Smile. Try to stand up.

"Of course. One more thing." Nod. Smile. Slump.

The phone rings, and I'm up and out the door. Nod. Smile. Wave. Breathe.

I honestly had no idea. Absolutely no idea Retta Bainbridge had a brother. No idea her brother Wayne Bainbridge manages the Piggly Wiggly. Retta was our realtor when we moved here, and she leads the exclusive book club in town that I was only allowed to join because they meet in our store. Wayne is as large as Retta, and while he doesn't share her extreme fashion sense, he definitely shares her love of gossip and opinion based on that gossip.

In the twenty minutes I spent in his office in the back corner of the store, where everything feels huge and dark and cold, he covered so many topics my head was spinning. Of course, that might be due to me not actually breathing.

Standing in front of the deli counter I find myself lamenting the deli selection in this one-grocery-store town. The food all looks old. Feels old. I swear the chicken salad's top layer is a different color than the one underneath. I turn away with a sigh, a sigh that can't possibly hurt anyone's feelings as no one has come to wait on me this whole time. "Peanut butter and crackers it is," I mumble as I push my buggy away from the deli.

"There you are!" Wayne Bainbridge hails me as he pushes through the swinging metal doors beside the meat counter. "Just had to wrap up that phone call. Figured you hadn't gotten away yet. Want to finish our talk?"

"I really have to get a few things and get back to work."

"Fine. I'll walk with you. Now what I need you to make sure of is that our float is not right in front of the band as we have some hearing issues among our cashiers riding on the float. Also, we cannot be behind any kind of animals that leave waste. Horses, donkeys, monkeys, or such. *Comprendo*?" His eyes bulging out and his hair swaying at me cause me to take a step back. I've just noticed—he has a calmed-down version of Retta's hair. It swoops up, then to the side under a decent layer of hair spray. Strong hair genes must account for the state of his furry forearms, which stick out of his short-sleeved, button-up shirt—though I've never noticed if Retta's forearms are exceptionally hairy.

"I'm really not in charge of the order of the parade." I make a quick turn down the cracker and cookie aisle.

"You say that, but everyone knows you know how to get your way." His laugh is loud, and I cringe before I really think about what he said.

"Wait, what? I never get my way."

He wags a hairy finger at me. "*Au contraire*. My sister keeps me informed on how you are taking over our little town." Still wagging his finger, he grins. "Very sneaky, verrrry sneaky," he admonishes me in a thick, bad German accent.

He talks me all the way through the store and even while I'm checking out. He's loud, and I can't help but feel that as this encounter is repeated around town, half his opinions will be credited to me. I'm beyond nodding or smiling or even acknowledging him. Yet, he himself deigns to take my groceries to my car over my protesting, "I can do it myself!" (Yes, I did sound just like a toddler as I pulled on the side of the buggy.)

With my escape finally in sight, as I'm getting in the driver's seat, he grabs my shoulder. I turn and he pulls me to himself, kissing me on both cheeks. With a salute he steps away. "*Ciao!*" he yells as he strolls along behind the empty buggy toward the front doors. I'm too stunned to move.

How on God's green earth did I not know this person existed until now?

"I met Wayne Bainbridge."

Shannon wrinkles her nose and shudders. "Lucky you. Thanks for lunch."

We each had a couple of round crackers with chunky peanut butter on them, but the lunch she's thanking me for is the Three Musketeers bar I bought each of us. We're enjoying them in the back, sitting on stools beside her worktable. After my first encounter with Wayne Bainbridge I knew *I* deserved chocolate, and who wants to eat a candy bar alone when you know someone who will enjoy, and deserves, one as much as you?

Shannon laughs as she unwraps her candy bar a bit more. "He makes his sister look normal, doesn't he?"

"Yes, he does. How have I never met him?"

"He and Retta still live on their family's farm. Not much of a farm anymore, they've sold off the pasture land, but still a nice old house."

"Neither one of them married?"

She gives me a "get serious" look. "They're like their own little club. Retta is the more social one, as she has to be with the real estate. Wayne usually stays in his office at the Pig or holed up at home. He invents things and reads. He's the one who actually started the book club."

"What?"

She nods and licks chocolate off her fingers. "Yep. But no one would read the books he reads, so he turned it over the Retta. That was when they got pretty selective about who they let join."

Okay, now I'm a little happier that they're so exclusive. Oh. That *we're* so exclusive.

At the ringing of the bell over the door, we both stretch to see who it is. "Hey, Patty."

"Hey." She plods back to us and stops at the table. "Oh, I love Three Musketeers," she says, looking at our wrappers on the table.

"Sorry. I only got two."

"No worries. I'd probably just throw it up. I throw everything up these days."

Patty's plain, round face with her plain, brown hair and her unhappy-looking body takes some work to get looking good. She did not put any work into it today. She apparently didn't throw out the huge old men's T-shirts she used to wear because she has one on today with an old Carhartt jacket some farmer thought was ready for the Goodwill. (And you know farmers never throw out a Carhartt jacket with any life left in it at all.)

Shannon and I lock eyes in a concerned look, and I get up to put an arm around Patty and guide her to the chairs up front. She doesn't look like she'd do well on one of the wooden stools. "Sit down. How are you feeling now? Are you really sick all the time?"

"Pretty much. Doctor says it happens sometimes. Could get

better, but…" She shrugs and takes the cup of water Shannon hands her. "Momma's bought us a house." Then she waves her hand as she thinks about it. "Naw, she didn't have to buy it, but she's giving it to us. Letting us live there, I guess. Some more property my granddaddy owned."

Seems every month or so we discover another property Gertie owns. When Patty and Gertie Samson showed up in Chancey last year, some folks recognized Gertie. She'd left here as a young woman when her moonshiner father was arrested in the hills near here. Apparently shine wasn't the only thing old Mr. Samson invested in. He owned a lot of properties and kept taxes paid on them through the years as he became a mover and shaker in South Georgia. Gertie had tried to set up an arranged marriage between Patty and one of Chancey's most eligible bachelors, Stephen Cross. Stephen's eligibility was purely based on his good looks and everyone's high opinion of his folks. However, no one knew that his family farm no longer belonged to his family, but to the Samson family. Keeping Gertie from spilling that secret caused his parents to agree to the marriage, but Stephen couldn't keep from rekindling the spark with his high school flame who'd had his baby, Libby's daughter, Cathy. So Patty got left out of the match—to her great relief. She decided to stay in Chancey, and Gertie decided to join her here.

Shannon and I sit down across from Patty. "So where's this house?" I ask.

"Around the corner from the library. It's not real big, but close enough Mama says for Andy to walk to work and for her to keep an eye on us." She lays her head back and as she talks her words fade out… and she's asleep.

We get up and tiptoe back to where she'd found us. "Maybe we won't get any customers for a bit and she can sleep." Shannon's eyes are wide and her voice wary. "She sure doesn't make being pregnant look good."

"No, she does not. But then it would be awful to be nauseous all the time. I'm not telling her, but my sister-in-law was sick the whole pregnancy for all three girls. It was horrible."

Shannon blinks at me, then her eyes well up and she gulps.

I grab her arm. "Shannon? Wait, you're not pregnant, are you?"

She vehemently shakes her head at me, and I take a deep breath. I smile at her and pat her arm. "Well, I better get some work done," I say as I get up and start toward my side of the shop.

Then I hear behind me: "I mean, I don't think so…"

Chapter 6

"That is the sleep of the dead." I whisper to Savannah as she tiptoes with me back to Shannon's worktable. Patty's been asleep for over an hour, and the bell over the door hasn't even made her flinch. "I remember one way I could tell I was pregnant was when I'd look at our blacktop driveway and think I could lie right down there and go to sleep. So, what are you doing here?"

"Where's Shannon?" Savannah asks as she walks around the table looking at the scraps of ribbon and stems.

"She, uh, went home. Nothing going on here, and she needed to do some things." Like get a pregnancy test, which meant she had to drive far enough away to not chance running into anyone she knows.

"And why's Patty sleeping up there?"

"She fell asleep there, and..." I shrug and try again. "So, you're out of school early." I've settled on the edge of a stool, but she's still wandering around. Not leaving my vicinity but not getting too close.

"Not really. Checked into study hall and then left." She circles a bit closer to a stool, then runs her hand across the top of it. "Always did it to get to cheerleading practice early, so no one cares."

"Are you missing being a cheerleader? You still might be able to join them."

She shakes her head and screws her mouth up. Her jeans ride low on her hips and her pink sweater just barely meets the waistband, which just barely fits the school dress code of no bare midriffs. The skinny jeans end at her ankle, and she has on flat tennis shoes with pink laces.

We hear a snort from up front, and we both grin. I step in that direction to check. "Nope, she's still out." I detour to pass beside my daughter and touch her back. "So, what's up?"

"Nothing. I just didn't feel like going home." She pulls away from me and walks to the other side of the table. "Susie Mae says she's starting work here tomorrow."

"Yep. Thought that way she'd be ready to help over Christmas break." I understand that getting a teenager to talk takes patience, but come on. My level of caring is quickly plummeting. I'm not used to being here all day, and I'm already itchy. Going around in circles with my daughter is pretty much beyond me at this point.

"Okay. Whatever." When my kids say, "Whatever," I hate it, but it does come in quite handy. She doesn't say anything to make me turn around. Whatever.

"Patty? Honey, I think it's time you wake up." I shake her shoulder, and she begins to come around. "I put your phone on silent, but it started vibrating a few minutes ago. I think Andy may be looking for you."

She sits up and blinks. "Oh, hey, sorry about that. Seems like if I sit down I fall asleep. Hey, Savannah." She cringes as she picks up her phone and reads it. "Andy and Momma are waiting on me to go see the house." She pushes herself to the edge of the couch and then stands up. "I do feel better. Doctor told me to take naps, but that feels so lazy, you know?"

"Not when you're carrying a baby. You need to cut yourself some slack." I look out the window and see Gertie and Andy walking our way. "Why don't you go upstairs and wash your face? Put on one of those pretty sweaters you bought last winter? We'll tell them you'll be right down."

She looks down at her shirt, and her mouth starts quivering, then she catches her breath. "Okay. Tell them I'll hurry." And she does, rushing back to the stairs before they can get inside the store.

"Carolina, I thought when you texted that Patty was over here taking a nap you'd wake her up after ten minutes or so." Gertie is tall, over six feet, and big, loud, and bossy, but she's another one I've come to be friends with in Chancey. I'd say I've lowered my standards, except I didn't really have friends before we moved here. Maybe this *is* my standard.

That's depressing.

"She says the doctor wants her to nap."

"Pshaw. Doctors these days." Gertie sits down where her daughter was seated.

Andy bounds in the door. "Let's go! We've got a house to see!" Then he frowns. "Where's Patty? You said she was here."

Yes, I'd texted him, too. Part of the charming duties of living in a small town. Let everyone know what everyone thinks they need to know.

"She's upstairs washing her face. She'll be right back down."

Andy grins at me, gives me a thumbs-up, and is off to the stairs. He's not one to wait anywhere much.

"Savannah, what are you doing lurking around over there in the bookshelves?" Gertie's voice demands an appearance. She's not much for playing the "waiting around to see if they want to talk" game. "Shouldn't you be in school or at some cockamamie activity folks think teenagers need these days?"

"Thought I'd come give Mom a hand."

Gertie and I share an eye roll. I take a seat. This could be interesting.

"Give your mom a hand?" Gertie says. "Oh, yes, I've seen

you in here *so* many times when things are busy like this! Come out here and tell me what's going on. I've watched you mope around long enough."

Savannah comes out, head cocked all the way to her left, arms crossed, and chin stuck out. Gertie only raised Patty who couldn't manage an attitude if her shoes were on fire. My teenage diva adds a raised eyebrow to the mix. "Mope?"

Gertie laughs, even slaps her knee. "You're funny. Think I'm intimidated by something the size of you? Sit down here and tell us what's going on. I've only got a minute."

And my daughter goes and sits down!

"Yes, mope," Gertie continues. "I saw you at the Christmas tree lighting. You hung around like a sick dog wandering between your parents. It's understandable since the movie's over, but didn't you get some offer to be in another one? I thought that was your *big* dream. From what I hear you've bragged from here to kingdom come about it."

From underneath my cloak of invisibility—at least that's how it feels—I see guilt flood Savannah's face and attitude. Her folded arms soften as her shoulders slump. She looks at her lap and a vehement shake of her head fades after one measly little shake.

Gertie watches, too, her eyes sharp, her nose even quivering. Then as the door closing upstairs sounds, she looks in that direction. "Sounds like we're ready to go." She struggles to her feet. "Hate these low, soft couches. Patty tell you she's moving into a house? Right down the street from Susan. Gonna go show it to them now."

Andy beams as he and his wife come up front. "Look at her! Looks like that nap did her good. Isn't she pretty?"

Patty blushes and looks even prettier. She'd washed her face, brushed her hair, and added a headband to hold it away from her face. Instead of her too-big T-shirt, she's found a mint-green sweater.

Gertie studies her. "Not saying that doctor was right, but maybe you should try taking more naps. Now let's go."

They all leave. I pull away my cloak of invisibility and laugh. "I really will miss Andy and Patty living here in the store."

Savannah sighs. "Yeah."

"So, honey, what's going on?"

She jumps to her feet. "Everything keeps changing, and what if I don't want to be in that movie?" Turning around she sits back down on the coffee table in front of me. "I don't want to be in that movie. Everyone keeps asking me about it and auditions are this weekend, but I don't want to do it."

I lean forward. "Honey, you don't have to. It all came up in a hurry, so don't feel pressured."

"Don't feel pressured? I've only bragged about wanting to be an actress for the past year, and now it falls in my lap and I don't want it? I have to do it." Her voice falls flat. "I have to do it."

Jackson was right. He said we shouldn't let her do it, but I argued we couldn't stifle her dreams. He said if it was her dream, she had plenty of time to make it come true later. Her big, blue eyes stare at me unblinking. She's waiting. Waiting for an answer. From me.

Sitting straighter I shake my head. "No. Absolutely not. Your daddy and I have decided you need to wait on doing something like this. You have your entire life to be an actress. Matter of fact, I'm calling Leif right this minute and telling him we won't allow you to audition."

She stays tightly crouched on the coffee table, eyes still large and skeptical until I'm done talking to Leif. I hang up the phone and look at her. "Okay. That's done."

She unfolds and stands, then she takes a deep breath. I wait as she goes to the counter and pulls her purse out, and then while she finds her keys. With keys in hand she goes to the front door and finally looks at me.

I raise my eyebrows in a question at her.

She opens the door, shrugs, and says, "Whatever."

Great. The princess is back, *AND* I have to tell Jackson he was right.

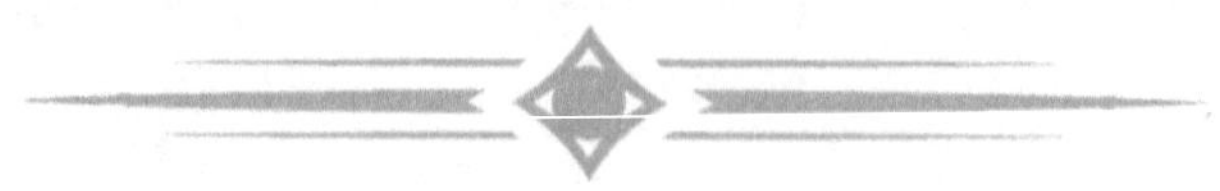

Chapter 7

"It's not even on Google Maps," Jackson mutters through the phone.

"I know. I told *you* that."

"Well, sometimes you're not so good at looking on there." I'd bristle at his comment, except he's right. I can hear his frustration. I've not had a customer in over an hour, so I jumped on it when Jackson called, but we've just gone round and round. He blows out a long breath again. "I just don't know what you want me to tell Will. They're grown-ups, and that's where they want to live."

"How are they going to get up that driveway when it snows? Does the cabin even have heat? Sure it's pretty in the summer, but all winter? You just need to talk some sense into him. They can move back into our house."

"I thought you wanted them out of there."

"But not to someplace out in the woods. It's just not safe. Wait'll you see it."

"Okay, good idea. I'll wait until I see it."

Shoot, that wasn't what I wanted. I wanted him to get involved before the weekend. The longer they stay in that place, the harder it will be for them to leave it.

"Whatever."

Then he thwarts Plan B. "And I don't think you should call

Missus and get her involved. But listen, I didn't call to get into all this. We're at a pause here in this project, and I'm going to be working from home until the new year."

"Our home? Here?" Okay, that just jumped out. Tone down the shock, Carolina. "Oh, that's great!" And maybe that was a bit over the top enthusiasm-wise, but…

Laughing, he says, "Oh, sweetheart. I'm so glad you're excited." He laughs again, adding, "I know it'll be different, but it'll be nice to be home through the holidays, right?"

"Right. I mean I *am* excited, just surprised. So when will you be back?"

"Tomorrow. I was thinking I'd turn the basement into my office."

"But what if the kids move back?"

"Carolina, they're not kids. They are *having* a kid. They'll be fine. I've got to go. See you by suppertime tomorrow."

"Okay. Bye."

We hang up, and one question sits top of my mind. How do I break it to him that we don't actually do suppertime anymore?

Jackson's call interrupted me finishing up Missus' list. After that close encounter with Wayne Bainbridge I decided phone calls would work just fine. I've sold some books and flowers, fixed Savannah's life, double-checked everything for the parade on Saturday, and worked on my Christmas gift list since we are now just over two weeks away from the big day.

I know this might shock you, but I don't exactly do my shopping early.

"Hey, Phoenix!" I greet the tall redhead who's sashaying in the front door. She sashays everywhere. "What are you up to?"

She looks around. "You here alone?"

"Yep. Getting ready to close." I'm feeling rather accomplished, so I smile at her as I walk out from behind the counter. "Come sit down."

We sit in the two wing chairs. She has on winter-white slacks and a navy blouse under a tailored jacket, with a bright green scarf hanging against her chest. Her hair is back in a sleek ponytail, and I'm in such a good mood I don't even compare my black pants and brown shirt or unkempt hair. Well, I don't compare much.

She sits on the edge of her chair, rests her folded hands on the arm, and leans toward me. "I'd like to find out about your rooms. At the inn."

"Oh, the B&B? What do you want to know?"

She shrugs but doesn't answer. I settle back in my seat. "Okay. There are three, all named for trains because we are a railfan B&B, you know for folks that want to come watch the trains on the bridge." I pause, but she only nods once. "There's the Orange Blossom Special, which is the largest, The Chessie, and The Southern Crescent. They're each decorated differently but nice. Well, I think they're nice. And they share a hallway bathroom."

"Are you booked through the holidays?"

"Actually no. We don't do much business in December. Chancey isn't exactly known as a Christmas town, although we are trying to change that. But we also don't need to advertise much once fall arrives. We were booked every weekend up to Thanksgiving. We're fine with having December off. Why?"

She clears her throat and looks around for a moment. "How would I go about reserving a room? Can I just tell you?"

"Sure. Laney handles our reservations, but I can let her know."

"Good. I'd much rather deal with you than her." She smiles at me and smooths out her ponytail. "I know she's your friend, but I find her a bit much."

"Understandable. So, do you have family coming to visit for Christmas?" Funny, but I haven't even thought of her having family. She's spent so much time with Colt and our family you'd think I would've asked about hers. She just seems so self-contained that I have trouble picturing parents or siblings.

"Maybe. But you're saying I shouldn't have a problem reserving a room, right?" She stands up, straightening her short blazer and tying her scarf under her chin.

"Right." I stand also. "But when? For how long?"

She lifts a hand at me and waves her fingers. "I'll get back to you."

She walks out into the late afternoon, and I watch her pass in front of the store windows. She's really nice, but even after spending time with her last week in Kentucky, she feels so remote. Turning the sign on the door from open to closed, I shrug. Colt likes her, so that's all that really matters.

Out the door I see lots of people around the gazebo. Shoot. My van is parked out front today, across the street. Monday is usually pretty slow around the square, so I took a primo spot. It's not so primo now. I'm going to have to go say "hi" to everyone. Working all day makes me miss life in the suburbs where you pull your car into the garage, close the door, and go sit on your back deck. I'm tired of being in public today, and yet in a small town you're always in public. Front porches. Sidewalks. Town squares. It's all so… so *friendly.*

After locking the front door, I turn, plunge my hands deep into my coat pockets, and hurry across the street. "Hey, guys! It's looking great!" Might as well fake it. Maybe I'll get out of here faster.

Athena Markum greets me from atop a stepladder. "Carolina! Come look!" The young woman scrambles down the rungs. "Come meet my husband!" She's in charge of decorating the gazebo as she suggested at the meeting last year. She's a professional decorator and actually participated in decorating the governor's mansion in North Carolina—or was it Virginia?— for Christmas. Charles did a whole, big story on it last year, and from what I hear he's running it again this December.

I pick my way over orange power cords strewn across the grass and scattered leaves. Wonder if anyone checked on the electricity needed for both this and the regular Christmas tree? Then I look around at the efficient young people. They seem to have everything under control. There are even thermoses of hot chocolate, and everyone is laughing while they work. Looks like an Old Navy commercial. Will and Anna are younger than these couples, but once they have the baby, maybe they'll fit with them. That's it. They need friends closer to their own age. Yeah, that's what they need.

Athena introduces me around the group. I know several from them coming into the store, but I try and remember names to ease Will and Anna's inclusion.

"Where are everyone's kids?"

"At home. We hired sitters so we could enjoy ourselves. Plus, we spiked the hot chocolate with some Fireball." She grabs my arm and pulls me forward. "Also, this way we could actually get something done."

Oh. They had definitely gotten something done. Pine boughs lined the railings. Tiny white lights embedded in the boughs shone dimly in the daylight, but they still added such a charming touch. Athena points out her husband who took her spot on the ladder. "He's putting up the final magnolia wreath on the outside. There are lights in them also, but they're not switched on yet."

Each post has a big wreath of magnolia leaves on the outside and the inside. The shiny dark green of the upper sides of the leaves is offset by the bronze of the suede-looking undersides. Then, toward the bottom center of each wreath a blue bow finishes it off.

"You were right," I say to Athena with a squeeze of our arms where she still holds mine. "Missus Blue is perfect."

At her emergency meeting about Chancey's woeful Christmas demeanor Missus had shared a memory of the gazebo being decorated when she was a little girl. She also then remembered how her father, the mayor, shut it all down. He proclaimed it a fire hazard, but honestly it sounds like he was the original Grinch. One of the older ladies recalled how Missus often wore blue, and Athena jumped on that idea for our accent color. Of course, we *must* have an official accent color!

It's a medium blue, kind of dusty-looking but rich. Athena used her contacts to buy simply miles of ribbons in it. Already it's being tied to pretty much anything that doesn't move around town, even though all the downtown establishments are supposed to be checking with the decorating committee before we do anything. I'm using that excuse to wait on Bonnie being in the store before I do anything.

"Come on. You have to see the inside." Athena pulls me up the gazebo steps. I'm glad she's holding my arm as we ascend because I can't swivel my eyes back down to watch my feet.

"It's amazing," I finally say in awe. "How did you do that?"

In the peaked roof of the round gazebo there is a wide, sparkling chandelier. The lights are small candles that look like real flames. I finally manage to look down at Athena. "That's not real fire, right?"

"No, silly." She laughs, and we walk to the center. "But it is real crystal."

"What? How did you—where did you—oh my goodness. I'm literally speechless." I pull away from her and go to sit on one of the benches around the inside edge. "And… it smells like cinnamon."

She sits beside me and points at the basket at our feet. "Cinnamon pinecones. We just spray them once a week or so." There are four baskets of pinecones; a woman is sitting on the floor tying a blue bow on one.

I look back up. "But that chandelier?"

"It was from a job I did a couple years ago. The owner scrapped it, and I took it. You should've heard Matt when I wanted to move it here! Then when I saw this gazebo, I knew it would be perfect." Someone calls her name. "Shoot. Carolina, I have to run." And she dashes off. I'm left sitting in the gazebo, thinking that this place looks like something out of a magazine or a dream. I can't wait to see it in the dark.

Walking back down the steps I pull out my phone and text Susan. I thought we had all week while Silas is gone to have supper together, but now with Jackson coming home, this is our one chance for a ladies' night. Although, if she really breaks up with Silas, I guess we could go to her house any time.

Yeah, right. Like she's going to break up with the hot movie star.

"Need me to bring dinner?" she texts back. I only answer "no" and then get into my van with a sigh.

I have a freezer full of cheap frozen pizzas I need to get rid of now that suppertime is real again.

Chapter 8

"I don't know how I worked all day every day at the library," I say to Susan as we move from the kitchen into the living room. We'd eaten at the kitchen table since she'd actually brought a salad to add to our quick dinner.

"Well, you have to admit you had more to do at the library probably. Less boredom." She sets her glass of wine on the end table, but instead of sitting goes to look out the front window. "Where did you say your kids are?"

"Bryan is over at Zoe's." I won't say, or even think about, how often he eats dinner over there, but that'll be coming to an end with our renewal of family dinners. "Savannah is back in with the cheerleaders, so they're at one of their houses doing homework. Did I tell you she's not doing the movie?"

"Really?" She comes back and sits on the couch beside her wine. "Is that what was stuck in her craw?"

"Yep. As soon as I told her she couldn't do it and called Leif, she morphed right back into her old self."

Susan laughs. "You'll be back to fighting in no time at all!"

"I know, but I think she's even more difficult to have as a best friend. So, how are things with Silas?"

She groans, rolls her eyes, and takes a drink of wine. "He keeps calling and texting. I don't know what to do."

"Does he have any idea that you want to break up?"

She doesn't answer, just takes another sip. "So, Jackson won't be going out of town for the rest of the month?"

See? Told you she's not dropping Silas. With a look I let her know I saw what she did there, then move on. "Nope. It'll be good to have him here, but I've gotta get used to it. Savannah, Bryan, and I have gotten pretty lax about things around here. Even the weekends have been crazy lately when he's been here. All fall we've been busy with guests, and then we were gone Thanksgiving week for the wedding."

She jumps, kicks off her shoes, and tucks her feet under her. "That's right. I haven't heard about the wedding! Tell me everything."

I hold up my glass and look at it. "Nope."

"Why not?" she cries.

"I don't have enough wine."

Leaping up she dashes to the kitchen. "You get started. I'll get the bottle."

"Trudging in the front doors of the old inn we'd all booked rooms in, we were met with my sister-in-law Abigail's screeching. It actually brought Jackson and me to a halt, which brought Will, Anna, Savannah, and Bryan to a halt because they were behind us. Seriously it sounded like she was being murdered." I laugh remembering it. "Abigail does not screech. She's old Virginia money, and she does not screech," I pause for emphasis.

"However, she was screeching to the point that we couldn't understand what she was saying, so we got our momentum back and hurried across the beautiful, polished wood floors to the small desk in the back. It really was stunningly beautiful. But just as Emerson saw us we finally heard a word that we completely understood. Bedbugs!"

Susan yells, "What?!" from the kitchen.

"Yep. 'Got a real situation here, guys,' Emerson informed us. He's a big guy, tall and portly. Looks like the executive he is. He has a very in-charge voice. 'Flight got in late last night, we came straight here and spent the night. Got up this morning to a pest company making its way through the place. Management asked us to move everything out; then we'd be free to come back tonight—'

"Uh-uh, I was all over that. Told the kids to take their stuff back out to the van right that minute and Jackson to cancel our reservation. By the time I turned around Savannah was already at the door with her suitcases. However, Bryan was sitting on a couch. I jerked him up hissing, 'Don't sit on anything! Go outside.' Will slouched, and I could tell from his face he was going to argue. I stopped that with a look and a swipe of my hand across my throat. Anna dragged him out of there by the ear!" I laugh and take the full glass of wine from Susan. "I don't think I've ever made that gesture before, but it was pretty effective!"

Susan motions with her hand for me to continue. "Don't interrupt your story. Keep talking."

"Abigail's main complaint, aside from the bedbugs, was that since the pest control people were there bright and early they had to have been called the night before. Before they'd brought all their stuff in. She was fit to be tied."

Susan exclaims, "Absolutely!" Then she laughs and asks with a wince, "So no elegant antebellum mansion for your stay and Thanksgiving meal?"

"No. Half of us ended up at a hotel out by the interstate, which was fine, but not what we had in mind. All our kids, including Anna and Will, stayed at the farm with Shelby and Hank. Which set Shelby off, but Hank told her to simmer down. He yelled, 'These are my grandkids and they are always welcome in this house!' Then he added with a finger in her face that she was the expendable one. Looks like the rose is wilting on that romance."

"What did she say to that?"

"She held her breath for a bit, then marched in the house. We were all standing out front as Hank had told us to bring the kids and their things to the house. Abigail and I both looked concerned about letting our kids stay, but before we could say anything, Emerson and Jackson were walking into the house carrying the kids' suitcases. Abigail's girls and Savannah didn't appear to have heard what had happened. They were huddled in a small circle and had their phones out, ignoring us. Bryan was off at the creek or something. He loves the farm, and he'd be fine staying there with Satan himself." I stretch to look out the front window. "Speak of the devil—not *that* devil—Bryan's home."

He pounds up the porch steps, across the porch, and in the front door. "Hey," he says then stops when he sees Susan. "Grant here?"

"Nope. Up at his dad's."

Bryan grumbles, then heads for the kitchen. "Can I have some of this pizza?"

"Sure," I answer.

Susan leans back to look in the kitchen door. "Hungry teen boys. I miss that." Then she yells, "There's some salad in the fridge."

"This is good," he mumbles, mouth full as he strides back in the living room, headed for the stairs.

"How's Zoe?" I call since he's already halfway up the stairs.

"Good. Got homework." And he's in his room, pizza in hand. We hear the door slam.

Susan breathes deeply then sighs. "I miss Grant. Teenage boys are so big, so noisy, so smelly. There's just nothing like them."

"You think he's still happy up there with Griffin?"

"And his grandmother. Don't forget Rachel. I thought he might choose to live with me, but Rachel treats him like a little god. He's getting the treatment she always reserved for her four children, over and above her grandchildren." She rubs her hand on the arm of the couch, then with a sniffle slaps her hand down. "No, not thinking about that. Back to the wedding. You were saying you and Abigail had reservations, but no one else did."

"Well, except for my mom and dad when I told them, but by then it was all a done deal. Us, my parents, Abigail and Emerson, and Colt and Phoenix at this run-down hotel, everyone else at the farm."

"Oh, that's right. I'd forgotten about Colt and Phoenix. How weird was that, her going back there? Is she actually divorced from that judge guy she was with?"

"Oh my—the judge! Not the wedding, but pretty much everywhere we went to eat, he'd show up. I'm not joking." Susan's mouth hangs open, and I laugh. "Halfway through most of our meals he'd show up. I don't know what kind of network he has, but it was good. Shelby did put her foot down on not cooking for everyone, and Hank said her food was so bad he agreed. However, he wanted family meals, so it would take a while to get us set up since there were so many of us. The inn we were going to stay at is pretty much the only nice restaurant in the area that could hold all of us so we ended up at Golden Corral, Denny's, or Cracker Barrel for every meal. You know me, I didn't mind since I wasn't having to cook or clean, but Abigail was pretty much comatose by the time the wedding rolled around. Thanksgiving dinner at Cracker Barrel was delicious, I thought. However, Abigail and Emerson did not adjust their wardrobe, so they looked a bit out of place in her dress and pearls and his suit sitting in the rockers on the front sidewalk beside the parking lot."

Laughing, I get up and jiggle my glass at her. She grimaces. "No, thanks. I do still have to drive down the hill home."

"Okay, but I'm having another one. You know you could have Susie Mae come pick you up."

"Oh, right, and have my mother's Sunday School class putting my drinking on their prayer list right next to my divorce and, well, Silas." Her weak laugh ends with a groan as I fill my glass and hurry back.

"So things aren't better with your mom?"

She shakes her head, lips pressed together tightly. "Maybe I shouldn't have started this whole mess, but I don't want to talk about that tonight," she says with a deep breath.

I sit my glass down and grab a crochet afghan off the quilt rack. "Want one?" She nods, so I pull another one off.

"Jackson's mother made these for you, didn't she?"

"Yes." I frown as I snuggle under the light blue cover. "It was sad being at the farm and her not being there. The house looks so different and so, well, sad. But Hank was such a jerk it helped. She's happy at the beach, and I'm happy for her. So, like I said, Savannah and Emerson's three girls were tight. They are all prima donnas. I must've said a blue million prayers of thanks that Savannah doesn't have a sister. They seemed to ratchet each other up on dressing better, skimpier, and more expensively than each other, and Savannah was right in the thick of it. They drove into Lexington to shop the day of the rehearsal, which was Black Friday, and invited Anna to go along. Apparently, Anna was dying of boredom at the farm. Will would go off with Bryan, Shelby was busy with wedding stuff, and Hank ignored her, so she agreed to go. I'd have gone and gotten her if I'd thought of it, but I was actually having fun with my mom and dad and Jackson. Even enjoyed Abigail and Emerson. Plus, you know I had a stack of books."

"Of course you did. Let me guess, the shopping didn't go well."

"I think that part was okay, except Anna wasn't shopping. She's eight months pregnant, so she just sat and watched them. However, I guess the cousins started treating her a bit like a maid, and I guess Anna acted like she did when she first came here, doing whatever anyone asked and not saying a word. Savannah said she didn't seem mad, so she just ignored it. Then they came straight from shopping to the church for the rehearsal."

I close my eyes and shake my head. "First of all, Savannah showed up in a dress that barely covered her top *or* bottom. It wasn't tight fitting, but that meant it pretty much flew around just promising a scandalous reveal. She had on false eyelashes from a makeup session they got at the mall. Emerson's girls have their own credit card! They paid for everything. The other girls' outfits were just as skimpy or so tight they left nothing to the imagination. Anyway Anna walked in behind them and went straight to Will. She tucked in behind him and before we even saw the other girls, she was sobbing. Absolutely heartbreaking. There we are in the sanctuary, the preacher, organist, and all, and the four floozies come marching in. They actually took the air right out of the room. Then Will yelled his sister's name, asked her, 'What did they do to Anna?' Anna looked a sight. Tired, pregnant, sweaty, and then there were the other four looking like they just stepped out of a magazine."

"That just doesn't sound like Savannah. She's always gotten along well with Anna," Susan says, shaking her head.

"I know. And Will yelling at her seemed to bring her to her senses. She looked at Anna and started going to her, but then one of the cousins said something like, 'Oh, come on. It was no big deal. She was *fine* until we got here!'

"Oh, Savannah went on a tear, crying all her makeup off apologizing to Anna and to Will. Her cousins argued back, loudly. Emerson finally herded his girls out to the vestibule, and Savannah and I went back to the farm where the caterers were getting the rehearsal dinner set up. She changed dresses and stayed close to Anna for the rest of the trip."

Susan rearranges herself on the couch. "So how was the ceremony? Any theatrics there?"

"Not really in the actual ceremony. It was pretty straightforward. Emerson and Abigail made their girls apologize when they showed up for the rehearsal dinner, and that went smoothly. Then the wedding was at noon on Saturday back at the church." I take a drink of wine, lick my lips, and grin. "That's where it got good. You know how the church ladies here do funeral dinners and receptions and such? Well, at Hank and Etta's church, where they went their whole married life and raised the boys, the women also do wedding receptions. Usually the couple gives the women's group a nice, big donation so it's actually a moneymaker. Shelby's been to dozens and probably helped cook for them, so she and Hank just assumed that's how it would be for theirs." With my grin growing, I shake my head.

Susan leans forward. "No? What happened?"

"First of all, the church was full for the ceremony, except there was no one any of us recognized. Colt didn't even see people he knew, and he only left earlier this year. Finally it dawned on us they were all old. Really old. Turns out the folks were there from nursing homes all around the area where Hank does his Hillbilly Hank routine. We found out later Hank's been showing off his new, young fiancée and telling folks they should come on over to the wedding." I can't help but laugh out loud. "And they did."

Susan laughs with me. "I can't imagine this turned out well."

"Oh, not well at all! So you have a hundred or so people all piling down to the basement for the reception. Before the ceremony, we'd all come from the farm where everyone had dressed. The church is really small, so we just went straight to the sanctuary until afterwards. Except when we get down there

there's not a church lady in sight. Not a one. Tables are not set. The cake was still in the box. There's not a cup of punch, not even a *cup* to hold any punch! Abigail and I made our way to the kitchen, and there on the counter is a lovely pink envelope with Hank and Shelby's names written on it in a fancy flourish. We notice when we lift it that it isn't sealed, so…"

"So you took out the note." Susan leans even farther forward. I'm worried she'll tip out of her chair. "What did it say? Where were Hank and Shelby?"

"The newly wedded couple had taken a ride around town in a friend's convertible while their guests got situated downstairs. So anyway, I take out the note and hand it to Abigail."

"Mom!" Bryan comes running down the stairs. "Mom, I need you to run me by Jim Blount's house. Our group paper is due tomorrow, and I still have to add my part to it."

"Now? Why didn't you ask me earlier?"

"Jim hadn't finished his part. He just got done, and his folks can't bring it. His dad works nights, and his mom just got his little sister in bed. If I get it to him, he'll put it all together. He says his printer isn't working, so I have to bring him my part on paper. And he has our notebook it has to go in. I just need to run this in to him."

I hold up the glass of wine in my hand and shake my head at him. "Call your sister and ask her if she'll come take you, but I'd ask her really, really nicely."

Susan stands up. "I'll take it for you, Bryan. The Blounts live near town, so I'll loop by their house. Besides, I need to get home." She turns to me and sighs. "I'm calling you when I get home or tomorrow to get the rest of this story."

"Okay. Thanks for taking it. You sure it's okay?" My phone rings as I follow them to the door, and I look down at it. "Oh, no. Missus after eight p.m." Susan just waves as they cross the porch. I roll my eyes as I go back inside and answer my phone. "Hello?"

"Carolina. Why did you take it upon yourself to upset Wayne Bainbridge? I will not, *will not*, accept not having a Piggly Wiggly float in the parade because you failed to control yourself." She stops long enough to tsk at me, then continues, "Flirting with Wayne Bainbridge. I'm appalled by your behavior, Carolina Jessup!"

Bypassing my seat on the couch I go straight for the kitchen. Please, please let there be more wine in that bottle.

CHAPTER 9

"Just going into Wayne Bainbridge's office is pretty much considered foreplay in his book. He's a perv from way back." Laney is seated across from me at Ruby's in the same booth we were in yesterday morning. It may be the same booth, but it's a totally different time. The school crowd isn't even here yet. The sun is barely up.

"Coffee is all, Libby. It's too early to eat," I say as she fills my cup.

"Not for me. I have a baby and have been up for hours. This is like lunch time to me," Laney says. "What muffins are done?"

Libby smiles, nods, and walks away without answering her.

"She look as tired as I feel?" Laney asks as she sits up straighter. "Cayden is killing me with not sleeping. I think twins at twenty-five is easier than one at forty-five. I'm thinking of moving my mother in with us."

"Really?"

"No. 'Cause she won't. I asked, but that godly, choir-singing woman practically cussed me out. If I do this mayor thing I might have to hire a live-in nanny."

"Back to me, okay? Wayne Bainbridge thinks I was flirting with him. Thinks his float's position in the parade depends on him accepting my advances. Missus wants me to meet with him to discuss it. Actually said he felt 'sexually harassed.'"

"So when is this date of yours with Wayne?" Laney asks with a straight face, then cracks up laughing. "Carolina and Wayne sitting in a tree, k-i-s-s-i-n-g!"

"Shut up. I'm serious." I look around. "Libby, can you bring her something to eat?"

Laney is crying she's laughing so hard. I'm going to give her some slack as I'm assuming she's punchy or her blood sugar has dropped. While I wait for her to calm down, I sip my coffee. Bryan needed to go in extra early due to that stupid paper, so I dropped him off at the school then came by here to meet Missus. Laney was sitting here half asleep when I walked in, just her and the big group of farmers at the front tables.

She managed when I got here to tell me Shaw didn't have to leave for work until nine, so she'd left the house when he got up. It gets quiet, and I realize she's asleep. Libby stops at the table, plate with muffin in hand. "Poor thing. I'll just sit her muffin down here. I can't imagine having a baby at her age. Just helping Cathy with Forrest wears me out."

"Cathy and Stephen still not working things out?" I whisper.

She shrugs and plants an elbow on the back of my seat. "Those two just beat all. Bill and I try to help them out, especially with Forrest, but sometimes I think they'd be better off if we let them alone to handle everything themselves. Ya ever think kids these days can get too much help?"

"Too much help? Like what?"

"Like us taking Forrest whenever Cathy has one of her lingerie sales parties, which means she's out gallivanting around town at all hours and then Stephen is at loose ends. And they have a fight and he runs home to his folks or she runs to our house. Or there's the phone and computer. There's always someone else to talk to or to tell your troubles to. Me and Bill when we had a fight knew better than to call our folks. They'd just tell us to work it out. If I went out or worked, Bill had to be home with Cathy. Vice versa for me. We couldn't afford a babysitter, and our folks were too old and tired to watch her. Besides, she was *our* responsibility, we felt." She sighs and shrugs. "And as for that phone and computer, we had to talk to each other. Not some strangers on Facebook. I just don't know." With another deeper sigh she adds, "All I know is I'm tired, but I'd do anything in the world to help that grandson of mine." She smiles at me. "You'll see soon, Carolina. That baby will just melt your heart."

She walks away to refill coffee at the front tables with smiles and pats on the backs of the many checkered shirts gathered there. Missus comes in the door and speaks to several of the men as she comes this direction. I kick Laney. "Wake up. Missus is coming."

Laney sits up abruptly. "Oh, Lord. I meant to be gone before she got here."

"Hey, Missus," I say brightly as Laney stretches her eyes, then rubs her face to wake up. However, when our attention is shifted to her, she still looks like she was sleeping on the table. Her hair is sideways, and one side of her face is mushed.

"Missus. Good morning, I was just leaving," Laney says as she straightens up and slides out.

"But Libby brought your muffin." I lift the small plate toward her.

"Y'all can have it." Then she stops. "Oh, are those nuts on top? I'll just take it." She grabs it and then scoots on toward the door, Missus and I watching her all the way.

Missus clears her throat, causing me to look at her. "Did you notice my sweater? The ladies out at Greens knitted it for me. It's Missus Blue."

"I see that. Very nice. I haven't been to Greens yet to see all their Christmas stuff." The Green family run a farm outside of town. In the summer they sell watermelons, peaches, all kinds of fruits and vegetables. In the winter they sell Christmas trees, and the women of the family sell craft items they make all year long.

Missus turns again for me to see her completely. She's wearing beige wool slacks and beige suede pumps with a low heel. (She'd pointed out that they were suede another time she wore them, or I wouldn't have probably realized it.) The sweater is not bulky, but sleek and straight. She has a blue and brown swirled scarf knotted underneath her chin. She's toned down the blondness of her hair, or maybe it's just the dye job fading except that I don't see any grey roots. I realize she's still modeling for me because I'm looking, so I sniff and look away and she glides into the seat across from me. "So, Missus, what is all this about Wayne Bainbridge? You *know* I wasn't flirting with him."

"I can only tell you what he said to me. You must keep his float in the parade. He's actually considering putting in another entry depending on you! A float from over in Canton, part of some Civil War reenactment group he belongs to. A *real* float. Not just a bunch of people on a trailer."

Libby brings her a new cup and then fills it. "Muffins, ladies?"

Missus vehemently shakes her head for both of us.

I ignore her. "What was that one you brought Laney?"

"Brown sugar pecan," Libby says at the same time Missus holds up her hand and says, "No. Not now. Carolina doesn't have time."

"Why don't I have time?" I demand, but Libby has already left. She knows who wins this argument.

"You are meeting Wayne and Retta in ten minutes for you to apologize."

Her words stop too abruptly. She sips her coffee and looks past me. I even look over my shoulder to see if something has caught her eye. There's nothing but Ruby back by the stoves, but when I turn back, Missus is pulling her phone out of her purse.

"Wait, apologize and what?" I ask. "There's more, isn't there?"

Missus ignores me by scrolling on her phone. Then my phone dings with a text. Fine, I can ignore her, too. Besides, she's crazy if she thinks I'm apologizing to that man.

Then I read the text. It's from Laney.

"Missus! You did this. This is your idea, isn't it?"

She finally looks at me. "You *do* own a B&B. Now finish up your coffee and hurry home. Your newest guests will be there any minute."

I look down at Laney's message again: "Bainbridges tenting their house for termites. Made reservation at B&B." She added the emoji of the smiley face throwing up.

"This is too much. They are *both* awful, and they're staying at my house?"

"It's the least you can do to save the parade. Now, scoot!" Her scrunched-up frown gets me moving, but I let her know with my own frown that I am *not happy*.

Like she cares.

Whatever.

Chapter 10

"You don't think it's long now, but wait until you meet him," I yell at Jackson through my phone. "A whole week, and I have so much to do this week."

"Good. Then you'll be out of the house, and I'll deal with them. I have to go, but I'll be home before dinner. Love you."

That's right. He'll be home. Dinner. Shoot. I was hoping he'd get delayed and have to eat on the road. As I pull across the railroad tracks I see Retta's big car in our driveway. It's really nice except for big advertising magnets featuring her picture on both sides. The other car is a little sporty car. It is too cute and can totally not belong to Wayne Bainbridge, and yet it's here and he's here. So...

They are standing on the porch, just waiting for me like an overgrown version of the twins from *The Shining*. I push through them, trying to smile as I open the front door and motion for them to go through.

Retta gasps. "That wasn't locked? How unsafe is that? My word!"

Her brother rolls his eyes and shouts, "Jumpin' Jehoshaphat! Don't start that here, too. We don't live in New York City, Ret. What would anyone want with this place anyway?" He marches in ahead of us both. "You've got internet, right?"

Retta finally feels safe enough to enter, and I reluctantly follow her. "Yes. Let me show you the rooms." This time I don't make the mistake of waiting for them to go first. "Here's the Southern Crescent room, Mr. Bainbridge. Most men like it best. Retta, would you like the Orange Blossom Special room?"

The realtor that sold us this house after it had sat empty for months sniffs around the room like she smells something off. I'm very picky about scents, so I know it smells just fine. However, she keeps smelling, so I step back to the dark green room I left her brother in. Remembering the flirting complaint, I stay in the doorway. "Everything okay?"

He frowns. "I suppose. My computer setup will have to go on that dresser there. You maybe got a card table or two?" He puts his hands on the hips of his brown polyester pants where his shirt is tucked in underneath a thin, green V-neck sweater. He squints at me. "Not sure this is the best setup. The reservations were all good at the hotel at the interstate, but Missus said you'd be right put out if we didn't stay here." He throws his hands up in the air as he turns away. "So, if it makes you happy."

"Can I see this other room?" Retta asks coming down the hall. "That one back there seems like it'll be awful bright on the corner with all those windows. I'm more of a sedate, peaceful person, and all that sunshine just makes my skin crawl." She steps into the Chessie room, and I try to keep my mouth closed. She is currently wearing an electric-blue jumper dress with a lemon-yellow blouse under it. Her neck and ample front are swathed in gold chains. Her hair is teased to the sky, which helps take your attention off her red, red lips and blue, blue eye shadow. She's turning back to the doorway as I step up to it.

"Oh, this is much better, but it's smaller, isn't it?"

Wayne shouts from his room. "Can we take these shutters down? Makes the room awful dark. I like to be able to see outside."

"Maybe you would like the Orange Blossom Special room?" I suggest.

"Naw, oranges and I are not *simpatico*, so that just sounds *verboten*." Then he looks up at me with a grin. "That's forbidden in German. I'm something of a language aficionado." Then he yells, "Retta, you ready to unload? I gotta get to the store. This room will be okay for me, I guess. Like Missus says, we have to do our part to help other business owners in Chancey while they try and get on their feet." With a little nod of sympathy for my struggling business, he goes toward the living room.

"Good, he's gone." With that, Retta bustles to my side and then with a jerk of my arm pulls me into the Chessie room. "You." She squints until her beady eyes nearly vanish into her blue eye shadow. "You keep your hands off my brother. We Bainbridges are pillars of Chancey society, and we will not be a part of any scandal involving a married woman with small children."

"My kids aren't small, and besides—"

She bends down so that her face is only inches from mine. "I said there would be no hanky-panky, and there will be no hanky-panky! Keep your hands to yourself, or to that poor husband of yours." She shoves past me down the hall, blue dress swaying like a caboose on the back of a runaway train.

I wonder if the Greens can make a voodoo doll.

"What is all this stuff?" Jackson yells at me from the bottom of the basement stairs.

I'm in the kitchen fixing dinner, so we all know what kind of mood I'm in. I yell back, "The Bainbridges' stuff. Remember? The people you said would be no problem!"

Retta and Wayne are still out. Savannah is at cheer practice, and Bryan is upstairs sulking. He's not happy about having to eat here either. I do have to admit, he took not going to Zoe's a little too hard. I might need to start putting a little more distance between those two.

I'm putting uncooked rice in a casserole dish when I hear Jackson stomping up the stairs. At the top he stands behind me, hands on his hips. "There's hardly any room for me to work down there. I got home early to set up things so I'd be ready for tomorrow. You could've had them put their stuff in the basement bedroom."

"Yeah, I tried that. They didn't want to. Said that storage should be our problem. I barely got them to bring it all inside." I lay defrosted pork chops on the rice then add canned soup, chopped onion, and water. "You know Retta, but her brother is even worse. You'll see."

I don't turn around, and he doesn't leave. Finally he walks up behind me, looking over my shoulder. "That looks good."

Bumping him back, I open the oven door and slide the dish inside. Then I turn around and hug him. "I'm sorry. My attitude stinks. It's good to have you home." I kiss him to remind myself that it *is* good to have him home and to let him know I mean it.

We're still hugging when he sighs and asks again, "So what is all that stuff?"

"Apparently when you tent a house you have to remove certain things. I looked it up and I think they went a little overboard, but they're just weird so I'm not surprised." We separate and he goes to the kitchen table to look through the mail. Picking up the most recent *Chancey Vedette,* which comes twice a week in the mail, he opens it to look through.

"Look at this," he says. "Phoenix has a big ad. Guess she's starting the dance classes up first of the year."

"That's a great time to do it. Hey, have you talked to Colt lately?"

"Not really since Kentucky. Why?"

"Phoenix asked me about renting a room over the holidays. Reckon she has some family coming in?"

The way he's staring at me I can tell he's never thought of her having family either.

"She was kind of strange about it. Said she'd let me know." I sigh as I wash my hands. "And here I thought all I'd have to do this month was Christmas stuff and wait for the baby. Now we have guests." I stop myself from saying anything about cooking dinner every day. I'm blessed to have a husband who works so hard, helps, and loves anything I make and I'm going to act blessed. Or at least try.

"Speaking of the baby, want to go see the kids after dinner? I've got to see this cabin."

"Sure. You want to text Will? Oh… wait. It'll be dark."

"So?"

"We might not be able to find their driveway." I lean on the counter and cross my arms as he squints his eyes at me and laughs.

"Are you joking? You've been there, we'll find it."

I shrug. "Okay. You'll see. Dinner will be ready in an hour."

"This is absurd," Jackson says.

Guess what?

We can't find the driveway. I am not smirking. I'm being supportive—from the back seat. Bryan claimed shotgun. Savannah said she had homework, and besides, she didn't think there'd be enough room for all of us in the house.

"Bryan, stick your head out the window and look for lights down the hill," I say. "Let me get out and look."

"No, I'll do it. There's not much shoulder," Jackson says as he unbuckles and gets out. He walks around the car, then up a little bit. He comes back and gets in the driver's seat. "I think it's right up here."

As the van creeps forward, Bryan yells, "I see lights!" Then, "There it is. Stop, Dad!" Half his body is sticking out the window, then he wriggles backward and plops back into his seat. "Yep, just turn here."

"This is absurd. I'm fixing this tomorrow," Jackson mumbles as we pull off the pavement.

"It's pretty wide but just hard to see from the road," I say. "Once you turn you'll be able to see it." There is little to no star- or moonlight coming through the tall trees, although most of them are bare. Some trees still hold onto their dead leaves, and there are enough pine trees to hide the sky as we descend into the little valley.

At the bottom we park beside Will and Anna's cars with Jackson still muttering, "This is absurd. Absolutely absurd."

Will opens the door before we even get near it. "Hello! You found the driveway. Come in!"

He's grinning from ear to ear, and I grab onto Jackson's arm. I pull him to me and whisper in his ear, "Our son is welcoming us into his first home."

Jackson pauses, then squeezes my arm, saying, "That's right."

I take a deep breath, and we step up onto the little porch, which Bryan has already crossed, plunging inside the brightness spilling out.

I release Jackson and grab Will. "Oh, it looks so cozy inside." I let him go, and I step through the doorway. Undoing my scarf I turn around enough to see my oldest son, standing straight and tall, shake his father's hand. Jackson grins and then grabs his son in a hug. "Well done, son. Beautiful place."

Like with that first coloring page they offer us from preschool, sometimes we have to ignore the blue pig, the lines colored over, and the fact that it's practically torn in half. We just need to smile and say, "Good job. I love it. I'm proud of you."

Anna is standing near the fireplace where a little fire burns. Her eyes are huge and she looks scared, so I rush to her and hug her. "It's so cozy, and you have a fire!"

I actually feel her release her held breath as I hug her. She jerks back. "Do you want some cookies? And we made a pot of coffee. Decaf." She scurries around the little kitchen area. Bryan isn't being supportive when he steps toward her, just hungry.

"Cookies? Sure," he says. "What kind?"

"They're just store-bought," she says.

"Our favorite kind!" I say with a laugh. "Oh, the ones with icing. I never buy these because I want to eat the whole package. And coffee would be wonderful. Let me help you."

We tour the cabin, eat cookies, talk and laugh, and laugh and talk. Bryan goes out to explore in the darkness and declares his brother's house the best place ever. He asks to come set his tent up by the creek in the spring and says his friends are going to love it out here. Anna rocks in the rocker they brought from her grandmother's house and smiles. Will sits on the little stone hearth beside his fire and smiles. They look at each other and smile, as do Jackson and I.

"Well, we need to go home," I say a few hours later as I stand. Tiredness had been creeping into Anna's smiles, and Will has early classes on Wednesday. "Thank you for the cookies and coffee." I pick up the cookie package and Jackson's and my coffee cups. Anna follows me to the sink while the guys stand around the fire talking.

"So has your grandmother been out here yet?" I'd waited to ask because it had been such a nice visit.

Anna sighs. "She's coming tomorrow. She bought us a cradle, and it was delivered to her house. Will's going to get it and her when he finishes with classes. We figured it was best if she's not driving the first time she comes here. Plus it's really prettier in the daytime, don't you think?"

The worry is back on her face, so I give her another hug. "It's just lovely, and it's perfect for the two, the *three* of you. Remember this, if you'd moved into one of the mansions up in Laurel Cove, Missus would've found something to complain about. You can't let her get to you."

"That's true. And it could always be worse." She giggles. "We could be living with the Bainbridges."

Rolling my eyes, I put on my coat. The guys are already outside. "Good luck at the doctor on Thursday. Let us know what he says. Getting close now." I lay my hand on her tummy. "I can't believe our granddaughter is in there. Can't wait to meet her."

Anna just nods, and fear slides into her eyes.

I squeeze her hand. "I'd tell you to not be afraid, but that's just impossible. I *will* tell you it'll all be worth it. She'll be sleeping right here all cozy and sweet before you know it." We step outside, and everyone says goodbye. From the front seats of the van we watch as Will steps to her and puts his arm around her. Warmth and light frames them and holds them.

Jackson and I meet eyes, grin, and then both take deep breaths. We allow the worry to creep into our gaze, then Bryan explodes from the back seat. "That is the best house ever! I wish we lived here!"

And we're laughing as we pull up the driveway into the darkness.

It's the best house ever.

CHAPTER 12

"I'm going down to the basement to get my office set up," Jackson says only minutes after arriving home. Sure, it's only minutes after we'd talked about watching a movie together, but who can blame him? It's also only minutes after we walked in the door to find the Bainbridges encamped in our living room watching YouTube videos on our TV. (I didn't even know our television would do that, though it might have something to do with Wayne's laptop and array of cords sitting to the side of it.)

Retta and Wayne were laughing uproariously as we came in and are still laughing, with no pause in sight, as I try to introduce Wayne to Jackson. Retta waves at us, and we go on into the kitchen.

"Hey there! You must be that Jackson I keep hearing about," Wayne roars from the living room just as the noise from the television is muted. We step back into the living room where Wayne is situated on one end of the couch with Retta on the other. They are both in robes and slippers. Wayne leans forward and shakes Jackson's hand. "Sorry about not getting up, but, well, this robe is a little short and I don't want to startle the women folk."

What is that supposed to mean? No pants? No underwear? I will never know since I will not look. Ever.

Retta slaps his arm and laughs. "Look there! You plum

scared the life out of Carolina. She looks like she swallowed a bug!"

Wayne is grinning as he spreads his arms. "Join us. Have a little powwow. We can go back and show you some of the funniest videos. We love watching them on the big screen. Here, watch this one." Like that, he's got another one started, and they are already laughing. Jackson just shakes his head and pushes me into the kitchen.

"They're insane," he whispers.

"You might say that. You go on downstairs. I'm going to call Susan and finish telling her about your dad's wedding, take a shower, then go to bed. What time are you setting the alarm for in the morning?"

"Six-thirty, I guess. I've got a conference call at nine, and I need to get ready for it." He drops his hand off the knob of the basement door and comes to hold me. The Bainbridges are rolling with laughter, and the crazy music from the TV is *so* loud. It only takes a moment before we are both laughing, too. "Kiss me," Jackson says. "This is crazy. I'll see you in bed."

We part, and I grab a bottle of water before heading upstairs. With a quiet "good night," I leave our guests to the kitten on the screen doing something with a vacuum cleaner. At the top of the stairs I knock then look into Bryan's room. He's lying on the bed, looking at his phone, wearing his earbuds.

"Hey Mom," he says as he looks up and removes one of the buds. "You going to bed?"

"Yeah. In a bit. No homework?"

"I'll get to it in a minute."

"Talking to Zoe?"

He shrugs and then looks back at his phone. "Some. Good night." Then, as I pull back and the door begins to close, he says, "Mom?"

"Yes?"

"How long are they staying?"

"This week. Why?" I'm sure they're bothering him, too.

"Just wondering. Good night."

This time I pull the door shut. Then stepping down the hall, I open the door to Savannah's tower. Her dormer room has its own short set of stairs leading up to it. I step up on the first couple and call her name.

She steps out of her bathroom wearing a long T-shirt. Her hair is wet, and it looks like she just got out of the shower. "Yeah?"

"Just wanted to let you know we're back." I move to walk on up the stairs, but she holds up her phone.

"I'm on the phone. Did you need something?"

"No, not really. Who you talking to?"

"Just a friend. So you don't need anything?"

"Nope. Okay, good night." Turning I jog down the steps, close her door, and pull my own phone out of my pocket. Everything got so busy last night that I still haven't told Susan the big, horrible finale to the wedding saga. "Hey, Susan," I say as she picks up. "So you can talk?"

"Yep, I'm all set. Susie Mae is in her room. I have my jammies on, and Silas and I already talked tonight."

I get undressed with my phone on speaker. "Any news on the breakup?"

"With Silas?"

"Of course with Silas. What other breakup would I be asking about?"

"I don't know. He's just so sweet. He says he misses me. I kind of miss him."

Because I'm pulling a sweatshirt over my head, I come out the other side not having said anything rude to my friend, who is acting like a teenager. No, worse than a teenager. Speaking her new language I say, "Whatever."

I can practically hear her eye roll over the phone. "Anyway,

I'm dying to hear about the wedding—well, the reception. What was in the fancy pink envelope?"

I flop on the bed and leave the phone on speaker. Easier to tell my story that way. "Okay. Remember, there are over a hundred basically uninvited guests from Hillbilly Hank's nursing home performances—a lot of old people ready for some good church basement reception food. Except there was no food. There were no tables or chairs set up, nothing but the wedding cake still in its bakery box. The big, fancy, pink envelope had Hank and Shelby's names on the front in pretty script, but since it wasn't sealed, and since the newlyweds were out riding around in a convertible and taking pictures, and in our official capacity as daughters-in-law—we opened it."

Susan laughs. "I've imagined and imagined what it could be."

"It was a beautiful card saying, 'Congratulations on your wedding day.' Under the printed message inside it was signed 'Best Wishes,' but with no name. There was a note inside, though." I take a sip of water and recite the note, not from memory but from the picture I took of it.

"'Dear Hank and Shelby, We want to wish you well on your special day, but you see, we just can't. Etta was and still is one of us. She cooked and prayed and worked alongside us for over thirty years. We think the absolute world of her and always will. She did not deserve what you two did to her, and you do not deserve our blessing of your marriage. That is what our cooking and serving on this day would be—a blessing. We also feel we've already given you our gift. The gift of silence. You see, most of us knew what you were doing to our beloved Etta and yet we kept quiet. Maybe we shouldn't have, but we did. So, you're welcome. We do hate if this causes a problem for your family, as they are most likely the only people in attendance today. We know most of the community will not be there.' Then it was signed The Ladies. But there was a P.S.: 'We do want to say if you'd asked we would've told you our plan for this afternoon, however you just assumed a reception was your due.'"

"Oh my goodness! I'd say that is unbelievable, but with how the ladies in town have been acting towards me for getting a divorce, well… But it's so…I don't know. Kind of perfect!"

"Isn't it? Abigail and I were both in shock. Before we could come up with what to do, Jackson, Emerson, Colt, and Phoenix found us. We just handed them the note. By that time the noise level was deafening in that concrete basement. The old folks were scraping out the metal chairs to sit down on. Abigail opened the refrigerator, and I tell you what, that was the cleanest church refrigerator I've ever seen. Same with the freezer. Reminded me of that line in *How the Grinch Stole Christmas!* about how there wasn't a speck of food even for a mouse left in the house. Etta's sons stood looking at each other. Phoenix read the note and then went to sit on the corner of the counter, closed her eyes, and proceeded to ignore us."

Susan hums in her throat. "Didn't she steal some judge from his wife? Maybe it was all a bit too close to home."

"That's pretty much what the rest of us were thinking. Anyway, the guys all stared at each other for a minute before we heard clapping and realized the happy couple was on their way down."

She breaks into a fresh fit of giggles. "This is just too much! Carolina, you need to tell all this to Leif and Tyler for their production company. What did y'all do next?"

"Well, finally Emerson pointed to the cake box. 'Guess we could serve that?' he said.

"Abigail came alongside me and put her arm through mine. She held her head up and said, 'You can. I'm not, and I have a feeling Carolina agrees with me. I don't see any paper plates or disposable forks, and I've reached my limit on what I'll do for your father. There's nothing to drink. It would take a good half hour to make coffee in that big urn *if* they've even left any coffee. The women of this church decided to take a stand, and I'm with them. Carolina, what do you say?'"

Susan jumps in and yells, "Good for her!" Then, after a bit, she adds, "So… what *did* you say? Tell me you didn't serve that cake."

"Come on! You know I did. But I didn't make coffee and I made the guys wash all the forks and saucers. Abigail ended up helping, too. I admired what she was saying, but the cake was just sitting there and, well, it was embarrassing enough. Believe me, Hank and Shelby both got earfuls from all those old folks who were counting on some good church-lady cooking and ended up with a tiny square of cake." I sniff. "It wasn't all that good anyway."

"I know you're right, but man… I wish you'd held out with Abigail. It's still a good story, though."

"Yeah, we couldn't get out of there fast enough. Jackson and the kids and I packed up and left that afternoon for Pigeon Forge. Got a hotel with a heated swimming pool and a nice restaurant. Emerson and his family headed toward home at about the same time. One good thing came out of it: despite the diva girls thing, I ended up liking Emerson and Abigail more than I ever thought I could. Their girls can be insufferable, but I'm not holding anybody responsible for the actions of snotty teenagers." I think of Savannah's histrionics in the Kentucky chapel. "Well, not too much."

"What about Colt and Phoenix?"

"I don't know. She disappeared after the cake cutting, and I didn't see her until we all got back to Georgia. She actually stopped in the shop yesterday and asked about renting a room for the holidays. So I'll be talking to her again soon, I guess."

Now that my story is over, I cozy up to one of our biggest sham pillows and wrap my arms around it.

"Speaking of the B&B, how's it going with the Bainbridges?" Susan asks.

"Ugh," I can't help saying. "Jackson finally got to meet Wayne tonight. He believes me now. Get this, they actually had reservations for a hotel, but Missus told them we need the business."

Susan sighs. "Cross your fingers that Peter comes home soon. She gets kind of crazy when he's gone, but before now we always had FM to reign her in."

I think fondly of FM, Missus' other and better half who has gone on ahead to his reward. I miss his no-nonsense attitude, especially when it came to Missus. "Aw, I hadn't thought about that. Maybe I'll text Peter again. Well, I'm going to get in the shower and go to bed now that you know the whole story about the wedding."

"Seriously, that needs to show up in a movie." There's one of those end-of-the-call lulls before Susan gasps and then blurts, "Oh, shoot! Carolina, I gotta go."

"Sure. Tell Silas I said hi," I say, half joking, but she responds, "Okay," as she hangs up. I'm left staring at the phone in my hand.

She's not going to break up with him. I think she feels more for him than she thinks, but that's between them. I get off the bed as a blast of laughter comes from downstairs.

I still can't believe Wayne Bainbridge is sitting on my couch in a shorty robe.

Now *that* needs to be in a movie.

CHAPTER 13

Shannon leans on her elbows across the shop counter. "I just can't imagine having them sitting in my living room."

Patty raises her eyebrows and adds, "Especially in their robes." She shudders and then swallows. So far she's held her breakfast of dry toast down, but we probably shouldn't push it with talk of Wayne Bainbridge's shorty robe.

Shannon wrinkles her nose. "Do a lot of guests do that? I mean watch your television and stuff. That just feels so weird to me."

"No, they don't. I was worried about that at first, but most are out until later. They have dinner in Canton or Dalton. They might come in and visit for a minute. Or they sit on the deck or porch, but no, most do not take over our living room."

Patty shrugs. "I guess with Wayne and Retta being from here they don't want to go out and sightsee."

"It's still weird," Shannon says. She stands and comes out from behind the counter. "I've got another order for that winery to get to. They're turning into great customers." She walks back to her work area and begins moving tubs of flowers.

"Momma will be looking for me," Patty says, but she doesn't move from her position against the outside of the counter.

So I ask, "How's the house coming along? When are you moving in?"

"Soon."

"Aren't you excited?" I step closer to her and rub her upper arm.

Her lip trembles. "Not really. A whole house to take care of?" She swallows again and waits a bit. "And a baby?"

"It has all happened pretty fast," I say.

Between you and me, I was hoping Patty and Andy would have more time together before they got pregnant. Andy and Gertie both love Patty, but they might just love her right into a nervous breakdown.

I give her a full smile. "But you'll be just fine. I'll help in any way I can, you know that. Besides, you'll have Susan just down the street. She's real excited to have you for a neighbor."

Patty perks up a bit. "Oh. Miss Susan. She *is* good with things, isn't she?" Then she actually smiles. "You think she'll help me? With the house and such?"

"Absolutely. You don't need to worry about all this. Just try and get to feeling better. Your anxiety sure isn't helping your stomach settle down."

"I do feel better now. Thanks, Carolina. Okay. I'm going to Momma's. I've been doing the shipping for Andy's Place, but it's getting kind of out of control. Who knew people would buy all this junk over the internet? And from all over the place?"

"Your husband, that's who. I'm glad it's going so well. Tell Andy and your momma I said hi."

She blushes and looks down, then strolls out.

The door is barely closed before I whirl around and dash back to Shannon. "So? Are you?"

She is bent over a pail of pine branches in a big, black bucket, and from that position she sighs. Loudly. Then she unbends and sighs again. "I didn't get a test. Just couldn't do it."

"Why?"

Shrugging, she clips pieces of pine from the bigger branch. "Was there someone you knew in the store?"

"No."

"Do you not need one anymore? Is it that now you know you're *not* pregnant?"

"No."

"Then…?" I take a breath, pick up a piece of the greenery, and lift it to smell. From behind the pine needles, I sneak a closer look at her. She's working her mouth, almost like when Patty was trying to keep her stomach from unloading earlier, but then she blinks to keep tears at bay.

"It's just not supposed to be like this. I don't want to know until Peter is here to know with me." She looks up at me, her mouth tight and her chin set.

"But… but…" I give up. "I get it. Totally get it, but what if he doesn't come back soon?"

"I'll deal with that when I have to. Right now, I'm just ignoring it. All of it. Until Peter comes home."

"Okay."

She pushes some buttons on her phone, which makes Christmas music fill the shop from the speaker up front. "I really have to get back to work, Carolina." She smiles at me. "I'm fine, really. It's good to be busy."

To the tune of "Walking in a Winter Wonderland," I walk to the front and look out on the gray December day.

Sure am glad I didn't tell her about the text I got from Peter last night.

"See you later," I say and then step onto the sidewalk. The gray morning looks to turn into a gray afternoon as I leave Blooming Books to head down toward Gertie's. Shannon left to make her flower delivery to the winery, but Bonnie arrived thirty minutes ago. She'd gone to some financial brunch thing with her husband, so I came in early. Things being slow, she told me to go do my errands and get something for lunch. Why I keep forgetting (refusing is more like it) to pack myself a lunch is beyond me, but here I am again. Hey, I might just go home and eat with Jackson. However, the way we keep getting on each other's nerves lately, maybe that's not such a good idea.

As I pass Ruby's I look inside, but there's no one I want to pop in and say hi to. There's a new little store that's opening just in time for the parade on Saturday, though, so I stop to look in the window. It's called a pop-up shop. I've heard about them, but I don't think I've ever been in one.

"Hey! Not much to see yet," a voice I recognize says as it comes up behind me. Oh, no. Susan's mother-in-law. The one who moved up into the big house in Laurel Cover practically as soon as she moved out.

I paste on the brightest smile I can muster before turning around. "Hi, Rachel." Then I see she has a set of keys in her hand and is walking straight for the door. "This is yours?"

"Yes. With Grant in school and busy with his golfing, I needed something to do. So, I bought the building." She opens the door and pushes inside.

"You bought the building? The whole building?"

She motions for me to come in, so I follow her inside.

"Why not?" she says, clearly taking offense at my tone. "You have a problem with an outsider owning property in Chancey? Or maybe you don't think women can own buildings?"

"No. No, not at all. I just didn't know it was for sale or..."

"Or you would've bought it? You think I jumped the line?"

"No! I just—oh, nothing." I fling around to go right back out the door. This woman is an argument on legs. But... I stop and instead of reaching for the doorknob, I put my hand in my jacket pocket and step toward Griffin's mother. "So, what are you going to do with it? I heard it's called a pop-up shop, but what's that mean exactly?" I've been talked down to by better people than her, and I really do want to know what's going to be here.

"Like you said, it's going to be a pop-up shop. People can rent the space for thirty days at a time to sell stuff. My daughter runs a couple for me down in Atlanta and one in Charlotte. This is my first time to do one in such a rural location, but I figured why not try? I already have it booked for this month and for January."

Trying to come up with how to ask without starting the accusations again, I'm quiet as I look around at the empty space. It's much smaller than our shop and not as nice. We have an antique tin tile ceiling and lots of old wood molding, which Gertie had painted white. Our window looks like it was meant for a display with a deep ledge and tall and wide glass panes. This looks more like it was an office. The front window and door are nothing special. The floor is old linoleum, and up above is a cheap-looking drop ceiling.

Rachel says, "Not much to look at now. I have the cleaners that Griffin uses in our house coming this afternoon, then the first store will move in tomorrow." I've described her as looking like a hanging judge. She's squat and heavy with heavy dark hair, heavy dark eyebrows, and heavy dark lipstick. I mean, the lipstick looks heavy the way her mouth is usually turned down. However, as she stares at me it turns up into a, a smile? "Don't you want to know what the first shop is?" she asks.

She knows that's the only reason I'm still here. And since it is the only reason I'm still here… "Sure. What is it?"

Her eyes narrow, and she slowly shakes her head. "No, no, no. Only a handful of people will be allowed to know, and you just aren't on that list. You'll have to come see tomorrow." She turns her back to me with an authoritative goodbye.

I jerk open the door and sail through. I try to slam it on my way out, but it's not a good, heavy, old-fashioned door like the one at Blooming Books. It's lightweight glass surrounded by an aluminum frame, which settles closed with an air of disappointment.

All my days. Rachel Lyles in Downtown Chancey. Susan is going to be thrilled.

"So I ordered moonshine for Emerson and Abigail and also for your dad and Shelby for Christmas," I say to Jackson, who might as well be on the phone with me in South Georgia and not sitting in front of me for all the attention I'm getting. "What do you think about Colt and Phoenix?" Then I wait. Any minute now, the question mark will register in his brain, and he'll look up at me.

"What?" Then he grimaces. "I'm sorry. What are we talking about?"

I'm propped against the washing machine across from where he's set up a long table to act as his desk. He's got another of the long, plastic tables holding plans, so he's taking up most of the main room of our basement. The washer and dryer are off to the side of the stairs, so Jackson left a small walkway around the end of the tables. All of Retta and Wayne's junk is stacked in what used to be Will's bedroom.

"We're talking about Christmas presents for our families. The pumpkin pie moonshine we took to Kentucky was so popular we decided to send it as gifts, remember?"

"Oh yeah, that's right." He sits blinking at me, and I know what he's trying to tell me.

I push away from the washer. "I'll let you get back to work. Speaking of work, though, I think I found Savannah a new job."

But when I turn at the bottom step to pause and tell him, he's bent back over his laptop.

Whatever.

At the top of the stairs I start to close the door hard and remind him I left, but he probably wouldn't even hear it. The house is quiet. The kids are still at after-school activities. The Bainbridges are somewhere that is *not* here, and that's all I need to know. Laney was here earlier doing books for the B&B, but I only passed her in the driveway. The only noise is the bubbling of the crockpot where I have tortilla soup cooking. I could vacuum and dust, but, well, I don't want to. We're going to get our tree Saturday, so I have two more days to clean before decorations start going up. Why hurry?

Oh, I know what I'll do. In the living room I sit on the couch and look on the shelf underneath one of the end tables for a book I put there last month. It came into the shop, and I brought it home to wait for Christmas.

And now it's Christmas.

It's a hardback by Anne Perry. She writes Victorian mystery novels, which are very popular, but I've only read her Christmas books and of those I've only read a couple. I like having a Christmas book to read during December, and this is perfect—a mystery set in Victorian England at Christmastime.

For a minute I debate making a half pot of coffee—or maybe a cup of tea, it is an English novel after all. No. I'm not letting anything get in the way of a few minutes of peace and quiet. However… now that I've thought of a cup of tea, it would be perfect. I get up to make that, and just as I'm coming back into the living room I start kicking myself.

A car is pulling across the tracks and up to the house, and it's not just any car. This car contains Missus. Missus, who's been to Will and Anna's. I look at my pretty book with its lovely Christmas cover and take a careful sip of my tea, steeling myself for the tirade that's marching my way. But something is strange. I'm actually not that disappointed. I really want to know what Missus thinks of the cabin, and I have news to share about the pop-up shop and Savannah's possible new job. Plus, Missus hasn't been filled in on Hillbilly Hank's wedding fiasco, and, well, I might as well admit it…

Chancey's just about ruint me. I'd rather chat than read.

I open the door to greet my guest. "Missus. Come in. I just made a cup of tea. Can I get you one?"

"Tea? Since when do you drink hot tea?" Missus has on a light blue sweater and navy slacks. She's wearing a dark red and blue plaid shawl and gloves in the same dark red. Her hair is disheveled, which she must sense, as she immediately steps to a mirror hanging at the bottom of the stairs next to the coatrack. "This new hairdo is impossible. Why that woman can't understand I want it to stay in place all week is beyond me. I give her permission to use hair spray." She tips her head to catch my eye in the reflection. "These young hair stylists act like I'm asking them to spray it with Agent Orange." In a high-pitched voice, she mimics, "Oh, but we want some movement in your hair." As her voice drops an octave, she explodes, "If I wanted movement, I'd just let it grow down to my be-hind like some hippy!"

She flips around at me. "Look at this. Look at it. I'm going back to Beulah Land and my weekly appointment. They know how to style hair so I don't have to think about it for days! You get a perm once every six weeks, show up for a shampoo and set once a week, and you never have to think about your hair again." Then she marches past me into the kitchen. "Not that you do much thinking about your hair anyway."

Wow. How good is reading my book looking now?

I follow her into the kitchen, but just inside she's standing still, bent toward the basement door. "I hear voices. God help us all, Carolina, *who* do you have living in your basement now?"

"No one. Jackson is working from home this month. Cup of tea?"

"I suppose. No, no tea. A glass of water. I'm supposed to be drinking more water."

"Okay. Here you go," I say handing her an empty glass.

"So it's self-serve now." She puts the glass up to the ice dispenser on the refrigerator. "Jackson could work somewhere else if the children move back here, correct?"

I whisper, "That's what *I* said, but Jackson said they need to be on their own." We move into the living room. She sits in a chair, and I settle on the end of the couch next to her. This way we can talk and not disturb Jackson. Right. More like not be heard by Jackson.

Dismissively she lets her shawl fall away from her shoulders. Just as dismissively she sniffs and say, "Jackson is a man. That cracker box is a sure recipe for divorce. Living on top of each other—and with a baby! They have no idea what they are doing." She lifts one shoulder in a half shrug. "We have no choice. What do you propose?"

"Propose? I didn't get any further than them moving back here. I have to listen to Jackson. He is my husband, and, well, he *is* going to be working here every day."

"Of course, Carolina, put the burden on me since I'm a widow and have all the freedom in the world."

"I didn't mean that!" I set my cup down hard, and tea splashes over the side onto the saucer. "I'm just saying they can't move here, so there's nothing we can do."

"Of course there's *something* we can do." Then her eyes lose focus, and she sits back. "However, forbidding them to live in that place we can cross off the to-do list. That did not go over well earlier today."

"Oh, I'm shocked." Carefully pouring the spilled tea back into my cup, I roll my eyes where she can't see. "I'm just afraid they're going to get settled there and think it's fine."

"Exactly!" she says, eyes regaining enough focus to pierce me. "And we both know it's *not fine*. I want to talk to the lady they are renting from. If she decides to sell…" Missus' cocked eyebrow has an air of menace, especially after she adds a smile that is a touch on the evil side. She leans forward to touch my knee. "But first, let's get this Christmas parade behind us. We want lots of happy children and parents on Saturday, right?"

I honestly don't think she sees the disconnect in her last few statements.

Maybe it's a lack of hair spray.

Chapter 15

Complaints about the days of clouds have been replaced with talk of freezing to death. Southerners are fond of thinking we're freezing to death. Not that the temperatures are actually below freezing, but it sure feels like it. I've not left the house without a coat in three days.

"Why isn't there any warmth in all that sunshine?" Laney says as she blasts into Ruby's on Saturday morning. Downtown Chancey is buzzing with excitement over its first annual Christmas Parade.

From where she's pouring coffee Libby apparently thinks Laney wants an answer. "Without cloud cover, heat accumulated during the day dissipates, making the nights colder. Mostly, however, it's the angle of the sun." She circulates, filling cups as she continues. "I think it's also a problem that we're here in the mountains, and it takes forever for the sun to get up over them."

Laney has stopped near the door and with a shake of her head says, "Whatever. All I know is those girls out there that aren't wearing tights or pantyhose are going to freeze their rear ends off." She comes over to where I'm monitoring the sign-in table. I'm supposed to be at the beginning of the parade route up on the hill by the church, but there was nowhere for me to be inside due to the church hosting Breakfast with Santa later, so I made an executive decision to park myself at Ruby's.

At least until Missus finds me.

Needless to say, I agree with Laney's assessment of the girls' rear ends. "I tried to talk Savannah into wearing her practice pants, but she refused." Then I tack on the mantra I've spouted all morning as folks complained about the cold, "At least it's not raining."

"Practice pants?" Laney is horrified. "It is *so* obvious you were never a cheerleader that it hurts sometimes. There are such things as cheerleading *standards*."

"Well, you're obviously wearing your fur on your float, right?"

"And cover my dress? Not in a million years. There are a blue million reasons to elect me as mayor, but there will be *some* voting on looks alone." She smiles and winks. "And leg. Lots of leg. I believe the public will respond to a candidate who dresses sedately during work hours, but knows how to shine on stage."

Ruby saunters out to my table and, leaning back on one hip, cocks her head at Laney. "Then let's see it. Show us this vote-getting dress."

Laney, snug in her fur coat, which she says is fake but no one believes that, smiles with wide eyes bathed in innocence. "Should I? The effect from the float promises to have such impact. Well, okay," she says, licking her lips and tossing her head of short, but teased to the sky hair.

Then the door bangs open and Jenna shouts, "Mom! Where are my practice pants? Everyone else is wearing them."

Laney turns around. "No one is wearing them, sweetie. They look bulky and, no." Then her voice drops. "And why do you have your brother?"

Jenna, the cheerleader twin, has on her black and gold outfit with the short skirt. She's wearing her letter jacket, and tucked into it is her six-month-old little brother. Cayden is an armful of adorableness, but he's not being adorable right now. Right now he's working up to a fit. Jenna is bouncing him, but he's tired of that. Now that he's seen his mother, he is definitely done. He's working up a squall to go with the squirming.

"Grandma had to help with the church's float, so she told me to take him. Dad is trying to get all the dealership cars figured out, something about one not having any gas, and Angie is too busy in the food truck. Here." She dumps him into her mother's arms then takes a step back, both hands now firmly placed on her hips. "Did you really not bring my practice pants? I don't have time to go all the way home. I'm going to freeze to death."

Laney hustles out the door with her daughter, holding her son away from her coat and dress, and talking rapidly. The door closes, and in the sudden quiet Ruby laughs. "Bet she's filling Miss Jenna in on all those cheerleading standards." She sits down beside me. "Can't you talk her out of running for mayor? We're going to have to put up with this kind of shenanigans for the whole next year."

"Yeah, right. No, she doesn't listen to anyone, not even me. Besides, we know Jed will run a peaceful race. That'll calm things down, right?"

Ruby blinks at me, then looks down at my spread-out papers. "Let me see the lineup."

I hand one to her with all my cross-outs and corrections.

After a quick look, Ruby holds it up. "What's this one here? Last one before the band and Santa Claus?"

Leaning to look at my own handwriting, I say, "Um, business float? Something Missus is taking care of. Speaking of which, I can't believe she's not here breathing down my neck."

Ruby laughs again. "You really don't know."

"Don't know what?"

"Missus ain't here because she's there." She points to the float position she just asked about.

"She's lining up the floats?"

Ruby rolls her eyes at me. "Not hardly." Then she stands up, pushing with both hands on the table. "Never mind. You just go on out and enjoy the parade. Shouldn't it be about ready to start?"

With a glance at the clock, I jump. "Yes, it is." I pull on my big coat and gather my notebooks. I have to dodge the lawn chairs lining the sidewalk as I dash down it. Alex Carrera's food truck is set up near the gazebo. The smell of coffee and hot chocolate makes me want to make a detour, but that'll have to come later. The police cars are lined up in front of the library where they will start the parade moving with their lights and sirens. I'm not cold yet, so I'm enjoying the bright blue sky and colorful huddles of coats and scarves. We've had a wonderful turnout, and I'm excited to see it all come together.

I can't help but smirk when, upon turning the corner, I see the cheerleaders all wearing practice pants. I also can't help mentioning it to my daughter in passing. "I see you *did* bring your pants."

She ignores me, and I hustle on. Jackson and I are meeting in the church parking lot. He's been helping get the sports teams on their flatbeds, and the colorful jerseys crammed together say he's done his job. I grab his arm and kiss his cheek. "Ready to go to Missus' porch party?"

His eyebrows jump. "You still want to go?"

"Yeah, she's serving shrimp and grits along with mimosas. It's the hottest ticket in town. Don't you want to go?"

Then I recognize the look he's giving me as the same one Ruby gave me a few minutes ago. "What?"

"I thought you'd've heard." He sighs and gives me half a smile. "Missus *is* running for mayor."

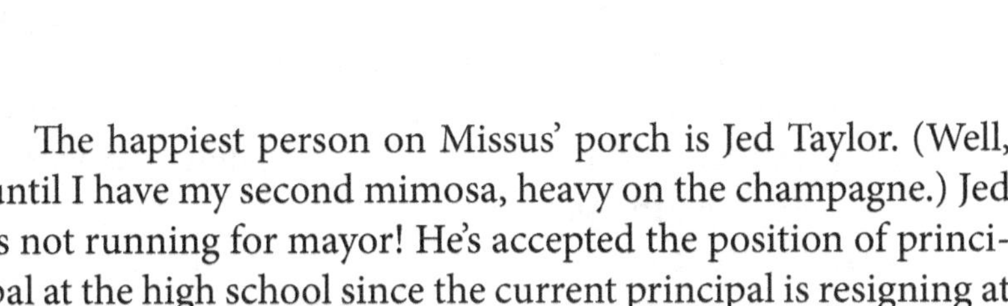

Chapter 16

The happiest person on Missus' porch is Jed Taylor. (Well, until I have my second mimosa, heavy on the champagne.) Jed is not running for mayor! He's accepted the position of principal at the high school since the current principal is resigning at the end of the year. Not only is he not running for mayor, but he's quitting effective January first. His term as mayor is over at the end of this year. That means it's a special election set for the end of next month. I can't help but believe Missus set this whole thing up, but who knows?

Despite everything, if you think I'm missing free shrimp and grits and mimosas, you don't really know me. When the first siren blasts and the parade begins to move, I tuck my arm in Jackson's and hurry down the sidewalks to Missus' front porch.

"Jackson! Carolina!" Folks wave as we turn up the walkway to her big, antebellum house with its wrap-around porch. The front railing is lined with people, including Jed and his wife, Betty. Jackson filled me in on Jed's new job on our walk down here, so we make our way to them to say congratulations.

Betty is scolding one of their five children as we walk up. This one looks to be in late elementary school. She's pleading to be let loose to run around with her friends, one of whom is seated beside her. Finally with a big wave of his arm, Jed decrees, "Go! Run around." The girls don't hesitate but leap out of their seats and dash off the porch.

Jed grins up at us, face relaxed and mood expansive. He waves his arm again. "Have a seat. These two have just been vacated. Servers will be around in a bit. Missus hired a catering service from Alpharetta." He leans forward, looking down the street. "Look! Here it comes."

Flashing blue and red lights whirl and the sirens make me dizzy, but it's a perfect start to our first ever Christmas parade. The officers throw hard candy from the windows of squad cars, and as kids scurry in the streets picking it up I have a brief moment of concern. Nothing ruins a first annual Christmas parade like a kid getting run over.

However, there is nothing to really worry about as the parents and officers are watching, and with the help of that first mimosa, I begin to relax. Sunshine glints off the small Shriner cars, and everyone laughs along with the candy-munching kids everywhere. The sound of the middle school band coming fills the air left empty as the sirens move around the far corner of Main Street. The route takes the parade around the block, behind the line of stores on Main Street, then turns back to the church and the parking lot there for dispersal.

We can't help but laugh as the middle school band plays the chorus of "Jingle Bells" over and over and over.

"Is that all they learned for the parade?" Jackson asks.

"Apparently," I nod.

We quickly pick out Bryan on the flatbed trailer with all the baseball teams on it. He and his friends are mostly shoving each other and roughhousing instead of waving at the crowd. Their mouths look suspiciously full. Weren't they supposed to be throwing out Tootsie Rolls?

Next are the younger cheerleaders on another flatbed. They wave and throw out candy as if it were pieces of gold. They have big bows in their hair, pink cheeks from the cold, and wide smiles. They are having the time of their lives.

Then the voices take on a bit of maturity as the high school cheerleaders march toward us, not a single one wearing pants. There's lots of leg, most of it bare. Maybe that was why they seem to have so much energy. They stop to do a cheer right in front of the porch and leave us echoing their calls for the team to "Go, Go, Go!" They also leave me beaming for Shannon at the compliments on the corsages the girls are wearing.

So Laney was right. There are cheerleader standards. Speaking of Laney—speaking of standards—after a little break in the parade her float appears.

Betty whistles. "Would you look at that!"

A smaller flatbed than the ones loaded with youngsters, hers is loaded with clouds. Fake clouds—along the edges of the trailer are big mounds of what looked like pillow stuffing. It's secured with roping that looks like heavy-duty Christmas tree tinsel. In the middle of the cloud sits a white convertible. The chrome reflecting the sunshine looks like more tinsel, and on the top of the back seat of the car (since becoming friends with Laney and Shaw, I've found out it comes in handy owning a dealership) sprawls Laney, sans fur coat. Her silver sequin dress and silver sequin heels blaze in the sunlight, and she looks like an angel being driven straight down from heaven. An angel not showing quite as much leg as the cheerleaders, but more than most angels you think of.

Big signs advertising that she's running for Mayor are blinding, seeing as they're edged in bright lights and the words are written in what has to be chrome paint. (Again, handy to own a dealership with a repair shop.) She's smiling and waving, right up until she spots me, champagne glass in hand, on Missus' porch. She gives me a stern glare, then spreads it to the rest of my fellow partiers. "Uh oh," I whisper to Jackson. "Looks like she's making a list and checking it twice."

I did notice, as her float moves on by, a pile of black and gold practice pants crammed into the corner of her float. Does Laney always get her way? I mean, of course the answer to that is yes. But was it by bribe this time, or physical violence or...

Next is the Piggly Wiggly float crammed full of people. Wayne has the place of prominence, sitting in the middle on a big, shaky stack of pallets. From them he's shouting at me.

"Carolina! Carolina! Take our picture!"

As he teeters on his grocery store throne, he preens for me, so I take some pictures. However, pieces of paper drift in the air around the float and in its path, obscuring the view.

"What is all that trash?" Jed asks. "Hope they know they're coming back to clean that up. Law, I can't wait until all I have to do it corral a bunch of teenagers."

"It's coupons," I explain. "Wayne said he'd already paid for the trailer and he didn't have enough budget left to throw away perfectly good candy, so he printed up a bunch of coupons. Not even very good ones."

Betty grunts, then pulls her head back to spout, "You mean the one person who could buy candy at wholesale is the one not giving it out?" She smacks her husband's arm. "You better follow up on making them clean all that up. Look at the mess, and cheating our kids out of candy to boot!" I'd noticed her younger kids were on the lawn in front of us. She yells at them. "Don't pick those up. We don't want his coupons!"

She leans back with a big smile. "I'm going to love not being the mayor's wife."

We all laugh, but then I pick up the sound of the high school marching band. There is a line of small floats going by, most from local businesses. However, the one I want to see is still out of sight. A group of people in jeeps roll by, big flags on them, tinsel wrapped around every bar. The people riding are decked out in tacky Christmas sweaters.

Then, after a group of horse riders, again decked out in

tinsel and sweaters, Missus' float comes into view. Pulled by a bright green tractor, all I can see at first is some kind of white structure built on the trailer. Then, as she gets in front of her house we can see it is the Chancey gazebo. I actually look up to see if ours in the park is still there. Of course this one is much smaller, but it's decorated exactly like the big one: magnolia wreaths, Missus Blue ribbons, lots of little white lights. Seated in the middle of the gazebo is Missus. No shock there, but all around her and even on her lap are small children. Then my eyes are drawn to the adults sitting around the edge of the float. It's Athena and her husband with the other young couples from the new development. A sign at the back of the float carries what I imagine is Missus' campaign slogan: "Chancey isn't just my home. It's my life." A young man on each side of the gazebo holds up a smaller sign, saying, "Missus for Mayor." It couldn't be more different from Laney's if she was wearing a choir robe and singing from a hymnal.

Jed nudges me and winks. "She's good, isn't she?"

Luckily the band launches into an even jollier "Here Comes Santa Claus" and I don't have to answer. By the time the fire truck rolls by with Santa Claus on top, throwing out small candy canes, I'm ready to take a nap.

Well, after some shrimp and grits, of course.

CHAPTER 17

"Follow me," Jackson says as we come to the end of the buffet table in Missus' dining room. He doesn't look around, just walks through the swinging door that leads into her kitchen. It's full of servers and cooks, but no one stops us—especially since my husband looks like he knows right where he's headed with a full plate in one hand and a topped-off mimosa in the other.

Walking behind him, I smile and thank the workers. Missus has a big, high-ceilinged, old-fashioned kitchen. The appliances are new and top of the line, though. FM did most of the cooking, and he kept it up to date. There's a catch in my throat thinking of how much fun he had in this room. How much fun he would've had today.

Jackson asks one of the women if she'd open the back door for him, and we walk out into the cold screened-in porch on the back of the house. All along one side is a bench, and he motions for me to sit, but I hesitate and stammer, "Uh, after being outside I was kind of looking forward to being warm?"

"Me too. Sit down, and you'll be warm in just a minute," Jackson says. He hands me his mimosa to hold when I free up one of my hands. Then he squats, and after some fumbling around there's a fan noise, then a push of heat against the backs of my legs.

"There's a heater under there?"

He grins as he sits, and I hand him his drink back. "Yep. FM and I used it when we were out here a couple times doing some project or another." He looks around and takes a moment. "I miss him. He was one in a million." Turning to me, he lifts his glass. "To FM."

"To FM," I say. I lift my glass and sip. "Now let's eat before our food gets cold."

Our moans of how good the food is and the whirring of the heater are the only sounds on the back porch for a bit. We both worked hard all morning and are hungry; plus, the food is magnificent. Rich, buttery grits with cheese and large, fresh shrimp. Pieces of green onion and red pepper add color along with small bits of ham. Tiny biscuits with salty ham and fruit cups laced with mint leaves make for a pretty and delicious plate.

"I thought my working at home would mean we'd get to talk more, but it's almost seemed the opposite," Jackson says as his shoveling of food slacks off.

"I know. Guess we have to work at it more. I keep thinking I'll talk to you later, and then there's always kids or something going on. And having the Bainbridges occupying our living room doesn't help." I straighten and take a deep breath. "Oh, I'm getting full, but this is so good. I'm warm, too. Maybe I'll just take my nap here."

The quiet after the busy, noisy morning is nice. We can hear voices from the kitchen and the house, but they mix with the heater and make a pleasant background. Our heads are leaned back against the screening, and the smell of old house and back porch take over as our food grows cold. My feet are plenty warm. As a matter of fact, they're beginning to feel sweaty. I stick them out away from the heater and cross them at the ankle.

A shout from behind us causes us both to sit up and look

over our shoulders, but there's nothing to see. Then Jackson smiles. "From the church. I bet Santa just arrived for breakfast."

"Oh. You're right." Leaning back again, I snuggle closer to him as he puts his empty plate on the floor to join mine. "I'm so glad our kids are too old for that."

"But next year we'll have a one-year old granddaughter who will be right there. Hard to imagine, isn't it?"

"So hard. Oh! Oh, yeah—" Now I'm awake. "You know Missus went up to Will and Anna's, right?"

"Oh, I forgot." He huffs. "What did she say?"

"She says they have to be moved out of there. That tight quarters like that are a sure recipe for divorce. That Anna will be too isolated and that driveway isn't safe. She…"

He grabs my thigh and squeezes it. "Guess I should've asked what did you say back to her? Could've guessed she'd say all that."

"Well, you know I pretty much agree with her."

He pulls away to look at me. "Still? After seeing how cozy they were the other night? After we talked about them being adults?"

"Yeah. I mean, I guess."

He throws up his hands. "Whatever. But I want you to know the only way I will consider them moving back into our house is if they ask—*they* ask—*and* if they have a good plan for the future." He looks at me again, this time with a stern eye. "That's the only way, got it?"

"Whatever," I echo him. "So what do you think about Savannah working at Andy's Place?"

Acknowledging my sidetrack maneuver, he nods, then looks away. "All right, I guess. Especially if it'll help Patty. Who knew there was enough shipping for them to hire part-time help? Plus, I like her being in town where you can keep an eye on her. I'm so glad she's not doing that movie. You think she'll ever go back to acting?"

"I do sometimes, then other times I have no idea what she'll end up doing." I ply my arm underneath his and snuggle close again, but my brain is working hard, telling itself I'm too tired to talk about Peter. I'm just too tired. Besides, there's nothing Jackson can do. It's not our problem at all. We didn't really become friends with him until last year. There's no way he should think he can count on me. I don't want to be his sounding board. Not at...

My husband murmurs, "Whatcha thinking about?"

Immediately I release the tension in my arm and attempt to let it roll off me. Not only was my mind going a mile a minute, my whole body had tensed. Jackson knows me well, and now my mind searches for something to tell him. There's no need to bring Peter into this nice moment. We seem to have so few nice moments together these days. I blurt out, "Just the shop and getting ready for Christmas. The kids are on board for getting the tree tonight. Even Will and Anna."

"Oh" is all he says. Again it's quiet, but this time it's not peaceful. Wait, I know why *I'm* agitated, but why is he? "What are you thinking about?"

His usual "nothing" doesn't come, and I think we're waiting each other out. That's how it feels, but that's just not like my husband. He says what's on his mind when there's something on his mind. Is it his job? His dad? The kids? Us? Now I'm more than fully awake. I scoot away a couple inches to look at him better. "What is it?"

He shakes his head. "Nothing." He stands. "Ready to go? Sounds like the party in there is calming down. Maybe we can get out without talking to Missus if we're lucky."

"Yeah, I'm not usually that lucky." He picks up our plates and steps to the door to open it while I get our glasses. Again I follow him into the kitchen. As the door to the porch closes behind me, I realize our screened-in getaway wasn't really an escape from the house and the people. He wanted to talk in private. But about what?

The worst part about being married to a person who doesn't keep secrets?

When they do.

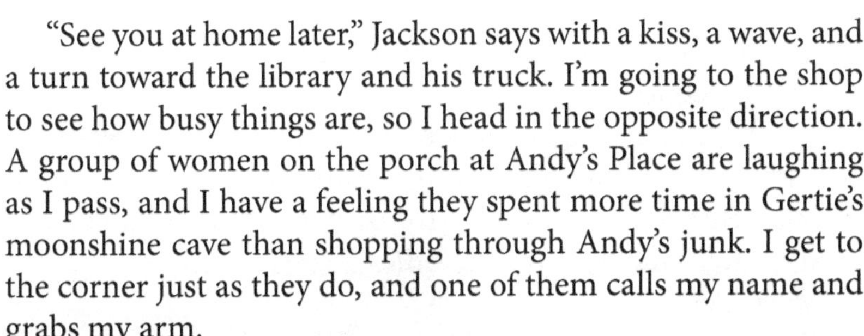

CHAPTER 18

"See you at home later," Jackson says with a kiss, a wave, and a turn toward the library and his truck. I'm going to the shop to see how busy things are, so I head in the opposite direction. A group of women on the porch at Andy's Place are laughing as I pass, and I have a feeling they spent more time in Gertie's moonshine cave than shopping through Andy's junk. I get to the corner just as they do, and one of them calls my name and grabs my arm.

"Cathy? Oh, hi, I didn't…"

Libby's daughter Cathy shushes me with a literal shush and a threatening glare before pulling me around to face her group. "Ladies, this is Carolina. She owns Blooming Books. It's a bookstore and flower shop all together! Isn't that a scream?" She actually screams. And laughs. She's laughing a lot, and her friends are, too. They have most definitely been to the moonshine cave. "Carolina, meet the best Sexy Belles ever!"

Now they are really laughing, as my face can't decide whether to do confused or alarmed. Oh, Sexy Belles! The name of the home lingerie company Cathy works for. So this is what an official Sexy Belle looks like and why I didn't recognize Cathy right off. Cathy is petite and usually dresses like she's still a high school cheerleader. She wears the same type of clothes Savannah does and bounces around a lot. The outfit she has on now looks like it's for a completely different kind of bouncing. Plus, she's wearing a wig.

The women are all in black, red, or hot pink. Those *are* the colors in the magnetic sign on Cathy's car. Some of their hair might be attached the old-fashioned way, but there are definitely more wigs than just Cathy's. And high heels. Another reason to not recognize Cathy: petite is not a good descriptor for her today. She's accented and augmented.

She still has my arm captive, and she pulls me along as we cross the street. "You have to come see our pop-up shop! It's amazing!"

"Oh. I'd been wondering about that. It didn't open when it was supposed to."

A tall woman (of course), with big, blonde hair (of course), and a corset atop her black leather pants and over a hot pink silky blouse (of course) huffs. "The owner tried to back out, but we don't fold that easy, do we, ladies?"

More laughter.

"Welcome to Sexy Belles on Main," the tall, blonde woman says, pulling open the door with a flourish. "Our pop-up shops are so popular. That granite-faced mountain of a woman who owns this place wouldn't know success if it was hiding in her eyebrow!"

I'm pulled in with the ladies and shocked at the difference from earlier this week. Every square inch of retail space is full of wigs, lingerie, makeup, bottles with labels I'm not reading, clothing, and purses, too. The moonshine fuels the Belles' rush to their favorite areas of the store to engage the shoppers. And there are shoppers. More than I would've imagined. I guess this is where the lack of a big display window would come in handy. People passing by can't see you in here. I wonder if they provide dark sunglasses and big hats to hide behind as you leave.

Or I guess you could just buy a wig. I don't have sunglasses or a big hat and I'm not buying a wig, so I just backpedal towards the door and ease myself out. On the sidewalk I can't help but grin and repeat the insult to Rachel Lyles to myself. "Granite-faced mountain of a woman who wouldn't know success if it was hiding in her eyebrow."

Oh, yeah. Susan is definitely going to want to hear that.

Our store is also jumping, so I get to jumping, too. Bonnie and Shannon tell me between customers that they've been busy all morning, except during the parade. Then of course we discuss the parade.

Bonnie points with her chin to a couple of step stools folded up behind the counter. "We used those and got to stay inside and watch through the big window. It was much warmer and much quieter that way." Lowering her voice, she says, "What about those floats! Missus and Laney's?"

With a little laugh, I agree. "They were something for sure." The bell over the door gets my attention. "Oh, hey, Susie Mae. Hon, you could've taken time to go home and change."

"Oh, it's fun to still be in my uniform. Besides, it's warm in here. I thought we were going to turn into icicles out there this morning!" She shoves her backpack under the counter. "What do you need me to do first?"

"Tell me how your aunt got you girls to take off the practice pants for the parade?" I say with a wink.

Her eyes are so big, especially with the fringe of her short, black hair framing her face. They widen even further as she looks at me confused. "How could we march in our pants? They're just for practice. That would just be so weird."

Bonnie laughs as she walks away, and Shannon yells, "Told ya!" from near the flower cooler.

"Shut up," I say just as two women walk in the front door.

Their looks tell me I spoke too loudly. "Sorry. Just a joke." Then I mumble, "What's a joke is that there apparently really are cheerleading standards that everyone knows but me."

I smile and leave the counter area to catch up with the ladies near the front window. "Can I help y'all?"

Their frost over my "shut up" line soon melts, and we talk about the intriguing display of Christmas books Bonnie has put in the front window. They point to two, and I take them out to hold at the counter for them. Being mostly a used bookstore, we have to sell books right from the window. We don't have copies of them on the shelves, but that's even turned into a selling point. People tell me that if they see something they might want in the window they know they have to buy it right that minute. These ladies are from a town nearby. They left their husbands at Andy's Place, wading through the junk rooms, but they figured the men had already headed downstairs to the moonshine cave.

"Excuse me?" I turn to find the ladies behind me. "Is there somewhere to eat other than that food truck?" one asks.

"Sorry, but there's really not. However, the food truck is wonderful. Alex's food is really good."

"But where do we sit to eat it?" she asks, while her friend laughs. "We're too old to sit in the cold holding food on our knees!"

"Thanks anyway," the other one adds, and they wander back into the bookshelves.

When Susie Mae comes to the front carrying books, with a customer in tow, I tell her to stay near the counter and the front door after she rings them up so I can go to the restroom. She's turning out to be a good employee and salesman. Her natural enthusiasm brings a lift to the shop and attracts shoppers.

After the restroom I stop at Shannon's worktable where she's been busy all day keeping the cooler filled plus making arrangements for a couple of the area churches.

"That's pretty," I say as I touch the flowers in the clear plastic container. She's explained to me before that these will then fit inside the individual churches' containers.

"Thanks. In December the churches all want fresh flowers. Not so much the rest of the year. They'll use flowers left from weddings or special occasion orders, or even fake arrangements, but in December they keep me busy."

"Everyone was saying how great the girls' corsages looked. You did an amazing job in such a short time."

"I shouldn't have thrown a fit about it, but thanks. Glad they turned out well." She's sticking tall gladiolas in white and red around the outside of another container and trying out different flowers and greenery around them. She's focused and obviously not in a talkative mood, so I begin walking away.

I'm startled when I hear from behind me, "Have you heard from Peter?"

"Me?" I turn to her. "Peter? Why?"

She flashes her eyes at me, but doesn't actually say 'duh.'

"Have *you* heard from him?" I ask.

"I asked you first." She's stopped work now and is staring at me.

"Yes."

Her sharp intake of breath and immediate watery eyes tell me she hasn't heard from him. Then she clears her throat, blinks quickly to disperse her tears, and asks, "Where is he? When's he coming back?"

"I don't know where he is, but I do think he's coming back."

She just stands there staring at me. "So what did he tell you?"

"He mainly just asked about everything here. Listen, I better go help Susie Mae. Looks like she's got a line." With a smile, I scurry up front. There, now Shannon knows he's okay. I hate myself for being vague, but really, how do I tell her the "everything" he asked about didn't include her?

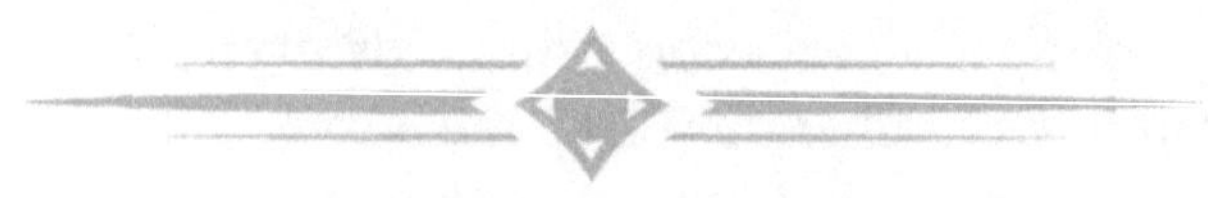

Chapter 19

"Libby was saying something about the lack of cloud cover explaining why it's so cold," I say as we pile out of the van at Greens. We're way out at the edge of the field. "And it may be cold, but look at all those stars."

Savannah glances up, rolls her eyes, and moves on, staring at the ground. Bryan stomps past me, his head intentionally tucked down against his chest. Jackson laughs and puts an arm around my shoulders. "You made them leave their phones at home, so they are not going to look at your stupid stars." He kisses the side of my head. "But I'll look at them with you."

He's still acting strange, but once I got home from work and we had supper, we were loading up to come out here and get our tree so we still haven't talked. I point up ahead. "There's Will and Anna."

Will gives his sister a nudge with his shoulder and his brother gets an arm punch as we catch up with them. Anna is tucked into his other arm, and she just looks tired. "Hey, sweetie," I say with a hug for her.

"Mom made us leave our phones at home," Bryan announces with the righteous indignation only a martyr being burned at the stake—or a teenager—can muster.

Will punches him in the arm again. "Good. Now that I don't

live with you I want to talk to you instead of the top of your head. But that does explain Savannah looking so sour."

"I'm not sour. Just bored. Come on, let's get this over with." She stomps on ahead, and we follow, Will and Anna bringing up the rear. We're still a ways from the well-lit tree lot with the bonfire. There aren't that many cars, but the parking lot is at the end of a big field. The building where the Greens sell their crafts is on the other side of the lot from us, so we have a ways to walk in the dark. As we walk I first see Savannah's head lift, then Bryan's does as well. Jackson gives me a wink, and we snuggle closer.

Our steps slow as soon we are all looking up as much as looking down. The night sky stretches dark and cold. The stars have no moonlight or city lights to compete with. As we near the tree lot and the bonfire, I inhale deeply. "Smells like Christmas!"

Bryan jogs past his sister toward the rows of trees out in the night air. His coat is hanging half off his shoulders, and his feet look too big for his body. Savannah slows a bit, and then she's walking next to me.

With a small smile she says, "It does smell good." Then she strides ahead, but I'm happy. That's all I'll get, a word of agreement and a bit of a smile, but it's more than a mom can expect. Or at least more than a mom *should* expect, because having expectations of teenagers is like buying lottery tickets to fund your 401k.

We walk the lot, and then meander back to the first tree we looked at. Jackson had hidden it to the side so it would still be there even with all the other shoppers milling around. We'd also found a small one for Will and Anna's house, which Will was carrying with us while we walked.

"Let's go sit by the fire while they get the trees," I say to Anna. She's had a wonderful time tonight, but is walking with one hand pressed to her back. She also has a glow on her face that isn't from pregnancy but from following Will and his siblings from tree to tree while wearing a heavy coat.

"Whew," she says as she collapses onto one of the stumps placed around the fire. She unbuttons the top of her coat and takes off her scarf. "I know I'll be cold in a minute, but right now I'm burning up." She looks around. "This place is awesome. Have you ever been in the craft building? Can we go in tonight?"

"Sure. I bet they have stuff for babies."

Her eyes light up. "I'm getting so excited about meeting her. The longer this goes on, the less afraid I am. I just want her to be here!"

We laugh, then with a shiver, she begins wrapping back up. "Grandmissus came to the cabin," she says through her scarf. "She wasn't happy."

"She's just concerned for you all. All three of you."

"Maybe, but we're happy. And you know what I finally figured out?"

"What?"

Her small face settles, her smile soft and eyes relaxed. "You were right. Grandmissus is probably never going to be happy. Not with what we do. She'll always want something more, not only for us but also for herself. Like now she wants to be mayor." She rolls her eyes and her smile turns into a grin. "Like *that's* a good idea."

"Maybe it'll keep her busy and she'll stay out of your business?" I say with a squint.

She rolls her eyes, then shrugs. "Maybe." She shivers again. "Can we go inside the craft place now?"

"Yes, let's. There's Jackson, I'll tell him where we're going and let Savannah know in case she wants to take a look. I don't know where she got off to. Probably ran into some friends."

"I found a sweater like Missus has from here for Mom, and I ordered one for your mom. They'd sold out of the larger sizes, but will have more by the end of next week." I lift my bag up at Jackson as we walk to the van and I tell him about my shopping. "I probably spent too much money, but everything is so cute. Wait'll you see the blanket for the baby. Anna loved it but said it cost too much. I got it after she left the store. I'll take it to the hospital and surprise her. Savannah never did come inside, but I got her a cute pillow for her bed so it's good she didn't. Did you get the trees on the van?"

"Yep. No problem. It was fun with the boys helping. Then we enjoyed hanging out at the fire with the other men while y'all shopped."

Anna and Will had headed to their car, and Bryan's walking in front of us, but Savannah isn't in sight. I stretch to look ahead. "You said Savannah told you she'd meet us by the van. I bet she snuck her phone in her pocket. Why else would she be out here in the dark?" Walking faster, I growl, "If she is out here playing on that phone, I'm taking it away for the week!"

Turning a corner I come to a dead stop and Jackson bumps into me. We both just shake our heads and start walking toward our daughter and another person mashed up against the side of our van.

Her father says, "Well, she's not playing on her phone."

"Nope. But I can't say I wouldn't prefer to see her on her phone instead of playing on Ricky Troutman."

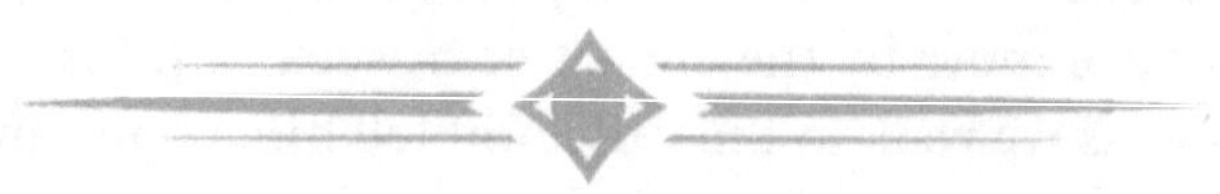

Chapter 20

"Breakfast with Santa was a wonderful event yesterday for not only our church, but for the entire community," the pastor says as he begins his sermon. "It was wonderful to hear all the laughter and see everyone working together. A huge thanks goes to Susan Lyles for overseeing it." He looks around for a moment. "I don't see Susan. She may still be downstairs cleaning up maple syrup and hot chocolate!" We all laugh at that, some more than others, and I manage to not roll my eyes. Laney, however, screws her head around to give me a smirk.

Silas made a surprise trip home last night.

Laney had informed me of it as we walked up the church sidewalk before service. They'd been having their family tree decorating at their mother's house around suppertime yesterday—Laney and Susan and their brother Scott and their families. I didn't ask, but I suppose that's why Ricky is home from college. Are you shocked that Savannah "didn't want to talk about it?" this morning?

Anyway, Silas arrived with the tree only half decorated to sweep Susan up in a huge kiss in front of God and everybody. Apparently Susan hasn't shared with her beau just exactly how her family feels about her and him. That was all I got of the story before we had to rush in and get into our pews since the choir was already singing.

I scribble "China buffet?" on a corner of my bulletin and quietly tear it off. Not quiet enough, since I get a frown from Jackson. Palming the piece of paper until I can pass it up to Laney, I put a serious look on my face and focus on the preacher...

...and on Bryan who is *not* sitting with Zoe. The Kendricks have been coming to our church lately. There they are. Zoe's not with them either. Oh, there she is on the other end of the row of youth on the front pew.

...and on Missus in another blue suit. This one is tweed, which looks very English-headmasterish. She looks mad, but then she usually looks like that. Wait, she's not looking at the preacher. Oh, she's staring at someone in the choir. Oh my word, Rachel Lyles is in the choir. Griffin's mother is everywhere! If that's who Missus is staring at, she doesn't look the least bit phased.

...and on Savannah who—is she asleep? I clear my throat— loudly. Nope. She didn't move. Somebody poke that girl. She's on the second row at the end way out of my reach. Ricky gave her a ride home last night and she was home by curfew, but she probably sat on the phone talking to him until morning. Using the psychic ability moms have, I force her to look at me. Yep, any minute she'll feel it. Any minute now... Okay, maybe that's not a real thing.

...and on Laney, who is looking at me again. Mouthing something? A tiny shake of my head says I don't understand. She says it again, her magenta-lined lips a perfect medium for mouth-reading, but...

"She wants to know if we want to go to China Buffet for lunch," Jackson says, leaning into my ear.

"Oh!" I smile and nod. She gives me a thumbs-up, then turns to listen to the sermon again. As do I. Well...

...Who *is* Missus glaring at? Why doesn't someone wake my daughter up? Are Bryan and Zoe even still going out?

"Oh, yes," Jackson says enthusiastically. "Carolina *so* enjoyed the sermon today. Didn't you, sweetie?" He's seated beside me in a booth at the Chinese restaurant. Laney and Shaw are across the table. Cayden is at the end of the table between the two men, sound asleep in his carrier.

"Don't talk so loud," I hiss at my husband. "You'll wake the baby."

Shaw points a half-eaten chicken wing at his son. "Naw, he sleeps through anything."

"Well, then," I give Jackson the evil eye, "just hush. So Silas showed up. Then what?"

Shaw laughs. "He laid a good one on Susan. Miss Prim and Proper, who used to sit and frown when I'd so much as try to grab a smooch from my own wife. I mean, we've all seen the two of them all over each other around town, but sitting in my mother-in-law's living room? You know how Abby Sue and Scott always were? Gladys always threatened to take a broom to them like two stray cats, but her perfect princess? Susan the Chaste?"

Laney leans back against the side wall and demands, "Who's telling this story?" Then she shrugs and leans forward. "But he is doing a good job. It was so awesome to not be the one on the end of Mom's disapproval. I'm not sure Silas had ever even met Momma officially."

"How did he know to find y'all there?" I ask.

They look at each other and shrug. "No idea. For all I know he's stalking her and has a tracker on her phone," Laney says. "Honey, can you go get me a bit more of that pepper chicken thing I like and maybe another crab rangoon? Jackson, you'd get Carolina a refill, too, I bet. What do you want, sugar?" She's batting her eyes at the men, then also at me, but at me her eyebrows jump, saying I should agree with her.

"Ah, yes, that's right. I'd like a crab rangoon, too, and, ah, some more of those green beans."

"They want to talk without us, but don't feel like walking all the way to the bathroom," Shaw says as he gets out of the booth and maneuvers around Cayden's carrier. The boy doesn't even stir.

We just smile at them and wait for them to get a few feet away, then Laney sighs. "That Silas, man. He's crazy about her. He acted like he belonged right there in the middle of all of us. I don't think Susan said another word the rest of the night."

"Was she upset? *Could* he be stalking her?"

Laney twists her mouth as she shakes her head. "No. It wasn't like that. She seems kind of crazy about him, too. But, I don't know. Anyway, that's not what I wanted to tell you without them. After Momma's, Shaw and I went to Gertie's for a quick drink since it was early and Momma was keeping Cayden overnight. It was busy as usual for that time on a Saturday night so I didn't notice him at first, but Colt was there. By himself."

"By himself? Are you sure?"

"Yep. On the way to the bathroom I went over to him. He was sitting at the bar not talking to anyone. I asked him if he wanted to join us. He just shook his head and turned back to his drink. He was still there when we left, and Gertie said as we were leaving that she'd had to cut him off."

"That doesn't sound like Colt. You didn't see Phoenix at all?"

Laney shakes her head. "I didn't want to tell you in front of Jackson. Figured you could decide how to handle that."

"Yeah. Thanks."

Just then the guys come back to the table. Jackson slides my fresh plate in front of me. "Shaw says Ricky isn't just home for Christmas break. He's home for good."

"Ricky left Georgia State? What about football?" I ask

quickly. I haven't mentioned Savannah and Ricky. Hope Jackson hasn't either.

Laney looks disgusted. Shaw shrugs and says, "Grades, I think. He just couldn't hack it. He also said that he doesn't like being so far from home. Scott's got both boys living back at home now."

"Ronnie's not still with his girlfriend? Wasn't he managing that gas station out on the blacktop?" We'd never known Ronnie well, and after his brother went off to college last summer to get ready for football, we really hadn't heard much of him either.

I'm getting the feeling that's going to change unless, like I'm hoping, last night was just a little flare of an old romance for my daughter and Ricky.

Laney chews and swallows before she answers. Shaw is busy rocking Cayden and cooing to him as he's started waking up. "Ronnie is still at the gas station. Doing well, I guess. He was at Momma's last night and seemed good. However, he and that girl did break up, and he moved back home around Halloween, maybe? Ricky and his mother got real close apparently while he was living down in Atlanta. You know Abby Sue is a real estate big shot down there, and she's convinced him he'd be good at it."

"Good at real estate? He's going to sell real estate?" We all hurry to finish eating as the rocking and cooing doesn't appear to be working for Cayden.

Laney nods, her cheek full of crab rangoon. Shaw adds, "He does have a seller's personality, especially after his time at school. He just seems more confident, wouldn't you say?" he asks Laney as he unbuckles his son and lifts him to his shoulder. He bounces him, and the booth bounces a bit, too.

"He's definitely more confident. Want me to take him?" Laney asks. Shaw just shakes his head. Cayden is snuggling into his dad and has closed his eyes.

"Is Ricky still dating that girl Charisse? The beauty queen?"

Laney and Shaw share another look, asking each other if they know. Laney answers, "I don't know. They were still together last time I heard, but she wasn't with him last night if that's what you're asking." She grins. "You interested in him for Savannah?"

Jackson and I laugh, and he moves to get out of the booth. Shaw does the same, but Laney grabs the back of his shirt. "Honey, I've got to go next door to the Dollar Store. You want to take Cayden to the car and just pick me up. I only need a couple things. Carolina, you wanna go with me?"

"I don't think so," I say. She's taken Cayden from Shaw and is securing him in his seat, so I wait with her. "Was Angie there last night?"

She cuts her eyes at me. "I don't want to talk about it. That girl…" She ends with a half growl, half sigh. Angie, only a senior in high school, wants to move into her older boyfriend Alex's apartment in Downtown Chancey, right beside Blooming Books. Her parents have informed everyone that that is *not* an option.

We catch up with the guys as they finish paying, and we head outside together. We stop as we almost run into a young couple coming into the restaurant. The young man has one arm wrapped around the girl who is tucked up against him.

"Oh, hey, Mr. and Mrs. Jessup," the young man says as he pulls the girl tighter, pulls his free hand from his jeans pocket, and offers it to Jackson who shakes it. Ricky slings his dark hair out of his eyes and smiles. "Good to see y'all again so soon."

Savannah smiles up at us from under his arm. "Hey, Miss Laney. Mr. Shaw. Mom and Dad. Come on. I'm starving," she says as she pulls Ricky with her into the door Shaw is still holding open.

Laney slowly turns to look at me. "So what was that? Good to see you again *so soon*?"

I cut my eyes at her. "I don't want to talk about it. That girl…" I replay her growl and sigh combination.

My all-time favorite statistic: did you know that ninety-seven percent of all people in liquor stores have teenage daughters?

Chapter 21

"What in the world is going on here?" By "here" Jackson means our home, as we cross the tracks after lunch.

Cars fill our driveway to the point we have to park up near the path to the walking bridge. "I have no idea. There's Missus' car. Of course, the Bainbridges' car is still here. Which reminds me, I need to nail them down on when they'll be checking out."

As we cross the yard he points out another car. "That's Phoenix's new little Mini Cooper. Can't believe she got Colt to ride in that."

I haven't mentioned Colt being alone at Gertie's yet. We'd been busy discussing Ricky's move home and the warm welcome Savannah gave him. "Looks like the living room is full," I say pointing to the front window. Then pushing in the front door I realize I'm more than right.

"Hello?" we both say/ask. Missus and Retta hold court in the room's bigger side chairs. Wayne is seated on the couch alongside Gertie. Athena and two more young mothers are seated on the floor. The biggest shock, however, is seeing Ida Faye, the librarian and my arch nemesis, in a dining room chair pulled in the middle of Missus' and Retta's chairs. That woman hates me, and here she is in my living room. Time to get to the bottom of this.

"So what's going on?" I look from Missus to Retta, nimbly skipping over Ida Faye. "Missus? Retta?"

"It's about time you got here," Missus says. "This is the Chancey Merchants Association. The CMA."

"Like the Country Music Academy?" I couldn't help it. "Y'all going to give awards?"

Ida Faye's jowls swing as she looks back and forth between the two women beside her. "See? I told you she'll be no help."

"What kind of help? What's going on?"

Gertie tries to turn around, which isn't easy on our low couch as tall and stout as she is. Jackson steers me to the side of the couch then in front of the TV. "I'll get you a chair."

He lifts it over Missus' head, then sits it in front of the television. Gertie nods at him. "Much better. Thank you, Jackson." Then she focuses on me. "So, this little group is kind of an offshoot of the chamber of commerce. We don't meet regularly, only when needed. When the chamber is hampered by too many rules and such."

"Like now!" Ida Faye shouts. "That smut shop has got to go!"

Missus raises an eyebrow. "That woman has got to go."

Heads around the room nod in agreement including Ida Faye's. I was kinda hoping that was who Missus thought had to go. Retta looks at me. "What say you, Carolina?"

"About what? What are you talking about?"

"The smut shop on Main Street," Missus explains as she looks down her nose in my direction. "I know you've seen it. It's been reported here that you were in it yesterday."

"Oh, the pop-up shop?" See, I knew they needed to hand out disguises. "Yeah, I was in there, but just for a minute. Cathy wanted to show it to me and wanted me to meet her friends."

Gertie hangs her head, then sways it back and forth a couple times. "They spent a lot of money on moonshine. It was busy yesterday after the parade, and I didn't pay 'em no mind. I did see that Cathy with them, but I never have given her the attention a mule gives a gnat." She looks up and squints. "Although she's about as pesky as a gnat. Hear tell you were laughing with her whole group right out on the sidewalk."

I stand up. "This is absurd. I have things to do. Retta and Wayne, y'all checking out today like you planned?"

Wayne grins at me. "Don't think so, but we'll let you know after the meeting." Then he screws up his face. "Sit back down and tell us what all's in that place. What did you buy?"

Gertie smacks his arm with the back of her hand. "Don't make me send you to your room, Wayne. But he's right, sit back down." She holds up her hand at me. "And don't tell us what you bought, just tell us if you feel it's appropriate to sit alongside your shop right there on Main Street."

I sit back down, mostly due to the pressure of everyone staring at me. "It's Cathy Stone. It's her business—I mean, she's been doing those parties for months now. Besides, isn't it just for a few weeks? Right?"

Athena rises so she's kneeling, back straight. "That's the idea behind a pop-up shop, and if we could be assured it would go away at that time, I'd possibly be okay with it. My concern," she looks at the other young women beside her, "our concern, is what if it becomes a permanent fixture of our town? What if it doesn't leave at the end of the month? Are there no rules to keep things, uh, you know, keep things better?" She slumps down as her words stumble off. "It's just having kids now and all…"

Missus tsks then tightens her mouth even more. Then she sighs and releases it with her thoughtful, wise, and oh-so feeling words. Yeah, right. "Exactly. The children. Being surrounded just yesterday with all those bright, trusting eyes as we had to go past that awful place on our float…" She fades off and sighs even louder.

Ida Faye and Retta roll their eyes at exactly the same time, and I can't help but grin. I look around for someone to grin with, but there's no one meeting my eyes. Except Wayne, and that's not happening. Jackson skedaddled downstairs as soon as he got my chair in place. Can you even imagine just walking away from something like this? How can he not be nosier? I finally ask, "Okay, so what do y'all want to happen?"

Missus smiles at me and nods. Oh, great. I apparently asked what she wanted me to ask. Then she looks down at Athena who lifts up, back straight again.

"We need stronger zoning. We need a leader who will take charge and not just let things happen. I'm sure Mayor Taylor is a very nice man, but he does seem rather ineffectual."

"Yes," Ida Faye agrees. "Ineffectual. Rules are in place for a reason. Chancey has gone too long without proper rules set in place. Rules with teeth."

Athena and her two friends are frowning, but not looking at Ida Faye. They've spent many hours in my shop complaining about the head librarian whose rules caused them to abandon story time in the public library. Well, they do say politics makes strange bedfellows.

Wayne speaks up. "I know I'm only here because this is our home for now, but I am manager of the largest enterprise in town, so will these rules, or laws, affect us out on the highway?"

Missus holds her hand up shoulder high. At first I think it's to shut Wayne up, but no, she's asking permission to speak. Oh, for the love of Pete.

How Gertie keeps a straight face when she turns to Missus and asks, "Yes, Missus? You have a comment?" I have no idea.

Missus reaches down inside a satchel leaning against her chair. "Here are some sample brochures for my campaign. I would like to get your opinions on if this is the kind of thing you feel might alleviate your concerns."

I mumble, "My concern is what happens when your head explodes from being so nice for so long." Sitting on my left, Retta turns to me and scowls. I fake-smile back. "Just joking."

Missus' pamphlet looks well done and fairly harmless, which is scary because it might actually get her elected. Just like in the parade, her campaign looks downright wholesome next to Laney's sequined dress with the slit up the side and the fur coat sloughed off behind her.

I wave the pamphlet. "Y'all might've talked about this before I got here, but has anyone talked to Rachel Lyles? She owns the place, and from what the Sexy Belles were saying yesterday, she fought them tooth and nail."

Missus bristles, and the fibers of her cowl-neck sweater seem to jump with static electricity. "No!" she snaps at me. "That woman thinks she can just waltz in here and turn our town into a red-light district. She's not someone we want to talk to. I'm sure *you* find her completely reasonable as she's related to one of your best friends, but *we* are taking a stand." Her moral outrage garners more nods from the room.

"Wait, Susan? Rachel's her mother-in-law, and Susan's getting a divorce from her son. Oh, wait, you're just wanting to connect her to Laney in the mayor's race. Okay, I get it. Never mind." I stand up. "I've got things to do. Wayne, Retta, do y'all want to check out now? I figure you want to get everything out of the basement during the daylight. Maybe all your *friends* here will help you?"

Only Athena and her group nod their heads and offer to help. Like I said, they're new here. Wayne leans back into the couch. "No hurry, Carolina. Missus suggested us looking into getting some painting done at the house since we're all moved in here anyway. Miss Laney just texted me back that y'all don't have any reservations up until past Christmas."

"Oh, Miss Laney said that?" I plant my hands on my hips and try to not look at Missus who is smiling at me from the side. Not taking sides in this mayor thing is apparently not going to work. I'm getting hammered from both directions.

Missus then adds words to her smile. "Doesn't it just make

sense since Retta and Wayne are already settled in here so comfortably? Oh, Wayne, did Laney mention seeing that picture on Facebook about this little meeting being here at Carolina's? I do hope she didn't get the idea this has anything to do with my campaign." Missus turns back to face me, and I finally look at her. Then I burst out laughing. Shoving a hand against my mouth and doubling over, I dash out of the room and then upstairs, leaving confusion and a halt in all conversation behind me.

In my bedroom, I close the door and sit on the bed.

Okay, I know you want to know what was so funny, but it was nothing. Literally nothing. I just had to get out of the room and couldn't think of a good enough exit line.

Things are completely out of hand when even sarcasm fails me.

Chapter 22

"Isn't it admirable to not choose sides? To stay neutral?" I moan into the phone to my mom. I'm still seated on my bed from when I escaped the meeting downstairs. Contrary to my usual practice of not wanting a house full of family, I called my parents begging them to come early for Christmas so I can kick Wayne and Retta out.

"I do think it's admirable. They're both your good friends," Mother commiserates. Again. I'm picking up some boredom in her voice.

"Not sure I'd say they're *good* friends," I grouse, "but anyway, you sure you don't want to forego Florida and just come straight here?"

"I'd be all for it, but your daddy is set on seeing all those Christmas lights in St. Augustine. He feels like everyone in the club has seen them but us. Plus, it's already so cold up here. We'll be there in just a few weeks to see the baby. How is sweet Anna? Due date still the same?"

"No changes in that. Did I tell you I took Jackson out to their cabin? It is awfully cute, but so tiny and so far out in the woods. I just wish they'd move here until the baby comes. Oh, I know! They can move into the B&B so the Bainbridges will have to move out. That's perfect! Two birds with one stone!"

"Honey…" she warns. I'd already told her Jackson's feelings

on the subject. "Besides, as busy as you are, how much trouble can these people be? Just ignore them. They'll leave soon, I'm sure."

"Not possible ignoring them." I stand up. "Well, I hear folks leaving. I guess I should go downstairs. Y'all have a good trip. Take lots of pictures."

"We will, and let us know if anything happens with the baby. I can't believe I'm going to have a great-grandchild!"

We say goodbye while I peek out, then tiptoe into the hallway. Yep, the living room is empty. I hang up, then slip my phone into my pants pocket. I've not changed from church, so I'm still in my black church pants and white sweater. There's a pattern on the front, so you can't see where I dribbled wonton soup at the buffet. Sneaking down the stairs, I dip and stretch to make sure the driveway is as empty as the living room of guests. Wait, Phoenix's Mini Cooper is still there, but she wasn't in the meeting, now that I think about it. I jog on down the stairs and then look into an empty kitchen. No Wayne rooting around in my fridge or Retta going through my purse. They are snoopers, I've also figured out.

Back to tiptoeing, I head down the B&B hall. Their doors are closed, so I sneak on past and peek inside the bathroom. No Phoenix. Maybe Colt picked her up here or something. I mean, what else could it be?

"Carolina?"

I step to the door of the Orange Blossom Special room, which I thought was closed, but it's only pulled to. "Yes?" I say as I push it open and step into the bright room. "Phoenix? What are you doing in here?"

She's sitting in the wide window seat, the afternoon sun making her hair shine. It's down today and fanned across her shoulders and arms. She has her knees up in front of her and her arms around them. She smiles, nods at the wing chair next to her, and says, "Have a seat. I really like this room."

"Me too, but… what are you doing in here? I didn't see you in the meeting."

She laughs. "I was waiting here for you and Jackson when all those folks showed up. I hurried back here. I guess you went to lunch after church?"

"Yes. So you've been here since noon?"

"Pretty much. I didn't think about you going out to eat. But no worries, I just sat in the living room and read your magazines. Probably even dozed some. This is a very peaceful house." She turns to look back outside. "That's why everyone wants to be here, I think."

"Sure doesn't feel very peaceful sometimes." I shift to be able to see out the window better. The view looks down our back hill, and in the distance I can see the river above the treetops. It's the prettiest view on the first floor. "So what did you come here for?"

"You know. To rent a room."

I cringe. Wow, good thing my parents didn't take me up on my offer. "Oh, okay. For when?"

She smiles at me through our reflections in the window. "Carolina?" Then her eyes travel around the room, and I follow.

"Oh! Is all that yours?" I'd walked right past three big suitcases, several grocery bags, and an armful of hanging clothes laying on the bed. So much for my powers of observation.

"Yes. It's all mine. I want to rent this room for myself."

"But, but what about Colt?"

She shakes her head at me, then lays her chin back down on one of her knees and resumes looking out the window.

Talk about being in the middle of something. I guess this explains Colt's solo drinking last night. "Is it really a good idea for you to stay here? I mean, Colt *is* Jackson's brother."

She shrugs but doesn't turn to look at me. "Colt will be okay with it. He's okay with everything." Then she does look at me. "Right?"

With a nod and sigh I have to agree. "He is pretty easygoing."

"Until he's not. Right now he's not being easygoing about moving back to Kentucky."

"Moving back? He just got the coaching job here. This town loves him."

"Carolina, everyone everywhere loves him. He's just one of *those* people. And he loves everyone loving him. Me?" She shrugs again and looks to the window. "Me? Not so much." She falls silent, and after a bit I think maybe she's fallen asleep. Quietly I get up and walk toward the door. She's sitting like a dancer or a gymnast. If I fell asleep like that, I'd have to be drunk and passed out then put in that position by a team of construction workers. Her hair forms a red sheet of shine, and my impulse is to take a picture. The sun on her hair, the white curtain, the peach pillows, and her cream knit sweater compose a portrait that looks like a drawing.

Instead, I back out of the room. She's right, it is peaceful.

But right now it's also sad.

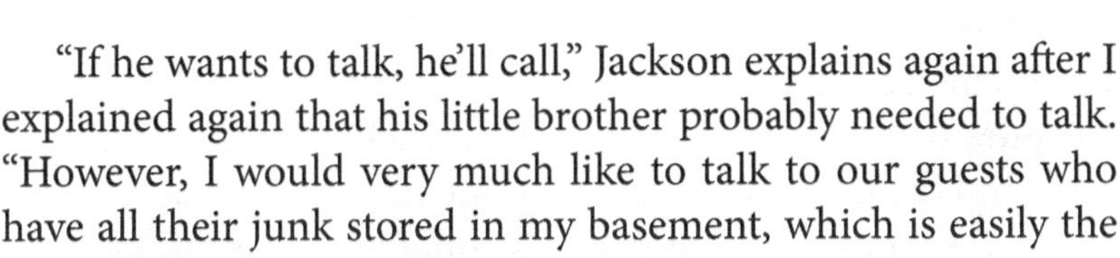

CHAPTER 23

"If he wants to talk, he'll call," Jackson explains again after I explained again that his little brother probably needed to talk. "However, I would very much like to talk to our guests who have all their junk stored in my basement, which is easily the least annoying thing about having them here."

"Please! Be my guest! I've tried to get them to leave, and they just ignore me." It's been two days since Sunday afternoon when Wayne told me they were getting some painting done and would be staying a little longer. That same night I'd told them they needed to be moved out by last night since we had company coming and I needed to get the rooms ready. I also told them the junk stored in our basement had to go even sooner than that. And yet…

They and their junk are still in place. So Jackson and I are having to unload our Christmas decorations from behind their piles of stuff.

"I think they've added more down here since they moved in. Are you letting them bring more junk here?"

Well, aren't I married to the stupidest person on the planet? Through my teeth I spit, "Did you seriously just ask me that? What is wrong with you? Are *you* letting them bring in more junk?"

"Wait. No." He sticks his head up from behind a stack of red storage containers. Mighty brave of him considering I'd gladly chop it off about now. "No, I know you didn't. I'm just…" He sighs. "Just this whole thing is out of control."

"Not because I've not tried to get them out. Maybe you should talk to them."

He cringes. "They just don't seem to listen, do they? What good will me talking to them do? But you're probably right. I'll try to talk to them tonight."

I swallow the words lining up in my throat, sharp words that are lining up just so perfectly badly—yeah, I've got to get out of here. "Going to check on dinner," I shout as I stomp out of the small basement room and move around and through all the piles without a look back. A look back, a moment's hesitation, and those words are coming out all over the place.

So, are you wondering how it's going with Jackson working from home?

"Hey. What's cooking?" Bryan asks when I emerge from the basement.

"Barbeque chicken for sandwiches. Why are you home so early?"

"I didn't feel good."

"And they just let you leave school? No call home?"

He grins. "Miss Laney was volunteering, and she gave me a ride home."

Oh. "So is it your stomach?"

"No. Headache and my nose is stuffy." He takes a Gatorade from the refrigerator and then folds into a kitchen chair. I hand him some medicine and feel his forehead.

"You do feel warm. Go lay down." I turn away from him to stir the chicken. Taking the lid off releases the spicy smells even more, and I lay a small piece to the side to sample.

"Hey, what about me?" my son, who is never too sick to eat, asks.

I take out another bite and lay it in the saucer to cool. "So what's up with you these days?"

"Nothing. Miss Laney came inside when she dropped me off."

I turn around, his bite of meat on the end of a fork. "Oh? Where is she?"

He takes the fork and shrugs.

"You don't know where she is? Did she leave?"

"She might've heard you and Dad fighting in the basement."

"Might've?"

He shrugs again, and as his face colors I try to think of what all we said. He chews and sits and waits for me to remember. Okay. Bainbridges. Colt and Phoenix. Oh… oh, and Peter. "Y'all heard us talking about Peter?"

He shrugs again, but it's a half-hearted shrug with a bit of a nod thrown in.

"Oh, man. Daddy and I just disagree about what he's doing, you know?"

"Sure," he says as he stands up. "I'm going to go lay down and watch TV." He walks out of the kitchen and then stretches out on the couch.

"Shoot." I dig my phone out of the pocket of my jeans. So who do I call first? Laney and try to get her to not say anything? Or Peter and tell him his time's run out?

"I'm leaving for book club," I yell down the stairs where Jackson is still working. "Everything is out on the counter for dinner."

Hurrying to close the door before he can ask anything, I catch my purse strap in it and have to open it back up so that

I hear him yell back, "You're leaving already? Book club isn't until seven, right?"

Really? Now he's paying attention? "I have some things to check out at the shop," I yell, then repeat, "Everything's on the counter for dinner." This time I get the door closed cleanly, and I'm to the front door and out of the house gulping deep breaths of fresh air.

It's dark already. I hate these short days. We're putting up the tree and outside lights this weekend, though, and that always helps brighten the long nights. Driving down toward town, Christmas songs playing and lights here and there, I relax and try to enjoy the season.

Peter. What is he doing? He keeps texting, asking me about what's going on in town, but he still hasn't asked about Shannon. Not one time. When I try mentioning her he cuts me off and swears me to secrecy. Finally this afternoon I told Jackson about talking to Peter, My thought was that maybe we could then talk about whatever is bothering Jackson, but that quickly became what was bothering him—me talking to Peter. More specifically, me not telling Missus and Shannon. For some crazy reason he thinks I should tell Shannon he hasn't asked about her. Of course, I have not told Jackson that Shannon thinks she could be pregnant.

This fall I learned my lesson about not sharing others' secrets, but this is feeling not so good, either. And now what in the world did Laney hear? Jackson and I have been picking at each other so much I don't actually remember what we said.

Laney is doing an event tomorrow night at the pop-up Sexy Belles shop. Yep, she's embraced it and all its hot pink signage. Their latest marketing idea is pairs of lips with an arrow on each street corner of our square. Anyway, we arranged to meet and chat in one of our cars since she's coming downtown to check things out for tomorrow and I have book club to set up for. Pulling in beside her across the street from the gazebo, I turn off the van and hurry to get in her car. Her cars are always nicer than mine.

"Hey there. Oh, it's toasty warm in here," I say as I slide into the passenger seat.

"Your seat warmer is on, too. I only have a few minutes. I see Cathy is already in the store to meet with me." She fully turns toward me. "So, what is Peter up to?"

"I honestly don't know much. He just needed some time to get his head together. Shannon and his mother and…"

"I don't care about all that," she says with a wave of her hand. "The bistro. What is he doing with that?"

"What? Why?"

"You know. Alex and Angie. I don't know what to do." Tears fill her eyes and she clasps her leather gloved hands. "That girl is so *nothing* like me, I always thought. The dark hair and Goth makeup. Not talking all the time and not being crazy about boys. Nothing like me and Jenna. But now she's turning into me!" Laney's actually frantic, and I'm a bit stunned. I've never seen her panicked like this.

I try to laugh a little, to calm her down. "But seriously, how can turning into *you* be a bad thing?"

She doesn't laugh with me. "Shaw is an entirely different creature than Alex Carrera. I knew I could make something out of Shaw, but Alex is smart and too cunning. He'll use her and drop her. I just know it. She'll be crushed."

"Hmm." I pull back a bit and think. "No, I don't think so. Crushed? Used? Neither of those fit Angie Conner." This time my little laugh is genuine. "Matter of fact you might be right. She *is* like you. Strong. Stubborn." I take a deep breath and motion for her to do likewise. "I still don't get what you want to know about the bistro."

She takes a second deep breath, and her eyes lose a bit of their watery shine. "I don't want Alex in town permanently. I saw him in the bistro the other day, and Angie is hinting at something like him opening his own restaurant. She could just be yanking my chain since that is something I do so well." She looks down, then back up at me with a bit of a grimace. "Sorry about booking Wayne and Retta for those extra days. I was just mad about your hosting that get-together for Missus."

"I told you—"

She stops me with a laugh and a hand on my arm. "See? I'm good at yanking chains. I know you're in the middle, and I won't mess with you anymore. I did tell the Bainbridges their time is up at the B&B, so hopefully they are leaving."

"No sign of that so far, but maybe there will be by the time I get home tonight." With a sigh I lean back into the warm, buttery soft leather seat. "You heard Jackson and me fighting."

"Yeah." She grimaces. "He wants you to tell Shannon about talking to Peter? Does she really not know? Hasn't she heard from him?"

"No, she hasn't. She knows I've heard from him. What I haven't told her is he hasn't asked once about her."

"Probably because he's still so hurt. When he sees her I bet it'll all be fine."

"Maybe. But as for the bistro, I don't know anything. He really hasn't said much." I point to the rearview mirror. "Cathy is looking this way. Guess she's spotted your car. I have to get things ready for book club." With my hand on the door handle, I turn to her. "Please don't say anything about me talking to Peter. He says he'll be coming home soon and I'll be out of the middle of all this."

"Okay," she says with a squeeze of my arm. "And just ignore all my nonsense about Angie. You're right. She'll be fine. I just remember how no one could talk to me about Shaw. I wanted him and I was going to have him. Luckily, he was the type that *wanted* to be caught. Guess I'm just not so sure Alex is the same."

She turns off the car, and we sit in the silence for a moment.

"Man," she breathes. "Makes me feel for my mom." Tilting her head to look at me, she asks, "You ever think about what your mom went through when you were a teenager?"

"All the time. Mostly about how I didn't think she knew anything I was doing. Now I see knowing a situation and having a play to make in the situation are two entirely different things."

"Amen to that." She opens her door. "Okay, now on to the smut shop." She grimaces at me again—this time not just a little one. With a sniff she adds, "Lord have mercy, I must want to be mayor something awful."

CHAPTER 24

Inside Blooming Books I turn on the lights. We read Jan Karon's *At Home in Mitford* this month, and I thoroughly enjoyed reading the first in the series again. I've read the entire series, which is set in a small town in the North Carolina Mountains, and I'm excited to get to talk about it with the club. I'm sure everyone loved it. There's just nothing to not like.

My only responsibility for food and drinks this month is to provide a table and make a pot of decaf coffee. With the chairs arranged and the coffee half done, I look around at the shop decorations Bonnie came up with. She settled on Dickens' *A Christmas Carol,* so everything is Victorian in theme, with lots of velvet and lace, candles and trees. She took familiar quotes from the book, stenciled them on sheets of brown paper, and then she shellacked them or something. They look like she just tore them out of a very large, very old book. We also ordered several of the books *The Man Who Invented Christmas* by Les Standiford, which details how Charles Dickens gave us so many of our Christmas traditions through the popularity of the small book he published himself.

Velvet ribbons in Missus Blue have helped our theme match the town. The business decorating contest ends this Friday, and on Saturday the awards will be given at a celebration at the train depot. The theme there is 1945, the year World War II ended and Chancey residents decorated the depot to welcome the soldiers home. I think we—well, actually Bonnie—have a good chance at an award. Chatter outside gets my attention, and I see the ladies arriving. Can't wait to talk about Mitford!

They didn't like the book. How can you not like that book?! When it was revealed that that was the consensus, I almost kicked them out of my shop. Well, I would have if not for the fact that the blackberry cobbler Dot brought was to die for, not to mention the homemade vanilla ice cream Helena brought to put on it. Real homemade ice cream—just for book club. I can almost imagine making a cobbler for this group, but homemade ice cream?

I've given birth to people I wouldn't work that hard for.

Rachel Lyles scored a couple of brownie points with the ladies after she got past their cold shoulders about the Sexy Belles pop-up shop. She's working for Missus' campaign to set stricter zoning regulations and left no doubt in anyone's mind that her family connection to Laney is strained and soon to be non-existent. Retta complained about Laney, too. She wanted to know if I knew she had thrown her and her brother out of the B&B. I tried, some, to say we just needed the rooms, but hey, Laney was getting thrown under the bus so much, I figured I'd just let her stay down there. Besides, have I mentioned the cobbler and ice cream?

Maybe it was a stomach full of rich cream and ripe berries with a good measure of sugar from both. Maybe it was the quiet of downtown after book club, as I locked the front door and stopped to look at the tree and gazebo shining in their own kind of silence. Maybe it was just being out of my house for a couple hours, but whatever it was, I felt peaceful and wanted to carry that home to the people I love.

Then—I actually get here.

Really fast, a few things become clear to me:

Colt cares about Phoenix staying here.

Wayne Bainbridge has an extensive collection of pornographic magazines.

Ricky hasn't *exactly* broken up with the beauty queen Charisse.

Bryan's illness has moved to his stomach.

And last, and probably least, no one turned off the crock pot after they ate.

"'Scuse me, Ms. Jessup," Ricky says as he tries to get around me in my frozen position blocking the front door.

Savannah is yelling after him. "And don't come back until you've really actually broken up with her!" In my direction she adds, "Mom, can you make Bryan throw up upstairs and not in the kitchen? He's gross!"

"Help your brother," her father demands.

"Oh, yeah, tell your daughter to help her brother while you screw yours over," Colt throws at Jackson from where he's standing only about a foot away from him. They both have their hands on their hips, facing off on the other side of the living room.

I'd move to let Ricky by except at my feet Wayne Bainbridge is slowly stacking up his magazines, which spilled everywhere when the bag he was carrying them in split in two. "Sorry, Carolina, just trying to keep them in order. Can you grab me a bag or two?"

I clutch Ricky's shoulder to step over Wayne and his magazines. Ignoring Savannah's tears I push past her into the kitchen where Bryan is standing over the sink. I do grab the crock pot cord and yank it to stop the cooking of shreds of BBQ chicken that are left, now black and sticking to the bottom.

Bryan is leaning over the sink. I feel his head, and it's warmer than before. I rinse out a clean cloth and hold it to his head. "Savannah, hand me a Gatorade," I say quietly, then I shout, "Jackson, get Wayne a couple bags and get him out of here. Colt, come here!"

The men enter the kitchen. Jackson gives Bryan a pat on his back then takes the bags Savannah hands to him. Colt stands at the end of the counter, waiting.

I tell Bryan to hold the cloth on his head, and then I motion for Colt to help him sit in a kitchen chair. "Come here," I tell my daughter, and I pull her into a hug.

She sobs for a moment, then pulls back, sniffing. "It's really not all his fault. We just kind of fell back together." She shrugs and half smiles at me, then leans down to side-hug Bryan. "I'm sorry I yelled at you. Do you need anything?"

Bryan shakes his head.

"Don't you have a test tomorrow?" I ask her.

"Yeah. Everything okay down here?" she asks but she's already heading out of the kitchen.

I give her a wave and turn to Bryan. He takes a deep breath. "I feel better now that I threw up."

"Just sit there and sip your Gatorade. If it stays down, I'll give you some medicine. Just sit there for a minute. Daddy's right there." Jackson and I make eye contact, and he sheepishly nods at me from where he squats near Wayne.

I grab Colt's jacket sleeve and pull him with me out the back door and onto the deck, then release his sleeve with a push. "Where did you think Phoenix was living? You knew she was at the studio every day, right?"

He squints and hesitates. "I didn't really think about it, just knew she moved out. But why would you let her move in here?"

"She said you wouldn't care. That you don't ever care. Maybe that's part of y'all's issues." I take a breath. "You are pretty easygoing, you know?"

"So? That's a bad thing now? 'Oh, Colt, you're just too easy to get along with!'" he says in a whiny, high pitch voice. We stare bug-eyed at each other, then we both laugh a bit, then a bit more.

He catches his breath. "Were those girly magazines he spilled all over the place?"

"That's what it looked like!" We start laughing again, and when Jackson opens the door to see what's up, his face is total confusion.

"What are you laughing at? Wayne and his collection are gone," he says in such a serious way that Colt and I laugh even harder. Jackson's eyes shift between his brother and me, and then he starts laughing, too. He chokes out in Wayne's cadence, "I'm trying to keep them in order!" Colt has to lean against the railing, and I sit down in one of the chairs, cold as it is. Jackson is doubled over laughing, and it takes a few minutes for us to finally get composed.

Colt reaches up to shake his brother's hand. "Sorry, man. Guess I should be saying thank you for taking Phoenix in. I'm glad she's here rather than down at the interstate by herself."

"No problem. I should've talked to you about it before now." He slides his eyes to me. "Carolina tried to tell me that, but…"

"But you've had a lot on your mind." I say, giving him a break. "I'm going inside to see how Bryan is. Probably be taking him to the doctor in the morning if his fever doesn't go away." I open the door, and the smell of burned barbeque sauce hits us with the wave of warm air. We all wrinkle our noses.

Jackson shakes his head at me. "It tasted fine. I don't know why it smells like that now."

CHAPTER 25

"So, where were you last night when Colt and Jackson were going at it?" I ask Phoenix. We've run out of other conversation over our coffee. We actually ran out of conversation around "good morning" and "how did you sleep?" but anyway, I have questions.

"In my room." She doesn't even look up from her phone to answer me. I'm getting the feeling she doesn't want to talk. Well, then she should've picked a different B&B, right?

"Did you know Colt was here?"

"Yes."

"Did you talk to him?"

"No."

People that don't have kids don't realize parenthood greatly reduces your repulsion at being thought annoying. Actually, it becomes kind of a superpower if you use it right.

"Think y'all will work things out?"

She shrugs.

"He's really a good guy, and he hasn't left for Kentucky yet."

No shrug. No nothing.

"You decorating the dance studio for Christmas?"

"We're not officially opening until January, but probably. Not with that Missus Blue, though." After another pause she looks up from her phone. "I do have something I wanted to ask you."

Part of me wants to pick up my phone and ignore her, but… "Sure. What?"

"What's Peter going to do with the bistro?"

That causes a pause. "Why is everyone obsessed with the bistro?"

That got a straightened spine and open eyes. "Everyone? Who? For what?"

Oh. Hmm. "Just people. Why are *you* interested?"

She sighs and narrows her eyes at me. "Okay, I wanted to run this by you anyway. You seem to kind of run things downtown." She holds a hand up at me when I shake my head and try to scoff. "Whatever. I'm…" She takes a breath and smiles. "I'm putting in a juice bar. That part is a definite go, but I'm also thinking maybe sometime in the future I could possibly add some food."

"Oh, that would be great. It's awful we don't have anywhere to eat or even pick up lunch."

"Healthy food. Salads, grains, things not available anywhere in this area."

"Uh, think there might be a reason for that?"

She answers with a cocked eyebrow, then goes right back to her phone.

Some people just don't appreciate good sarcasm.

"No, sorry, Phoenix. I think it's a good idea. As for the bistro, I don't know anything."

She still isn't looking up, but she asks, "That Carrera kid? The one with the food truck, is he looking at opening up there?"

My silence causes her to shift her eyes in my direction. "I don't know anything about that," I finally say with a jump to my feet. "I've got to go get dressed. Talk to you later."

The house is quiet with the kids already gone, the Bainbridges moved back to their house, Jackson in the basement, and Phoenix? Well, she might be the quietest guest we've ever had. Interesting talk this morning, though. A juice bar sounds interesting.

Although I have no idea what one actually is.

Shannon reads loudly from her phone, "A juice bar that serves customers fresh-squeezed fruit juice drinks and smoothies is a fantastic new business enterprise to put into action, as more and more people are striving to lead healthier lifestyles."

"Guess that explains why I didn't know what it was. I mean it's pretty self-explanatory, but still… to just sell juice?"

Bonnie is stringing a set of old-fashioned lights on the coffee table between the couch and the chairs. She talks while she works—unlike me. "Smoothies are great, I guess, but the ones that taste good often have a lot of calories and sugar. Natural, but sugar is sugar."

"Expensive, too," Shannon adds.

"Hey, maybe if one day she offers healthy food Ruby would stop experimenting with healthy muffins," I say as I head to the door. "But speaking of Ruby's, I'm heading over there for a quick cup of coffee with Susan before taking Bryan to the doctor. Want me to bring anything back by here?"

"Yes!" Shannon says. "I'm starving. Just bring me one sweet and one savory."

I stare at her remembering how a queasy pregnant stomach calms with starches, but she doesn't give me any hint. She still refuses to talk about anything until Peter comes back. And, no, I haven't, and am not, going to talk to her about Peter not asking about her. They're going to have to work all of that out without me. Jackson won't even talk to me and we're married.

Why he thinks I should talk to her, well, whatever. "Bonnie, you want anything?"

She stands and leans her fist on her jutted-out hip. "A smoothie. Why'd you have to start talking about them? But nothing from Ruby's, thanks." Looking back down at her handiwork, she asks, "What do you think?"

She's turned our large coffee table into a Victorian village. Small ceramic buildings are posted up and down a little road. Along the edges she buried tiny white lights under mounds of cotton, which looks like snow.

"It's perfect. Where did you come up with all this?"

She is quiet, looking down and licking her bottom lip. Softly she says, "It was my mother's."

"Oh" is all I say as I hear the hitch in her voice. Shannon must've heard it, too, as she's coming up toward us in the front of the store.

"Your mother's?" she asks. "It's really beautiful."

"Mother was not an easy person to deal with. When she died Cal just boxed her things up and shoved it all in a storage unit." Her face is sad as she looks up. "I'm an only child, so I got it all. That was over ten years ago." She breathes deeply. "Cal has never complained about what it costs for the storage unit, but I decided ten years was enough and finally started going through it." She looks around the store. "I'd forgotten about all her Christmas stuff."

"It's wonderful you're sharing it with us, but…" I step closer to the table. "But what if something gets broken? We do get busy at times."

She shakes her head. "No, I want it out for people to enjoy. I don't want it in my home, but here is perfect." She suddenly looks up. "If it's okay with both of you?"

Shannon and I share a look and laugh. "Are you serious? It's way more than okay," I say.

Shannon agrees. "I love flowers, but that is the end of my

decorating ability. You've turned this place into a wonderland. A Victorian winter wonderland."

Bonnie takes our hands. "Thank you. I really do love it here. And getting that storage unit cleared out is helping me in so many ways. I actually feel lighter." She waves me on. "Go, and I will take a muffin. Sweet one. It is Christmas after all!"

And it feels like Christmas outside. The cold has a bite this morning, and there are a few flurries playing in the shafts of sunlight. They shine like glitter, and although they melt as soon as they touch anything, it's still snow.

Susan is waiting and already has coffee. Libby nods at me that she'll meet me at the table, and she does, talking before she even reaches us.

"Can you believe Missus acting like Cathy is running some cathouse on the town square?" Libby spouts as she flips my cup upright and fills it. "I was right embarrassed when Cathy started this lingerie business, and Lord knows I'd rather eat sand than go into that shop, but why all the ruckus? Just let it play itself out. Want a muffin, Carolina?"

"Yes, and some to go in a bit. What should I have?"

"If you're feeling exotic, I'd go for the white chocolate, ginger, and orange. It's got a tang of spice, then sweet. It's been popular today. There's also chocolate chip and a bacon one with Pepper Jack cheese. It's not hot, though."

I shove off my coat behind me. "Okay, exotic it is."

Susan scrunches up her face. "I already regret asking, but what's the healthy option?"

Libby matches her scrunches. "Bran or oat or something crunchy. I've served a few, and only thing I have to say is people keep leaving little bits of it half chewed up on the plates. Something that won't exactly crunch is my guess. Want one?"

"I'll think about it. I'll try a bite of Carolina's. I do feel a bit exotic," she purrs.

Libby and I both roll our eyes, then she walks off.

"So, speaking of exotic," I say, "how's Silas' commercial going?"

"Fine. Laney told you about him showing up at Mom's?"

"Yeah, she was right tickled to not be the one in trouble for once. Shaw was right tickled, too. What were you thinking?"

"Thinking? Oh, you think I'm thinking? Funny." She closes her eyes and sighs. "I can't think straight when he's around. It's exhausting. When he's not around I eat ice cream. Lots and lots of ice cream. Hence the interest in the healthy muffin." Laying her forehead in her hands, she moans, "What am I going to do?"

"No idea. Are you sure it's just your hormones? Maybe you really care for him."

"He's an actor. He's so young. He's not right for me at all. It's just how he makes me feel, and that can't last."

Libby is back with my muffin and more talk. "So back to Cathy's business. You were in there. What's it really like? Is it really X-rated?"

"I wish someone else in this town would go in so I wouldn't be considered the one source of information. But no, I mean, I don't know. I was only in there for a minute. I didn't look around much, just saw wigs and lingerie. Same stuff we've all seen at her home parties."

Susan shrugs and frowns. "But that was in someone's home. With people we knew. Not out in public."

Libby nods at her, then leans closer and whispers, "Either of you going to the thing Laney is doing there tonight? Some kind of speech?"

Susan and I look at each other. Of course we've both told Laney we'd come, but… "Probably," I say and Susan echoes me.

Libby jumps on it. "Okay, then I'll meet you at your shop? I can't go in there by myself, but with you two, I can." She straightens and hollers Ruby's name. Then she sticks a thumbs-up high in the air.

Ruby shouts, "I'm in, too."

"Oh, good," Susan says. "We've got ourselves a posse." Then she grabs my muffin and takes a big bite. Spitting crumbs she tells Libby, "Bring her another one."

CHAPTER 26

"Let's go in there," I say to Bryan as I pull into a small parking lot. He woke up feeling pretty good, without a fever, and by the time we got to the interstate headed to the doctor he was feeling even better. Some kind of twenty-four-hour bug, I think. I canceled the appointment and took him out to an early lunch instead. He'd slept hard and Jackson let him sleep until right before I picked him up, so he only had half a bagel before we left. His biggest complaint on the drive was that he was starving.

A starving teenage boy is a good sign. I didn't let him eat too much, but he's looking good and talking. I think he's going to make it.

Hence the detour. "Have you ever been to a juice bar? Phoenix is going to put one in her studio."

"Cool. I've been to Smoothie King. Remember? It was near the school back in Marietta."

"Oh, I do remember that, but I never went in there." I park and we go in. I settle on a combination juice that's pretty good. Bryan chooses a strawberry smoothie, and we walk back out.

"Anywhere else you want to go before we head home?" I ask him.

"Nope. I guess I can't go to basketball practice, can I?"

"No. No school, no practice. Glad you're feeling that good, though."

He shrugs as he opens his van door. "Basketball is okay. I just wanted to see people." We drive for a bit before he says, "Weird Will being a dad, isn't it?"

"Very weird."

"Zoe says she's never having kids."

"Well, she's really helped a lot with her little brothers and sisters."

"I guess." He pauses, but a quick look at his profile tells me he's still thinking about it. I take a sip of my drink. He shrugs. "She might change her mind."

"You're right. She might."

"She thinks a lot about things," he says.

"Really? Like what?"

"Oh, like having kids, well, not having kids, and what she wants to be and stuff."

"She still want to be a nurse? I remember her mentioning that a long time ago."

"Yep. I told her she ought to just go ahead and be a doctor 'cause she's so smart." He finishes with a bit of a laugh.

"What's funny about that?"

"She blew up at me. That I thought being a doctor was better than being a nurse. She got all over me. Like I said, she really thinks about things."

"What did she say?"

"Just that a nurse had to know as much as a doctor about so many things and that being in control wasn't anything special, it was about helping people. And she wants to travel. Like around the world." He turns to look at me. "She said a nurse can work anywhere."

"She's probably right about that."

He nods. "Oh, she is. I looked it up."

"Do you want to travel around the world?"

He looks back out the front window with a sigh. "I don't know. Feels like I should, though."

"Why should you feel like it if you don't want to?" I ask with a smile.

"Well, if I want to be with Zoe it would make sense."

That took care of my smile. "Oh, well, she's talking about a long time from now. I mean, after college and everything."

"Yeah, I guess."

"But you like Zoe that much?" We're pulling onto the ramp for the interstate, so I can't really look at him. That's probably for the best.

"Maybe," he says. "I guess I'm just trying to think about things more." He sighs loudly. "You know I'm going to be an uncle soon."

My smile jumps back, but when I look at him he's all seriousness.

My heart crunches for him.

Life is such serious business, but he's still just my little boy.

But then, little boys *are* where men come from.

Chapter 27

"Remember the last protest we had in Chancey?" I ask, pacing in front of Blooming Books' display window. "It was when the coffee shop, MoonShots, was going to be open on Sundays."

"Oh," Andy speaks up with a big grin. "That was my dad and his church. Although I don't know if you'd call it an actual protest. Think they officially called it a 'prayer gathering.'" He's bouncing on the balls of his feet as he mans his post, looking down the street where news camera lights flood the area even more brightly than Laney's campaign/billboard truck. "This here? This here's a *real* protest."

At another knock at the back door, everyone yells, "Come in," and Susan pulls open it open.

Susie Mae bounces inside in front of her mother. "Isn't this exciting?" She rushes to where the other young people are gathered around the front door.

When I got here I parked around back because Shannon had texted me something was going on and the street was full of cars. By the time I got inside, Libby and Ruby had walked down from the café and were chattering about how Missus and a bunch of her campaign workers showed up to protest Laney's event at the pop-up shop. Jackson and my kids showed up a few minutes later as they'd heard about the excitement and didn't want to miss out. Andy and Patty came down from upstairs, and now that Susan is back from picking up Susie Mae, we're all planning on walking down to see what's happening.

Laney was supposed to talk at seven, and it's almost that time now. I've texted her, but she's not answered. Wonder if she'll even show up. As we walk down the street, everyone we see is like us. No protestors or signs. Just nosy people, like us. The kids push forward, gravitating toward the lights where we figure the camera is. I don't see a television van, but maybe it's around the corner. The crowd isn't tight or hard to get through. Matter of fact, a lot of people seem to be walking in the opposite direction, like there's nothing left to see.

And they're right.

In front of the store, the gazebo from Missus' float is sitting on a couple of pallets in the street. Jackson points at a machine off to the side, like I've seen in big warehouse stores that move pallets of boxes. Walking around the gazebo are about a dozen people. I see Athena and some of her neighbors and friends and then some older people from town. They are all smiling and holding signs that ask questions about the zoning laws and Chancey's future. Our police officers are also smiling and talking to people. Apparently, this is it. I'm surprised the television people are still here. Then I look closer. There's no station markings on the camera, and the man holding it is Athena's husband. And the lights set up behind him are big and bright, but just on a stand shining onto the gazebo. What's going on?

Susan and I are noticing all of this at the same time, but before we can compare notes, the front door opens. Cathy, clad in black pants and a black leather jacket with hot pink and red accents, steps out first. She then holds the door for Laney to walk out. Laney is wearing black and pink, but definitely not leather and not in the least bit provocative. She smiles and waves, then from behind her steps Missus. I guess they were having a talk inside.

Missus is not wearing black or pink or red. She's wearing… say it together, children… blue.

Athena hands Cathy a portable microphone. She clears her throat, frowns, then begins speaking. "Thank you for coming. My store, my catalog store, Sexy Belles, is always available by contacting me. I've decided to take down this pop-up site." She frowns as she shoves the microphone toward Laney, who first moves as if to take it, then pauses for Missus to push in front. Which, of course, Missus does.

Missus smirks at Laney, who only gives her a raised eyebrow and a bow of her head as if in acquiescence. As if.

Missus speaks, loud and strong. "I—no, *we* know what is best for Chancey, and I'm happy Mrs. Stone has realized it also. This is an important day for our town, and now we must make sure the zoning laws reflect what we know is right for all of us. I will be watching closely, as I have for so long, but soon I will be watching in my official capacity as mayor. Thank you." She hands the microphone to Cathy, moving it right past Laney's outstretched hand. She then moves to block Laney out.

Susan mutters, "Uh-oh. Laney's getting mad."

Laney gives Missus the evil eye, but jerks around to smile at Cathy and grab the microphone. "Hey y'all. Thanks so much for coming out to hear me talk. I'm just thrilled to see each and every one of you. You know, at first I was for keeping this store open merely because my opponent in this race wanted it closed. Isn't that silly?" She wrinkles her nose and laughs, even rolling her eyes at herself. "So silly!" She takes a breath and with an easy sashay steps in front of Missus and closer to the people watching. She has on a wide black skirt that swirls around her black boots. Her jacket, also black, is short and fitted but open so that her white, pink, and red striped silk shirt shows. She puts a hand on her hip, and her face turns more serious.

"But doesn't that seem how things are lately? People *for* something merely because of who is *against* it. Or vice versa." Then she makes a face and rolls her eyes, and we join her in laughing at her, and at ourselves. "Another truth?" she asks with eyes wide, scanning faces. "I didn't have one single solitary idea about what to say here tonight! Not a clue!" She winks and adds, "However, I did know that I wanted to see just exactly what they were selling in this store that caused so many people to get their panties in a wad!" Her hand flies to her mouth. "Oops, I said 'panties'!" She's got the crowd with her now as we all laugh and relax.

She takes a breath and lets it out. "Well, folks, what I saw were some right pretty things. Sure, some are kind of naughty, and I gotta admit, I'm uncomfortable with them being sold right here on Main Street where just last week Santa Claus rode by on a fire truck. That's just the truth." She pauses and gives us a coy look. "It's also the truth that I bet Mrs. Claus would love to find some things from Cathy's store in her stocking." As we laugh she preens a bit, then shakes her head. "So folks, be sure and pick up one of Cathy's catalogs and fill up the stocking of your deserving sweethearts. Believe me, that'll be more fun than listening to silly old politicians talk, right?" With a flourish of thanks for the applause, she hands the microphone to Cathy, then gives us all a big wave followed by a blown kiss.

Jackson and I look at each other and shake our heads. He leans forward into my ear. "And we'll have this moment to remember when she runs for governor."

Ruby grabs onto Jackson's arm and pulls him toward her so that she can whisper in his ear. He listens to her, then straightens up. He waves and shouts, "Ruby says she's opening up in five minutes."

Libby groans, but turns to follow her boss toward the café. Susan meets my eyes and smiles. "My sister beats all, doesn't she?"

"Jackson says we'll remember this when she runs for governor."

Susan shudders. "Please don't put any thoughts in her head." Then she brightens. "There you are! Well done," she says as she and her sister embrace.

When they release, Laney sees me and puts one arm around me. "So glad y'all were all here." Then she bends down a bit and lowers her voice. "Did you see Missus' face?"

"She'll be okay. You both won," I say.

Laney clucks her tongue. "Not quite. When we met inside—me, her, and Cathy—I was so fed up with it all and so tired, well, I told Missus I would drop out of the race tonight."

Susan and I gasp. "What?"

She shrugs and widens her eyes in amazement. "Then when I saw the crowd and I had that microphone in my hand, well, I just couldn't let all you folks down." Looking around she asks with a sly cut of her eyes, "Ya think Missus will be mad?"

Chapter 28

"One thing about you working from home, I sure get my days started off earlier." It's still fully dark out, and Jackson and I are having coffee in the living room. Savannah's alarm was going off as we headed down the stairs, and Bryan had just hit his snooze for the second time. "I don't get up much later, it just feels like I get moving earlier."

"I love having this time to sit with you before getting to work." He pauses, and the way he sits still, I think he's going to finally tell me what's bothering him. Then he chuckles. "Sure was a scene at Ruby's last night."

"Sure was." I don't bug him about talking because he did say he's really preoccupied with stuff at work and has said twice in the last couple days he didn't feel like talking about it "yet." I cock my head when I hear Bryan's alarm turn off again, but then I hear his feet hit the floor. It's hard having guests just down the hall because I can't yell up at him, but it sounds like he's up. "I thought Missus was going to throw her cup of decaf at Laney, and she probably deserved it. Sashaying in there all apologetic about not quitting due to the people deserving a choice. She is so full of it."

Jackson scoffs. "But come on. Missus and her fans staging that whole protest with fake cameras and everything. Putting that stuff on the internet about TV crews being there. That wasn't exactly playing fair."

"And why are these new people so on her side? Athena and them are all smart people, supposedly." I listen and then whisper, "Phoenix is up. I heard the bathroom door down there close. Have you gotten anything else out of Colt? Is he really thinking about moving back to Kentucky?"

"If Phoenix would've gone with him, I think he'd already be back there." Jackson sighs. "Emerson and I moved away for college and didn't go back. Colt went right back home after school and has been there ever since. Being a winning football coach made him a little like a god to the town. I think he mainly misses knowing everyone and everyone knowing him. Plus, he and Dad got along pretty good."

"But I don't think it would be the same with Hank married to Shelby now, do you?"

"No, and I mentioned that to him." The bathroom door opens, and we hear Phoenix walking in our direction.

She sticks her head in the living room door. "Good morning," she says then she walks on through to the kitchen. She pours her coffee and then retraces her steps back to the Orange Blossom Special room.

As her door clicks shut, I whisper, "Wonder how long she's going to stay here?"

Jackson shrugs, then slides forward in his seat. "I'm going to go downstairs and get started. I have another conference call at nine."

After he leaves, I shift to be able to look out the window at the graying of the sky. It looks cold, and I shiver just as the heat kicks on. Behind me I hear Savannah coming down the small staircase from her room. She slams her door behind her, then she's loping down the main staircase. "Hey, Mom."

"Good morning."

At the end of the stairs she drops her book bag and comes to sit on the couch. "Okay. So, Ricky broke up with that girl. The really pretty one." She rolls her eyes and breathes. "Whatever." She places both hands on the thighs of her jean leggings and frowns. "So, he's asked me out on a real date. I don't think I've ever been out on a real date. We always just go to parties or games or with groups, you know." She is still frowning, but her eyes sneak little looks at me, checking out what I'm thinking, and I can see she's trying to not be excited.

"Yeah, y'all don't date like we used to," I say. "But maybe kids do when they get older? It's kind of a show of respect, I guess. Is that what you think Ricky is thinking?"

She studies that thought for a bit, then nods. "I do. Like, he messed up not breaking up with her, but well…" She dips her head, fiddles with a hank of hair, and shrugs. "Neither of us were really thinking a lot, you know. We ran into each other at Greens, there was the fire and the trees, and it was just so romantic. You know."

"I know. But don't let yourselves get carried away with all those feelings, *you know*?"

"Mom!" she says as she jumps up. "Okay. So I'll tell him 'yes.'" Then she's humming as she flits around the kitchen getting her breakfast, and I'm happy for her. Not gonna lie, it makes me nervous as a cat on a hot tin roof to have her dating someone she has such chemistry with—a boy who's been off to college no less.

However, having a happy teenager is downright addictive. It's also fleeting, so I'll enjoy it while I can.

"Mom!" explodes from upstairs. "You didn't wash my uniform!" Bryan comes stomping to the top of the stairs. "We have a pep rally today. Didn't you know that?"

I twist around to see his hand, stretched out over the banister in my general direction holding a uniform I can smell from here. Well, maybe I can't actually *smell* it from here, but I can imagine how it reeks.

"Why didn't you put it in the hamper?" I ask as I stand up. "And don't yell at me."

He holds his yell to a small roar. "You said *you* would, remember?"

And I do—sitting on the edge of his bed the night he was sick, smelling his uniform without seeing it and saying I'd take care of it. "Okay, that's right. Throw it down. I'll wash it and drop it off before lunch."

"Thanks," he says as the two black and yellow pieces fall to the floor and he goes back into his room.

The happy child is still buzzing around the kitchen. We exchange smiles (just like in a Disney movie), and I go down into the basement to throw a load into the washer.

"Hey, I forgot to wash Bryan's uniform. How's work going?" I say as I pass Jackson's table turned desk.

"Okay, I guess…" He doesn't quite put a period at the end of it, but I've fallen for this before. This *maybe I'll say something, maybe I won't* thing. So I don't look at him, just start tossing clothes into the washer. Of course, I don't say anything, leaving lots of blank space for him to fill.

"Listen," he says, and his chair creaks as he turns it my direction. "There've been layoffs across the railroad."

"Really?" My heart actually skips a beat and I only half-turn to face him. I try to stay nonchalant. "What's going on?"

"Just the railroad business on the East Coast is screwed up, so there's belt-tightening all over."

My throat is dry, but I swallow and take a breath. "How about your office? Atlanta?"

"We're good." Then he shrugs and adds, "For now, but…"

"So that's what you've been thinking about?"

"Yeah. Hey, I've got to get back to work, so I'll let you get back to the wash."

We smile at each other and turn back to our tasks. When I

start the washer, I detour by his chair and give him a hug. He hugs me back for a second or two, then looks down at his work.

I hate when someone finally tells me what I've been wanting to know—and I immediately don't want to know it.

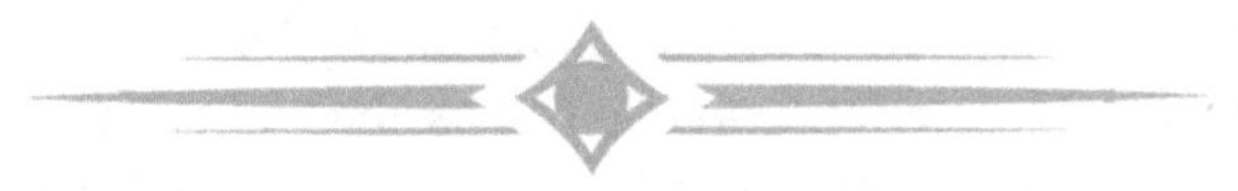

CHAPTER 29

"What is that? Don't you hear it?" Bonnie asks me again.

And again I shake my head at her and lie. "No. I don't hear anything."

Shannon doesn't even look up. I understand she's working on an elaborate arrangement for the grand opening of the depot's Christmas display tonight, but come on. She's got to hear that!

"Sounds like there's someone next door," Bonnie says. Then she gasps. Her eyebrows fly up, and she blurts, "Oh! Is Peter back?"

Now *that* got Shannon's attention. However, she only scowls at us and goes back to work. With raised eyebrows of my own accompanying some jerky nods, I encourage Bonnie.

"Shannon? Do you know if Peter is back? Could that be him next door?" Bonnie reads my non-verbal clues so very well. The man I'm married to would be standing there asking me if my head was itching or if my foot had fallen asleep.

"Oh?" I query. "Could that be what it is?"

Shannon gives me a look. "I thought you didn't hear any-thing."

"Well, whatever Bonnie heard. I mean, I don't think she's *lying* about it."

"No, I definitely heard something. I think I'll go check." She plops down her feather duster and steps to the door with such purpose I'm too stunned to yell 'no'. Which is a good thing because Shannon says it for me.

"No. I'll go," she says. "I need a breath of fresh air."

"Good idea!" I silently offer Bonnie a high five. Bonnie accepts it and steps back as she pulls open the door. Shannon doesn't even give her a good eye roll as she walks past.

The door barely falls shut before Bonnie is halfway across the floor to me. "Is it him? Is he back?"

"I think so. I'm pretty sure. He texted me last night that he'd see me today, and now there's all that noise from next door."

"Wait, you heard all that? You two were making me think I was losing my mind. Why didn't you say something—oh, oh wait. What do you mean, *he* texted you? Why is Peter Bedwell texting you?"

"He just is. Whatever. But about the noises, I was waiting for Shannon to notice them or something. Thought she was never going to wake up." I walk back up to the front. "I don't see her."

"Uh-uh, young lady, not so fast. Peter and you have been in communication?" Sometimes Bonnie's school teacher side comes out, and it's not pretty. Well, not when it's directed at you. "Does Shannon know? Don't try to worm yourself out of this. After all that's gone on, why would you be the only person in town in contact with the mysterious missing man?" She purses her lips and looks so disappointed. "You know Missus is not going to take this lightly. He's her son, Carolina."

"She and Shannon both know I heard from him. But, but it's complicated."

Now only one eyebrow lifts as she looks down her nose, really, truly down her nose, at me. "It's complicated? Well, tell me just *who* complicated it?"

I wave an arm next door. "I just sent her over there, didn't I? I do wish she hadn't been wearing those purple tights, but that's what she looked like when he fell for her the first time, right? I'm almost positive he's coming back to Chancey, so…"

Bonnie plops down on the arm of the couch. "Honey, you need to stay out of this little romance." She sighs. "Or whatever it is. They don't exactly match. You do know that?"

"But I think they were both happy when they were together."

She looks at me, wrinkling the nose she is no longer looking down. "Do you?" Then she stands and lifts her arms in an exaggerated shrug. "Possibly I'm wrong," she says before walking to the back of the shop.

There are certain people that say something like, "Possibly I'm wrong," and you know they do *not* think they are wrong. Bonnies proves that she's one of those people by whipping back around to face me. "So what did he want to talk to you about? Shannon?"

"Not exactly. Listen. It was nothing. For all we know they're next door making up." I march around to dart into the aisles, but I can still hear her doubtful "we'll see" over the shelves.

"It's just workmen," Shannon announces, pushing through the front door hard enough to make the bell on top dance loudly. "Said they're, 'Working for *Mr. Bedwell* to clean it up.' Had big trash bins throwing everything away. I grabbed us some chips." She dumps several bags of snacks on the table.

"Seems a waste to be throwing away perfectly good food," I say as I meet her at her worktable.

"That's what I told them, but they just shrugged and said it wasn't their call. I did see stashes of food in some boxes toward the back, so I bet they're taking the good stuff home instead of throwing it away. Actually, there's not much left in there anyway." She's quiet for a minute while Bonnie and I sneak peeks at her. "Looks like he's wanting to sell it. You know, maybe Peter isn't coming back."

Bonnie stares lasers at me.

I ignore her. *She's not my teacher.*

Grabbing a bag of cheese curls, I retreat back to the bookshelves. Bonnie asks Shannon about her big flower arrangement as I sneak around to the counter. I'm humming and making little noises, rattling the chip bag, but you know, sneaking. Sliding my purse out from under the counter I step to the door. "Okay, I'm heading home. See y'all tonight at the depot!" I wave goodbye, fling open the door, and disappear out it.

I'm kicking myself before I even get across the street to my car. Why in the world am I protecting Peter? I know it's no leftover romantic idea. I honestly just want him to be happy. To come home and be happy. Why is that so much to ask? Everything was fine before he went crazy and popped the question to Shannon. He needs to get over his pride and come home so that the two of them can start over.

I sit in my car thinking as the clock ticks to noon. Sunlight sparkles on the candy canes and snowflakes hanging on the light posts. The tree and gazebo actually have families around them, and there's a photographer taking pictures. I don't remember anything like this being set up before. Maybe it's a church or a scout group? The woman doing the photography is not too tall, but she carries herself tall, if you know what I mean? She has a dark blonde ponytail with a white fur cuff around it. It matches the fur on her cute vest. Her turtleneck is a light coffee color, and her leggings are the color of darker coffee. She has on worker boots and genuinely seems to be enjoying herself. It's hard to tell how old she is. She's dressed young, but something in the way she moves makes me think she's older than the parents she photographing.

From the direction of her house, Missus strolls over to the people and then makes her way to stand beside the photographer. They hug when the woman finishes with the family group in their formal stance. She excuses herself with a squeeze of Missus' arm as she moves to take some candid shots of the children. Now that I can see them better I realize the families are some more of those in Athena's group, though I do not see Athena or her husband. As the photographer walks toward the gazebo talking to Missus, I decide that I don't think I've ever seen her. She's striking. Definitely older than I first thought, but still very healthy and happy-looking. She walks with a lot of confidence, and the way she puts her hand on Missus' back looks like they're familiar. I'm trying to remember the last time I saw Missus hug someone. She and the photographer walk on the other side of the gazebo, where I can't see them, and I start my car. It's cold, I'm hungry, and I'm going home.

Shoot. I'm entirely too distracted by this Peter thing. Here I sit with a perfectly good bag of cheese curls, and I forgot to even open it.

Chapter 30

"You sure you don't want to come?" I ask Bryan again. I can't get used to going to things just Jackson and myself. The days of corralling the kids and loading the van rarely happen anymore, and most the time I don't give it a second thought. But nights like tonight, going somewhere fun, with Christmas lights on the porch and tree trimming planned for later, it seems strange to just be the two of us.

Bryan, however, has had his fill of family. He hasn't said it, but he has that look teenagers get when they don't know if they can take one more dad joke or one more impromptu hug from a mom wearing jingle bell earrings. "I'm good," he says from where he's sprawled on the couch with my bag of cheese curls, a Coke, and football on the TV. He doesn't look at us, but he also doesn't shout, "For the love of all things holy, will you people just leave me alone for a minute?" So I'm calling it a win.

Jackson tries to pull the front door to, which pushes me onto the porch. "We'll be home in an hour or so to decorate the tree!" I yell through the diminishing crack.

"He knows. Believe me, he knows," Jackson says. Then he wraps both arms around me. "I'm glad to be out on the town with just you. The kids will all be here later, right?"

"Right." I smile at him and reach for his hand as we pull away a bit to walk down the steps toward the van. Dusk is my favorite time of day. The smell of wood smoke hangs in the air as our feet stir up the dead leaves in the yard. Washes of purple and blue are lined with ribbons of orange, and I pull us to a stop to look out over the river.

"You see a headlight?" Jackson asks as he stretches to look across the bridge.

"No. Look at the sky. We don't have to have a train to make things pretty."

He shrugs, then grins. "No, but it always helps." I let him go on to open the van while I watch the orange ribbons begin to fade. It's a beautiful night for such an important event, though I can't help but feel a bit of worry. I still haven't heard from Peter. Hopefully he's not planning on surprising everyone at the event at the depot. The older ladies have put so much effort into this.

With their first reminisces last year of how World War II ended right before Christmas in 1945 and trains crossed the country loaded with soldiers going home, they've collected memories: soldiers, family members, and townspeople telling of how much the decorated Chancey depot meant that Christmas.

The heater is going full blast. Jackson crosses the railroad tracks in our yard, looks both ways, and says, "This should be really interesting tonight. That Christmas of 1945 was such a huge deal. I'm glad you got us a copy of that book about it. Can you imagine how happy everyone was? President Truman gave all the federal employees four days off to celebrate. And that lady you told me about was right; the trains were completely packed. Hard to imagine…" His voice trails off as he imagines those days when trains were the main form of transportation and every little town had a depot.

Marigene, the sweet lady I told Jackson about, who reminded everyone of all this last year at our first Chancey Christmas meeting, is speaking tonight. I can't wait to hear her story again.

I've only seen what they've done to the outside of the depot. They closed the museum a few weeks ago and haven't let anyone in. Peter was the one who got the museum organized and cleaned up when he came back last year, so I'm sure he wouldn't dream of upstaging this, right? He's just not like that. "What?" I have to say when I realize Jackson asked me a question.

"Will and Anna coming to the depot, or just up to the house to decorate the tree?"

"Oh, just to the house, I think. So glad you got those reflectors in place for their driveway. Although I think they're getting used to it, so it's not as scary… or dangerous."

A sweet rendition of "Mary, Did You Know?" comes on the radio. As we listen to the words about a mother holding her baby, I can't help but think of Anna soon holding little Frances.

Jackson looks at me. "You're okay now with them living in the cabin? Not going to start plotting with Missus to get them to move?"

"Plotting with Missus? You make it sound like some episode of *I Love Lucy*." Reaching for the radio, I turn up the music to let him know I'm trying to listen to it, then turn to face the window. I think Missus buying the cabin has definite possibilities, but it's not like a *plot*.

We cross the tracks on Main Street and pass by our shop, Ruby's, the pop-up shop, and Phoenix's dance studio. It's not quite dark, but the holiday lights are all on. The best part about dusk at Christmas is getting to see the decorative lights and the unlit decorations at the same time. Pine branches are tied to the street lights with that blue ribbon, and shiny, red plastic poinsettias line Ruby's window boxes. Phoenix's bright lime green and orange ribbons and decorations with lemons, limes, and oranges showed up yesterday afternoon. Wonder if the fruit is fake? It looks completely out of place in our old downtown, but it's still pretty. Rachel turned over the pop-up shop for the Boy Scouts to sell Christmas trees out of. Cathy and her Sexy Belles got the place cleaned out in record time, and the scouts moved right in. I'm not sure I've ever heard of an indoor Christmas tree lot, but you can't say Rachel Lyles isn't trying to improve her reputation in town. As Main Street ends in front of Andy's Place, we turn left. "Park on the other side of the depot," I tell Jackson. "Shouldn't be too muddy."

We usually park on the side of the depot where the park is or closer to the shops, but tonight everything is happening on the track side. The museum's main door is on what is really the rear of the depot, but it's on the sidewalk and across from the library. The side facing the tracks used to be the main entrance, but with no more trains stopping, it became the junky back, but it won't be after this grand reopening. I'm not sure if it'll become part of the museum or what. Guess we'll find out tonight.

We park at the end of the lot as we don't want to take any of the close spots for the many older people attending. Jackson jumps out, exploring and talking. "This is where you'd get on the train, that area between the building and the track. It's so close to the track I bet that's one reason this entrance isn't used anymore."

"Plus the floor had water damage and was considered unsafe, I heard. That was the first thing that had to be fixed."

We stop for Jackson to look along the side of the old building.

"See how this porch and entrance are higher than the museum part? I don't know why they built it that way. Doesn't seem to make much sense." The area we're going into, the one that's been closed off for years, has a crawl space underneath it. We climb the wide rows of steps that line the entire front of the building. At the top is a porch with carved wooden benches like church pews on it.

"I don't think these benches were here before," Jackson says.

"They look original, though," I say, and an old man sitting on the end of one speaks up.

"They're original, all right. Made just for this porch. Ordered by my grandfather Haskin Chancey when this depot was finished. Part of a bargain he made with the town. He'd provide seating if they'd make it high enough to see down the track." The old man is wearing suspenders, which I can see because his big winter coat is spread open to let his belly, which is straining the buttons on his white dress shirt, stick out. He laughs, and his belly shakes. "He loved to watch the trains. I'd sit right here with him." He caresses the worn wooden seat beside him.

"Is Chancey named after your family?" I ask while Jackson asks permission to sit on the bench beside him.

"Why, there ain't ever been a Chancey that needed someone to name something after them. We just name things Chancey like it's the name God wrote for it in the Bible."

We laugh and Jackson says, "Well, it has my vote. Your grandfather was a wise man. You really can see all the way down the track. I never knew that, or I'd've been up here way before this." He leans over toward the man. "I like watching trains, too."

"They had all this roped off, like it was gonna fall down." The man shakes his head and then leans forward as he pulls his cane around and plants it in front of himself. "The men that made these steps and this porch knew what they were doing." He stomps his foot. "Solid as a rock. Just that girl of the judge didn't want folks remembering my family no more. Bad enough the town was named after us in her eyes."

I wave to a couple walking inside, then turn back to ask, "Girl of the judge? You mean Missus?"

He laughs, then coughs because of it. "You mean Shermania? Calling herself Missus! That girl's got guts, I'll say that. I've got to get inside." He gets forward momentum with his cane and some rocking to help him stand. Jackson has a hand under his elbow. "Had my daughter drive us over here today for this." He stops and looks at the stairs, then over to the tracks. "Lot of good men left right here and never got to come home." He stops and takes a shaky breath. "Good that somebody did something about it. Disgrace for it to be all closed up."

Jackson gives him an arm to hold onto. "You said these are the original benches, but they sure don't look like they've been sitting out in the weather all those years."

"Nope. When the judge closed this off after the passenger trains stopped, I took 'em. Loaded them up in a truck in the middle of the night. I told folks round 'bout where they could be found if they ever did the right thing and opened this back up." He starts laughing and coughing again and doubles over. "Whew," he says, straightening up. "Yep, they've been in my basement just a-waitin' all these years."

As he goes inside in front of us, Jackson looks back at me. "Now there's a story in all that somewhere!"

"Yeah. I've never heard anybody around here named Chancey." I push into his back. "Hurry, I'm freezing!"

We enter a warm, bright room where about thirty people are milling around. There's lots of talking, laughing, and hugging. This must be what it feels like living in Florida—Jackson and I are the youngsters in the crowd. I see our friend from the porch being helped into a seat by a woman who is probably his daughter, and even she looks older than me. Jackson tugs me over to a wall full of pictures. I gravitate to the ones with people in them. He gravitates to the ones with trains. We both study the ones of the depot in its busy days.

It doesn't take me long to get to the end of the wall of pictures, though Jackson has barely moved from where we began. When I get to the end, I look around. Missus is here; she doesn't have her fan club with her, but is standing next to Ruby and Libby. Gertie and Andy are here, but I don't see Patty. She doesn't like crowds, especially now that she's sick all the time.

This is only meant to last an hour, so the only refreshments are punch and cookies. But they are homemade cookies, so I head that way.

"Carolina! Merry Christmas! Can I get you some punch?" Pearl Bennett asks. "Be sure and have some cookies. We have about a billion more underneath."

"Underneath?"

She hands me my full cup of green punch, then lifts a corner of the tablecloth. "See those bins? Every one of them is full of cookies. I told Mama there was no need to ask *every* Sunday School class to bring some, but she didn't want to run out. Said it would look bad on our whole church."

I take a sip of the very sweet, very cold punch. Pearl's family has been in Chancey forever as far as I can tell. Plus, running the beauty shop, they know everything. "Hey, we met that man over there out on the porch. Says his name is Chancey?"

She looks then shakes her head. "His name isn't Chancey. That's Junior Blackwell, his mother was a Chancey. They live over near Toccoa now." She smirks at me and lowers her voice. "Bet he told you about the benches?"

"Yeah. He said he took them?"

"Middle of the night! I've never heard of Judge Bedwell being so mad. He ranted and raved, but to most folks Junior was a hero. Not much love lost for the judge."

"When was that?" I ask. I survey the platter of cookies and pick a thin wafer with what looks to be lemon zest grated on top.

Pearl sighs and scoops another cup of punch to sit out in front of the bowl. I move around the corner next to her and out of the way of those looking for liquid refreshment. "Early seventies? I was still in elementary, but I was one of those kids that sits with the women and listens to the gossip, you know. I remember the women being glad to see the judge get bested by someone. He was still ruling the roost around here. From what

I remember the Chanceys didn't take to listening to anyone." She looks up. "Hey, Momma, come here a minute."

The matriarch of the Bennett family is a big woman with big hair. She talks her whole way over. I've heard of Momma Bennett, but I've never met her. Her daughters run Beulah Land Beauty Shop and her granddaughter has on and off dated Bryan since last winter, but Momma Bennett doesn't go out too much, except church, from what I'd heard.

"Law, Pearl, get me a chair. When is this shindig gonna be over? It's time for me to be home with my robe and slippers on."

"Here, Momma," Pearl says as she guides her mother back behind the table to a chair. "This is Carolina. She and her husband own that B&B up in the Cogdill House, and her son—"

With a wave of her arm, her mother stops the introduction. "Shush all that. You know I won't remember it in no time. Hand me some cookies, any kind." She looks up at me and shrugs. "Sorry, darlin', just I've got that old-timers and nothing sticks in this head for more'n a minute."

Pearl nods, adding, "Unless it's from way back. Momma remembers all that. Carolina was wondering when it was the Chanceys left town and what they were feuding with the judge about." She looks at me and excuses herself to the punch bowl where a line is forming.

"Nice to meet you, Mrs. Bennett. I was—"

"I heard what you want to know. Let me talk while I eat these cookies. Then I'm leaving." Her thick hair is gray with what looks like maybe a silver-blonde rinse on it. It's been done on big curlers and as she studies the cookies in her hands, the curls bob. Thin, arched eyebrows drawn on with a light brown pencil don't move as she closes her eyes to think. She chews then nods as she thinks of what she wants to say. And then she starts talking. Mrs. Bennett talks half the time with her eyes closed like she'd love to go to sleep right here. Then she remembers her handful of cookies and jerks awake. She eats and crumbs tumble out, but she keeps telling stories, which don't really make sense to me. I listen until her words start to run together, and I think she might actually be asleep. She's slumped enough in the chair so that she won't fall over, so when a little snore slips out, I tiptoe away.

With punch cup in hand, I step to the side wall and look around. The walls are painted a mellow gold, and with the shiny hardwood floors, the soft light from the old-fashioned wall sconces makes everything golden. There's a small podium, and Marigene and a couple others look to be getting ready to start things. Next to the podium is a table holding the large flower arrangement Shannon had been working on this morning. It is stunning.

There's evergreen and red poinsettias fanned out to form a dark backdrop for thirteen beautiful, large white roses that are just beginning to open. Next to each rose is a small piece of yellowed paper with a name written on it in old-fashioned script. The thirteen men from the county who were killed in World War II are the focus of this evening, and Shannon's flowers do them honor. As I look around the room, tears welling, I realize this is where many, if not all, those young men spent their last few moments at home.

I feel their presence. To put their dreams and lives to the side to fight on the other side of the world is unthinkable to me, and yet they came here on some cold winter morning or humid summer day, walked out those doors and down those steps to get on the train that took them to the end of their young lives.

As Marigene taps the microphone, Jackson finds me and bends to look in my face with a look of concern. I smile and shake my head at him. Then I focus on those thirteen roses while Marigene welcomes us and starts to speak.

Chapter 31

"Welcome to the reopening of the Chancey Depot Parlor and Porch," Marigene says. She waits to gage a reaction to the name. Her eyes are alert and wise. She's small, but not from being stooped or diminished. She's one of those women you find working in her garden in the heat of the day, still smelling of powder. Her voice is low but clear and makes me think of a chilled glass of homemade eggnog. Too rich, too thick—just perfect. She smiles and continues, "Yes, I'm happy everyone approves. As you can see we are decked out for Christmas now as our depot was back in 1945 to welcome not only our soldiers home, but also to spread cheer to those passing through. I'll leave all the history of what was known as 'Operation Santa Claus' to our next speaker. His presentation tonight will be very brief, but he will be doing several longer talks in the upcoming days, right here!" She claps her tiny hands and beams. "That's right! We will be offering the Chancey Depot Parlor and Porch for events and gatherings such as this one tonight. With a very handsome donation from one of our leading families, this is all possible." She pauses and looks into the crowd and then at the empty seats behind her. "But, uh, more about that in just a minute. For now I'll ask Mr. Russell Westerly to come give a preview of his upcoming talks on 'Operation Santa Claus.'"

She moves back and primly sits on the edge of her seat. She

gives her attention to the man at the podium, but the lines between her eyes and the set of her mouth say something isn't right. Leading family? I'm sure I'm not the only one thinking it's the Bedwells, but why would that be a problem? Oh, but where are they? Where's Missus? She was here earlier. There's a buzz and shifting as people turn to whisper to each other. Momma Bennett is wide awake, and Pearl is talking in her ear. Poor Mr. Westerly has lost his audience. Luckily he's one of those speakers who doesn't seem to need anyone actually listening to him.

Jackson leans over to me. "What's going on?"

I shrug and take another look around the room. "I think Missus is supposed to be up there." Our friend from the porch is scowling, and his daughter is patting his back. As difficult as it is for him to get around, he still looks like he's about to leap out of his chair. Maybe that's why Missus left. Maybe she didn't want to cause a scene with Mr. Blackwell since he feuded with her father. Momma Bennett appears deep in thought, and I do remember her mumbling something about some folks holding onto grudges for a long, long time. Pearl is nervously dipping cups of punch to add to the dozen or so already sitting in front of the bowl, but she's too far away to ask what's going on. Usually I can count on Laney and Susan to give me a reading on what's happening, but they aren't here tonight. This is a different crowd than we're usually around. Jackson and I are only here because of his love of trains. Libby and Ruby are not in my sight as they are behind people at the door. Or maybe they've left, too.

There's a smattering of clapping as Mr. Westerly turns away from the podium. Marigene steps up to the podium. "Thank you, Mr. Westerly, for sharing your knowledge this evening. Now, I've asked Reverend Charles to read the names of the men we are dedicating this place and this evening to, and then he will say a prayer."

The remaining whispering fades and the pastor's voice reading the names adds weight to the air. When he reads the name James Chancey, my head tips up in surprise. So that's why this was so important to the man on the porch. I see the big man wipe his eyes and take a deep, shuddering breath. Then I close my eyes as Reverend Charles says, "Let us pray."

By the time he says, "Amen," sweet smiles replace the furrowed brows, and more than Mr. Blackwell wipe their eyes. Lights on the tree in the corner by the front window twinkle, and the roses release fragrance to compete with the smell of Christmas cookies, evergreen, and candle flames.

Marigene steps back to the podium, and her voice is husky. "Hearing our loved ones' names called in this room was special, wasn't it?" She looks around to nods and smiles.

"Can I say something?"

It's the man from the porch. I was right. He *was* preparing to stand, and he's now on his feet. "I don't need no microphone. Just need to say how much I appreciate you folks from Chancey doing all this. Miss Marigene, you are so right. To hear my Uncle James' name read was so very special. I was just a kid of ten when—" He gets choked up and has to clear his throat to continue. "I was just ten years old when my uncle, a kid himself, hugged me right here in this very room. Then I sat on the porch out there, on that very bench I was seated on earlier. In that very same spot, I watched his train pull out and roll away from me, from his family. His home." Not stopping due to tears this time, he says, "This here is holy ground for me…" His daughter puts her arm on top of his forearm, which is straining as he leans on his cane. He shakes her hand off. "No. I'm going to say it. It's all nice the so-called leading family has money to put into doing this, but it sticks in my craw. Them always acting all high and mighty! I'm half-a-mind to take my benches back tonight!"

The murmuring raises to a new level, but it's not angry,

more like folks that came to see a show and who haven't been disappointed. Jackson and I meet eyes. "Told you there's a story here," he says.

Marigene looks sternly at Mr. Blackwell. His daughter shrugs in apology at her, then Marigene smiles sadly and shrugs back at her. Marigene turns away from the podium, to talk to the others behind the podium. I say to Jackson, "Looks like without the 'leading family' there's not much left to do."

"I need to go home!" Momma Bennett decrees. That seems to echo others' thinking as the crowd turns toward the doors to the porch, then they open and, well, I don't think anyone is leaving quite yet.

Well, maybe me. Maybe I'll leave. Yes, I would very much like to leave now. Because stepping into the room is Peter in a suit, clean-shaven, with a starched shirt. His tie is Missus Blue. The folks heading to the door part, and he walks to the microphone, his mother right behind him.

"You've got a lot of nerve—" Mr. Blackwell begins. He actually lifts his cane and points it at Peter.

Peter holds out a hand to Mr. Blackwell. "Thank you, Junior. Thank you all." He looks taller, bigger, more confident, and his voice carries not only with sound, but also with importance. Missus standing behind him looks, well, satisfied isn't a big enough word. Peter thanks everyone again, for what I don't know, and continues. "We are proud to announce the opening of the Chancey Depot Parlor and Porch. There was some thought that we should call it the Bedwell Parlor and Porch, but our family has never sought praise or notice. We are proud to give this holiday present to our town."

Another round of murmurs begins, but his new voice of authority brushes it away. He smiles and makes eye contact around the room. "Now, it's late, and we *all* have Christmas things to do with friends and family, right?" With a laugh he raises his hands as if he's doing a benediction at the end of church. "Merry Christmas, and everyone have a good evening." He steps away from the microphone, and the room swirls with people moving in every direction. Pearl motions for me to come to her, so I tell Jackson and go back to that side of the room.

"Here, take this container of cookies. Give them out in the store or eat them yourselves. Hell, throw them away for all I care. Momma wants to go home, and I want to get out of here."

"Are you okay?"

She sighs and says, "Momma makes me nervous. Always has."

"Are you upset about, well, that?" I nod my head toward the podium area.

Pearl actually looks in that direction. "That? The Bedwells running things?" She pauses and takes a deep breath. "Not really. Not surprised either. Who else in town cares enough to give money to fix things up? They wanna run things? *I* don't really care, but some folks have long, long memories, like Junior Blackwell. He won't be taking those benches, though." She turns away to offer another container of cookies to someone, but I grab her arm.

"Why won't he be taking them?"

"We screwed them to the porch this time." With a quick grin, she goes back to dispersing boxes of cookies.

I bend down to say goodbye to Momma Bennett. "It was nice to meet you. Merry Christmas." She doesn't look in my direction, just stares toward the front. As I go to leave she grasps my forearm. She's wide awake, and she's staring intently enough to make me follow her stare. She's watching Peter and Missus.

"Law, honey," she says. "I never realized how much that boy looks like the judge." She sighs and squeezes my arm tighter. "'Fraid he's started acting like him, too." She releases me and closes her eyes. She mumbles, "I've lived too long. Things just never change. Pearl!"

I back away from her to have Jackson come up on my side.

"So Peter finally showed up. Did you know he was coming tonight?"

"Me? No. Well, I hoped he wouldn't, but… let's get our coats and go."

Jackson shows me his right arm, where our coats are slung. "I hurried over to get our coats when I saw everyone wanting to leave at the same time. Come on."

We turn toward the door, but right there in our faces are Peter and Missus. Peter reaches out to shake Jackson's hand, then reaches to kiss my cheek, but I only give him my hand to shake. It doesn't faze him a bit. "It's so good to be back. Didn't this all turn out well?"

"What?" I say. "Clearing a room by taking credit for all this hard work?"

At the same time I'm talking I hear Jackson say, "Delaney? What are you doing here?" and I see him hug a woman standing next to Peter. Took the fire right out of my words.

"Delaney, this is my wife, Carolina." We shake hands. Jackson explains, "Delaney and I met the morning of the parade."

Our hands are still clasped, and she leans toward me. "And *you* did a marvelous job that morning. It was a fantastic parade." She has a very soft, classy Southern accent and a genuine smile. She's wearing a soft gray dress with gorgeous jewelry. Okay, I'll just say it, she looks rich. And why does my husband know this woman well enough to hug her? I drop her hand and turn to him, giving him my questioning look, which, wonder of wonders, he gets right away.

He grins at us both. "Delaney was taking the group pictures, and I helped her get folks arranged. She helped me get those kids on those floats!"

"Oh! You're a photographer." That's where I'd seen her before. Earlier in the park.

Missus then steps closer to add, "A very *well-known* photographer and an old family friend." She doesn't look bothered at all about what's going on around her. Satisfied is the word that comes to mind again, as if this is exactly how she planned it. I look in Peter's eyes, and he just looks back. He doesn't wink or roll them or even let them crinkle a bit at the edges. We break eye contact, and he moves closer to Delaney. They look at each other, then they both look back at us.

"You forgot one thing about Delaney, Mother. Photographer, family friend," then he holds up their clasped hands, "and my fiancée."

CHAPTER 32

"His what?" Anna and Savannah yell at the same time.

"Shhh, I promised your daddy I wouldn't say anything." It's taken nearly an hour for me to get alone with the girls to tell them. Because that promise was, well, stupid for Jackson to believe. Besides, the look he gave me when I headed upstairs with them to supposedly show them some Christmas presents said that he knew what I was doing, so it's not like I'm actually breaking a promise, right?

All the kids were there when we got home after a mostly stunned drive. Stunned and frustrating as I tried to jog Jackson's memory of Delaney's last name. He extracted my promise to not cloud our family time with the drama, and I agreed because I needed time to process it.

We'd decided to do finger foods while we decorated the tree. Bryan made pigs in a blanket; Savannah mixed up a bowl of spinach dip and heated up the dish of buffalo chicken dip I'd left on the counter. Will and Anna made their first ever batch of sausage balls, and it was all hot and waiting on us when we walked in the door. Jackson and Bryan had put up the tree earlier in the day and even strung the lights, so all we had to do was eat, enjoy our traditional Christmas CDs, and decorate the tree.

I actually forgot about Peter. Then, soaking in the fully decorated tree with the house lights off, it crept back to the front of my mind. And I had to tell somebody…

Which is how we came to be standing in my bedroom with me quickly telling them all I know.

"She's a family friend and apparently they dated in college. She looks like she's got money, but I didn't find out her last name so I can't Google her."

They both groan, and Anna moves to sit on the bed. She leans back on her arms and her belly just looks huge. Her shirt stretches and she looks down. "Watch, I bet you can see her moving around."

Savannah sits beside her, eyes glued to possible movement from her niece. "But what about Shannon? How can he already be engaged? They were living together just a couple weeks ago."

"Exactly. Shannon is going to be devastated," I say. "Should I call her and tell her before she hears it at church tomorrow?"

Anna shakes her head, chewing on the side of her mouth. "I don't know. Did Peter and Missus act like they're going to tell everyone? I mean, were they just telling y'all?"

I step into the bathroom and look in the mirror. "I don't know. Honestly, it was kind of a blur after they told us. My mouth literally dropped open, and I didn't say anything. Then we left." Staring in the mirror I shake my head and sigh. "Guys, they looked so great together. She seemed nice." Coming back into the bedroom and seeing the baby dancing and Savannah in awe makes me smile.

"Go ahead, you can touch," Anna says.

Savannah gently lays her hand down. Then she laughs out loud. "I just can't wait to hold her!"

"Join the club," Anna and I say.

Abruptly Savannah sits up straight. "Wait, she's a photographer? Is she the one at the parade?"

"Yeah. That's how your daddy knew her."

"Oh." She grimaces. "She was super nice and so pretty. She didn't look that old until you got close, you know?"

"That old? She's my age. But, yeah, I know what you mean."

"Did she have a ring?" Anna asks. She's moving around to try and get Francie to move some more, but is having no luck.

"Oh, did she have a ring! It was magnificent. Something about it being from her family or something. Like I said, it was… whatever." I reach out a hand to pull my daughter-in-law up. "Come on. Let's go back downstairs. Will and Bryan should have the hot chocolate done by now."

We all stand, but Savannah holds us back. "Wait just a minute. Mom, did you tell Anna about me and Ricky?"

"No."

Anna waves a hand in the air. "I think I saw enough last week at Greens beside the bonfire." She nudges Savannah. "Y'all going out?"

Crossing her arms and pressing them to her, Savannah dips her head, then tilts it to look up, her eyes huge. "He asked me out on a real-live date. Next Friday." She's grinning, and her face is flushed. Anna and I connect glances.

"Sounds nice. Where are you going?" Anna asks as we walk to the door.

"He just told me to dress nice."

"Sounds interesting…" Anna says as she opens the bedroom door, then she yelps. "Oh, Bryan!"

Bryan also jumps back. "You scared me." Then he holds up my phone. "Mom, you left your phone downstairs, and it's blowing up." I take it from him, and he turns to lope down the stairs. Over his shoulder he says, "It's been ringing, but ya also got some texts. Looks like Peter and Shannon got engaged. That's cool!"

For a moment I look at the girls, then quickly open my phone. "Oh, no. *Oh, no.* He's right. Word's gotten round it's Shannon he's engaged to. Oh, no…"

Anna winces. "'Oh, no' doesn't quite seem strong enough." Then she stops mid-stair. "Wait. Why didn't Peter or Grand-missus tell *me*? I'm family." She stomps down the stairs, Savannah and me following, then Savannah stops behind me.

"What are you doing?" I ask over my shoulder.

"Nothing. Just texting Ricky to be sure and come to church in the morning. This is one Sunday no one will want to miss."

I sigh and walk on down to where Anna is explaining everything to the guys. Folks say the biggest crowds at church are on Christmas and Easter. They've just never been around when big gossip hits a small town on Saturday night.

CHAPTER 33

"Well, it's kind of your fault."

"My fault! How in the world could it possibly be my fault?" Jackson asks as he parks the van in our usual spot at church. Savannah was right. Lots of folks are here already. But maybe it's because the choir is performing the Christmas cantata today.

Right.

I persist in my argument. "If you hadn't made me promise to not tell anyone, then Laney and Susan would've had the right story from the get-go."

"And your name would've been all over it. Did you think of that? Maybe you should just say 'thank you.'"

We get out and walk toward the sanctuary. There isn't Sunday School today, just the cantata. The choir practices for months for the long performance, and it's usually pretty good. Several of the smaller churches participate in ours since they don't have enough people or space to do their own, so it's really a big community thing. It'll be done twice, once this morning and again this evening. That way the other churches can have their own service this morning then see the cantata tonight. It's quite the production and there's always a crowd, but this feels different.

Usually people rush on in to get seats so they don't have to sit up in the balcony, but today little gaggles gather across the lawn in prayer.

I'm joking, they're not in prayer.

My own gaggle motions for me to hurry. Jackson reluctantly releases my gloved hand from his.

"Save me a seat," I say with a smile. I add a wink. "And it's really not your fault."

He sneers at me then blows me a kiss.

Laney grabs my arm. "Get over here. So you're right. It's not Shannon!"

"I know I'm right. I met her. I heard it from Peter's own lips."

Susan shakes her head, lips pursed, and eyes livid. "I'm going to kill that daughter of mine. She once again played town crier! She walked to the depot to get some pictures for that infernal blog of hers. She got there late, ran into Libby and Ruby who were already outside, and they told her Peter was engaged. She took it from there. I don't know if she just didn't hear correctly or if they didn't know what was what. Either way," she takes a deep breath, "I'm going to kill her."

"I tried calling Shannon last night, but she didn't answer. Wonder if she'll show up this morning."

Laney scoffs. "Are you crazy? Although her church *is* small and out of town. Maybe no one there knows."

Susan rolls her eyes. "Oh, yeah. They don't gossip out in the country."

"No," I say. "She's singing in the cantata."

Their eyes widen. Laney cringes. "This cantata?"

Nodding, I bite my lip and look toward the front steps. "Guess we should go on in and face the music. Has anyone seen Missus or Peter?"

Laney says, "Nope. Mom just texted me that we need to come inside. She hasn't spotted either of them."

We start walking, and the other gaggles do, too. I nudge Susan with my elbow. "Silas still shooting his commercial?"

"No. He's here this weekend."

Laney huffs. "He home waiting for you in that nice, warm bed?" She murmurs, "And you complaining about your daughter."

Susan ignores the last statement and steps ahead of us, but with her nose in the air, she says, "He's inside."

Laney and I share a look. "Inside where?" I ask as we begin up the stairs.

"Inside the church. Saving me a seat just like Shaw and Jackson are for you."

She pushes on ahead and is headed down the center aisle when Laney lets out a bit of a laugh/sigh combination. "Thank goodness I had Momma looking for Missus and Peter. It kept her from spotting Silas and asking the ushers to throw him out!"

I slide into the pew beside Jackson, whispering in his general direction. "This cantata might have a cello, flute, and solos, but I don't think it can hold a candle to the entertainment in the pews. Here comes Peter and Missus, and Delaney is with them."

"Really? That would be amazing." I hear Anna breathlessly exclaim as I walk up behind her and Will.

"Hi," I say. They're speaking with Delaney, and I figure I might as well get it over with.

"Carolina, Miss Delaney is going to do our baby shoot. Can you believe that? She's, like, famous!" Anna turns to me with wide, shiny eyes. Guess we now have a local president of the official Delaney fan club. She asks, "You know each other, right?"

"Yes," we both say. The fellowship hall is crowded for the cantata after-party. I don't think they actually call it that, it's something much holier sounding, but that's what it is. Little quiches, fruit salad, and mini muffins are being served, along with a table of Christmas cookies coming from the same containers I saw last night under the table at the depot.

Delaney reaches out to hug me first, but of course I meet her halfway. This *is* the South, y'all. She's wearing a navy dress, and her hair is pulled back into a low ponytail. "I met your lovely daughter, Savannah. She does you proud. And here you are expecting your first grandchild. You are a blessed woman, Carolina."

"That I am. Did you have something to eat?"

"Oh, I'm fine. Thank you. What a wonderful cantata!"

We talk about the cantata and the church and other stuff, but I'm on autopilot. All I can think about is how absolutely charming this woman is. How perfectly she seems to fit in Chancey. Which makes me think of Shannon. She did not sing in the cantata after all, and she's not answered my calls or texts.

Then I see Peter headed our way. "Oh, I'm going to get some coffee," I say abruptly by way of an exit line, but when I turn, there stands Jackson holding a fresh cup up to me.

"I got you coffee."

"Thank you," I manage to grit through my teeth.

By the time I take the cup, Peter has joined us. "Carolina, Jackson. Good to see you again." He leans over to kiss Anna's cheek and shake Will's hand. "Won't be long now, will it?"

"No," Will says. "Only a couple more weeks. Welcome home—oh, and congratulations on the engagement."

"Thank you. We'll have a party soon at the house to make a more formal announcement."

"The house?" I say with a look at Anna. I can't ask, but she's family.

Anna frowns at me, then her face clears. "Oh, the house? Peter's house? Um, is that where you'll be living or are living…?"

Delaney smiles wide. Peter laughs and shakes his head. "Not

hardly. That house was just some silly project. Why I spent so much time and money on that hovel is beyond me. No, we're moving into the Bedwell house. Mother is moving into the wing she updated for you two."

Anna and Will's shocked looks must be echoed on Jackson's and my faces because Delaney and Peter look at us all, then frown at each other. Then the four of us take breaths and find our smiles. Anna reaches over to hug Delaney. "What a surprise! That's wonderful news. Grandmissus did make that such a nice place for us. You'll, I mean, she'll love it."

Jackson shakes Peter's hand again. "Congratulations again. Well, I think we're going to go. Right, Carolina?"

"Yes," I say as Jackson puts his arm around my shoulders. "Bye. See you soon."

We walk straight across the room, not stopping until we're next to the opposite wall. Then we turn and take a minute. We are both staring across the room saying nothing, then we look at each other.

"Did I hear that right?" Jackson asks.

"Yes. I heard the same thing and one phrase keeps running through my mind: The King is dead. Long live the King." I crush my empty cup and toss it into a nearby garbage can. "Or should it be, 'The Queen is dead. Long live the Queen'?"

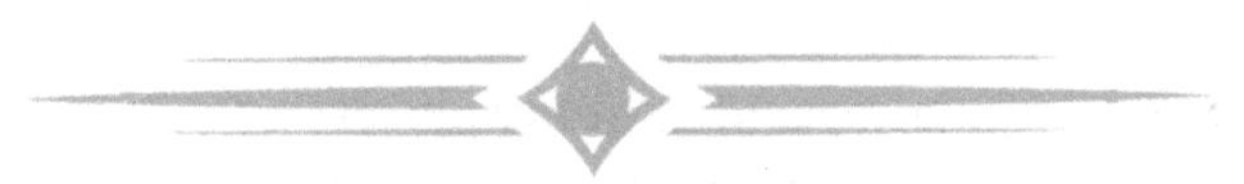

Chapter 34

"Falcons play at four. Come over for chili," Laney says as we leave the church fellowship hall. "We're having the family over."

I hear, "Sounds great," before I can say it myself. Laney and I twist to look behind us. We stop, and traffic weaves around us. Susan is standing there with her arm looped through Silas'. He sheepishly smiles at us with a silent "hello." Susan's eyes are narrowed and burrowing into her sister's, daring her to say they aren't invited.

I really don't like when people dare Laney. It never works out well.

Until now. Laney swallows, then actually relaxes her shoulders and takes a step back. "Of course. Kids, too."

Susan blinks. Her mouth opens, but nothing comes out. Finally she nods and says, "Okay."

Laney looks around us. "We're blocking traffic," she says and pulls me around to hurry outside. We don't hurry fast enough to keep from hearing Silas say loudly, "Great. I love soccer."

I start laughing, and Laney is laughing, too, by the time we get outside. We chuckle all the way down to the parking lot at Silas and his lack of football (real football) knowledge, but also the way the family lighting the advent wreath almost had a knock-down, drag-out fight over which kid got to light which candle.

"What can I bring?" I finally ask. "'Cause I love soccer, too!"

"I don't care. I've got the basics. Some snacks or a dessert or even nothing is fine. Not like anyone is going to starve." She straightens her long coat, which matches her dark plum dress. Her lipstick is the same plum; her heels, too. It's a good color for her, so I tell her that.

"Thanks. I did an overhaul of my closet with that wardrobe lady from the movie." She makes a face like she smells something going bad. "Everything's pretty, and very expensive, but it all feels so old and dull." Then she sighs. "But every time I wear something I like, that really brings out my assets, I get in trouble."

"In trouble? With who?"

She begins walking and sighs. "I take it you're not on Instagram?"

"No. Isn't that more for the kids? Just a bunch of pictures?"

"Kind of. But as a politician I've been told I have to be on there. And, well, every time I wear something fun I am very much on there. And it's not nice." She wrinkles her nose. "You should've seen it after the parade."

"Oh, the silver dress with the slit up to, well, you know." I pull her into a bit of sunshine. I've once again left the house without a coat.

She looks around and whispers, "That was really why I was going to drop out of the race. People can be so mean online."

"Well, I think you look beautiful in this, but if you don't like it, then wear what you want."

She hugs me. "Thanks. I'll think about it, but it's only for a couple months. Then I can be who I want to be, right?"

"But what if you win?"

"Silly rabbit, of course I'm going to win. Why would you think I might not win? Thought you were my friend."

"But you said…"

"Right, when I'm mayor I can wear whatever I want." She

looks to the side. "There's Shaw. We'll see you later." She hurries off, her stylish coat flapping behind her like a cape.

Jackson is waiting in our van, and as I step inside, I laugh. "Missus and Laney think they can change who they are overnight to get votes and folks will buy it."

He puts the car in reverse, and as he looks over his shoulder he says, "That's why long campaigns are good. It's hard to fake it for a long time. This time they've only got to get to the middle of January."

"But honestly? Do they think folks buy it?"

He grins as he stops backing up. "Yes. Those two believe folks will believe whatever they tell them to."

"That's true. Where's Bryan?"

"Kendricks were there. Um, they've invited us for Sunday dinner, and I said yes. Just didn't feel like Chinese buffet today."

"Oh, Laney invited us over for chili and to watch the Falcons at four and I said yes."

We look at each other for a moment, and I shrug. "I guess if you eat at the Chinese buffet every Sunday, folks eventually feel sorry for you."

Wrapped in my robe I creep down the stairs before the first light of day. I woke before the alarm, which will wake Jackson in about fifteen minutes, and lay there for nearly a half hour so I decided to come downstairs. Smelling the Christmas tree makes me smile. I go straight to the switch connected to the tree lights and turn them on. The house is so quiet, and to have it alone is worth being awake this early. I pull an afghan from the couch and snuggle beneath it in the chair closest to the tree.

Yesterday was the loudest day I've ever experienced. The cantata was wonderful, but powerful and not very contemplative. Or maybe that was just me not being very contemplative. Then there was the after-party in the fellowship hall with the general fawning over Delaney LaMotte. Did you know she's *famous*! Straight from there we plunged into the chaos of the Kendrick home. Kimmy and Kyle's better control over their brood in public does not seem to have caught on at home. Or maybe I've just forgotten what three kids under the age of six sounds like. No, Kimmy is louder than I was on my worst day. Kyle is a better husband and father than before, but he's doing that on the back of jokes. Yes, he's become the grand champion of dad jokes. He laughs so loud. So very loud. And the kids all laugh so very loud, too. All of this could've been forgiven with a good meal, but it was frozen lasagna—cheap frozen lasagna, with cold garlic toast and raw baby carrots. And we had to wait for the lasagna to cook. I'm sure you know a pan of frozen lasagna takes an hour to cook. I suggested doing some of the cooking in the microwave to give it a boost. Did you know cheap frozen lasagna comes in an aluminum pan so you can't put it in the microwave? Well, it does.

Jackson said he kept looking for a camera from some reality TV show: put nice, normal people in extreme conditions and see how they handle it. However, it was nice to watch Bryan and Zoe. They laughed at all the jokes, played games with the kids, and helped with dinner. I hate to break it to my son, but I realized yesterday that Zoe sees him as *just* a friend. Poor guy.

The three of us did get to run home to change clothes before heading to Laney and Shaw's. I grabbed up the container of Christmas cookies Pearl had given me at the depot, we put on jeans, I put on a red turtleneck and Jackson his Falcons jersey, then we were out the door again, Bryan in tow. Grant had texted that he was coming to his Aunt Laney's for the game, so Bryan was willing to leave Zoe and his unrequited crush behind.

Jackson's alarm buzzes upstairs and makes me jump. I get up to put on some coffee. Last night I put the Christmas mugs in the cabinet, so I pick a couple and set them beside the coffee maker. The backyard looks blue as the light begins to come up the hill. The lights of the tree reflect in the door leading outside, so through that reflection I look down the hill and toward the river.

Patches of the water shine silver through the black trees. I pull my robe around me tighter by hunching my shoulders. My hands are buried in its pockets.

Laney's house was as loud as the Kendricks'. Her whole family showed up, and even she had to admit Silas was a good sport, making fun of himself and his lack of football knowledge. He subjected himself to a lesson from the guys in the backyard during halftime. Again, one of my favorite parts was watching Bryan, this time with Grant. They were like the boys they used to be, running and laughing, trying to tackle Grant's cousins Ricky and Ronnie. Laney's brother Scott was there not only with his boys, but also with their mom, Abby Sue.

Last time I was around Abby Sue was last Christmas. She's tiny with long, blond curls and the hots for her on-again, off-again husband. She lives and sells real estate in the northern Atlanta suburbs. She moved there when their boys were little. They stayed here with Scott, who would not even consider moving from Chancey. Scott's mother and his sisters helped with the boys. It may sound crazy, but this arrangement has worked for them. Abby Sue comes around just often enough to get her itch scratched. While she's around, they scratch a lot. All the time. Everywhere.

It's embarrassing the first few times, then you get kind of used to it. However, I don't think any of us will ever get used to Susan and Silas acting out. With Scott and Abby Sue there's giggling and joking back and forth, it's yucky, but kind of cute. Susan and Silas it's uncomfortable because it feels intense. Silas watches her, studies her, like he can't get enough of her. I was wrong, he won't just go away. And watching them together, I'm not sure she wants him to.

But while all that noise and the wide array of people kept swirling in my head instead of sleep last night, Shannon is why my eyes wouldn't stay shut.

I finally got a hold of her mother, who said to not worry about Shannon. She's out of town for a while. That's it. Out of town for a while. That's all she would say. She said Shannon will contact me later this week, but that she's covered everything with the flower shop. Her mother sounded happy, like Shannon had won a trip to Hawaii or something. What in the world is going on?

And before you ask, no, I never did find out if Shannon is pregnant.

CHAPTER 35

"Momma says we're moving the baby shower to the new house," Patty announces as she comes down the back staircase in the shop.

"Anna's shower? Like the one Thursday night? This week?" I'm seated at my card table going through the box of used books Andy delivered over the weekend. "I thought it was in Gertie's cave?"

Patty sighs loudly enough to make me smile. She's such an Eeyore. You know, the sad donkey in Winnie the Pooh. "Naw, Momma said that's not right. Not with me expecting now." Patty slogs around to stand in front of me. She plants a hand on her hip and looks down at me. "Momma said that if we want a big fancy shower for *our* baby, then we have to throw a big fancy shower for *your* baby. Momma says that's just how things work."

"Nooo," I say as I get up from my metal folding chair. I'm thinking, Yeah, that is pretty much how it works, but I say, "Don't be silly. We *all* thought a shower in the moonshine cave would be such fun." No, we didn't.

I lay one arm across her shoulders and walk her to the sitting area. "Is your house even ready for something like that? Y'all invited an awful lot of people."

"I know. Momma thought it'd be a good way to promote her business, but now…" She pats her stomach.

"Now things are different," I say. Susan and Laney had been planning on throwing a baby shower for Anna when we all received the first round of email invites from Gertie and Patty. I say the first round because every update has meant a whole new invite, each of course stating it would be held in "Gertie's Moonshine Cave in Andy's Place. Come early to shop!" No, I'm not joking.

"Momma says if we don't do something nicer then my shower will be held in some church basement or even here in the shop." Patty sighs again and then pushes herself up. "I'm meeting Mr. Spoon upstairs at the *Vedette* to get some real nice invitations printed up to hand deliver before Thursday." She's almost to the door when she says, "Momma says if—"

I cut her off. "If you don't do nice invitations, then for your baby shower there will only be email invites."

She turns to me, surprise widening her eyes and opening her mouth. "So it's true? You think that, too?"

"You better go before you miss Charles. He might already be down at Ruby's."

She nods and plods out the door.

I would've really liked to have been able to tell her that her momma was dead wrong, but I'd be lying. I'd already been congratulating myself on how easy Patty's shower was going to be.

Darn it. Momma's right again.

Heading back to my box of books, my back is to the door when I hear the bell ring. Expecting it to be Patty back because she forgot something, I yell, "Hey."

My heart practically stops when I hear Jackson respond, "Hey."

I flip around. "What are you doing here? What's wrong?"

He's standing just inside the door, and his face is grim. I reverse course to go to him.

"It's work. There are going to be layoffs in our office."

Cold clutches my heart. "Have you heard anything specific?"

He shakes his head. "No, but I couldn't concentrate. Needed to get out of the house." He walks past me toward the back of the shop. "What are you doing?"

"Marking books." I catch up and turn him to give him a hug. "It's nice to get a visit from you. Bonnie comes in in a bit. Want to go get a cup of coffee at Ruby's?"

He chuckles and steps back. "Think I've had enough coffee. I made another pot after you left and drank most of it. Besides, I'm meeting Colt."

"Doesn't he have classes?"

"He has a study period, and we're going to talk about working together maybe."

"But what about him moving back to Kentucky?"

Jackson shrugs. "We're just talking." He walks around Shannon's clean worktable. "So nothing else from Shannon?"

"Nope. Everything was cleaned up when I got here. There's a cooler full of her orders for early in the week, and her dad is going to deliver them. Then she's got the florist in Collinswood covering for her. They do that for each other since they're both basically one-woman shops."

We stand at opposite ends of the worktable, him looking down at the table, me looking at him. "When do you think you'll hear anything?"

He shrugs again. "There's a meeting in the office on Thursday. Guess we'll find out if my project is to remain on hold or cancelled altogether."

"But that's not your fault."

"No, but it means there's not a lot for me to do." He taps his knuckles on the table. "Well, I'm going to go meet Colt." He smiles and walks toward me. "But I sure could use another one of those hugs of yours." We hug tightly, then break apart as the bell over the door rings.

"Hey, Jackson," Gertie says. "What are you doing gallivanting around in the middle of a workday? Taking vacation?"

He shakes his head at me (like I would tell Gertie anything), then turns quickly toward her. "Just working from home and thought I'd come see how things look downtown in the daylight. Gotta go." He tells us both goodbye as he strides out the door, then turns down the sidewalk.

Gertie leans back on the counter. "Not good when a man is checking up on his wife when he's supposed to be at work. Either he thinks she's up to no good or he's up to no good. Which is it, Carolina? What's going on with you two? I saw him tell you not to say something."

"Nothing. Shouldn't you be busy enough with the shower you've decided to upgrade?"

"Oh, I've hired a party planner and given her full use of Patty. Works out good that Savannah taking Patty's job."

"Savannah is only part time," I say. "She's supposed to be helping Patty, not doing her job."

Gertie shrugs. "So what I do need is to hire someone to get the house in order fast. I've got a crew over there painting. They're finishing today, but I need to hire someone to get things furnished and decorated." She pauses and tips her head at me with her eyebrows raised.

"Me? I don't have time to do something like that."

Standing up straight and uncrossing her arms, she scoffs. "Time? You don't have the *talent* is the biggest problem with that suggestion. Thanks for offering, but no, thanks. Bonnie. When does she come in today? Or, you know what? Just give me her phone number. That'll be quicker."

"Bonnie isn't going to be interested in doing that on this kind of time, but I'll let her tell you that. She'll be here any minute." I turn my back on her and try not to stomp back to my box of books.

I only get one book written down before I hear the bell ring and Gertie say, "There she is! Just the woman I want to talk to."

Trying to block out their conversation to keep from hearing more about Gertie's opinion of my decorating ability, or lack thereof, I manage to get to the bottom of the box before I realize I didn't write down the authors' names. Multi-tasking for me means doing neither job well. I also only half heard what Gertie was saying, but Bonnie will tell me the high points and we can laugh about it later.

I'm halfway through getting the authors listed when Gertie yells, "Goodbye, Carolina. Quit sulking. Maybe your blood sugar is low. Want me to bring you a muffin?" She doesn't even give me a chance to say, "Yes, I *would* like a muffin," before the door closes and she's gone.

Bonnie, however, is already standing beside my little table. "I assume you heard all that? I told her I'd call her to let her know, but I needed to check with you first. Can you cover for me this week?"

"What? You want to do it?"

Her face lights up. Bonnie's pretty, but usually in a rather private-school, teachery way—very held together, polished, not too expressive. Now, though, she's really excited, and it changes her whole appearance. It even makes her look younger. "I've always wanted to be a decorator, but my parents said I couldn't make a living doing it. I got a teaching degree instead, and it was easy to get a job wherever we moved for Cal's career. Then I decided I was too old when I retired." She takes a big breath and lets it out. "For something like this to fall in my lap? Oh, Carolina, it's a dream come true."

"Then, well, of course I can cover for you this week. Shannon's not here, so we don't have the flower business to worry about, but…"

"Oh, thank you!" She has her phone in hand and immediately walks up to the front as she's dialing. "It's a go! I'll meet you there," she blurts into the phone.

I rush to the front before she can leave. "So, um, I don't know how to log the books in or the other stuff you do here."

She waves a hand in my direction. "I'll stop in before you close today and give you a run-through. It's so easy. You'll pick it right up. I should've shown you before. It *is* your shop!" She laughs and is flying out the door before I can say anything else.

But honestly, what exactly is there for me to say?

CHAPTER 36

If Sunday was the loudest day, today has been the quietest—except for that flurry of news this morning, of course. Susie Mae isn't scheduled to work after school on Mondays because they're so slow. That's how bored I've been: I'm wishing for Susie Mae to talk to.

Midafternoon, Bonnie sailed in full of news of the adorable little house and all the plans she has for it. Before heading off to shop in Atlanta, she ran through what I needed to know about our computer system. I didn't tell her I'd pretty much figured it out in the hours and hours I had to fill with something.

"I'm closing early," I declare to the empty building. But what if Jackson loses his job? I can't help thinking. What if this becomes our livelihood? What if I miss someone who wants to buy a lot of books and they couldn't get here earlier because they had to work? Speaking of Jackson, what did he and Colt talk about? Why won't he call me back? Is it a good idea him going into business with Colt? Isn't Colt too much like their dad? What if Jackson is home all the time? Why haven't I paid more attention to our budget? I need to think. I need to go home. I'm closing early.

But what if…

I slam my hands onto the counter and push against it, my eyes closed. "I'm going to drive myself crazy."

The bell rings. My big customer who's going to buy a lot? Then my eyes jerk open. "Oh, Rachel. Hi."

Susan's mother-in-law gives me her judgy look, which is her normal look. "Hello. Looks quiet in here."

"It is. Mondays are like that."

"Really? Maybe you should run a special or something." She walks into the rows of bookshelves.

"Maybe I should. How are things going with your pop-up shop? I imagine selling Christmas trees in December isn't the kind of business you need to really run specials on, is it?"

"Right you are. However, since I donated the space to the Scouts, I'm losing money. What book are we're doing for book club next month?"

"*Big Little Lies* by Liane Moriarty, but I don't have any copies left." I wander a little closer to the shelves. "So you'll still be here in January?"

"Suppose so." She pulls out a book. "Have you read any of his?" She holds up *Devil in the White City* by Erik Larson.

"Oh, yes. That is really good." I move into the aisle. "His are non-fiction, but they read like they're made up. That's his best, I think." I pull out another. "And this one of his is good, too." We move through the shelves talking about books, and when we walk out to the front end of the store, I'm surprised to see how dark the shop windows have grown.

"Oh! What time is it?" I say as I turn to the clock. "Only four-thirty. Guess it's overcast. Plus, the days really are pretty short now."

Rachel carries her stack of books to the counter. "You're not usually here in the afternoons, are you?"

"No. Bonnie's got things to do this week." I feel more comfortable with Rachel than ever before, but she still makes me bristle. She just made a statement, with no judgment. It's all in my mind, I tell myself as I move behind the counter.

"Might be tiring for you actually having to work full days.

Not like sitting around up there on the hill waiting on people to need a room in this one-horse town."

I was obviously being nice too quickly. I let myself bristle away. "Yep." Ignoring her I ring up the books only to finish and have her tell me she has credit on them.

"You know? The credit system you have in place. Or is that Bonnie's system? Should I wait for her to come back? Maybe we could call her."

"No. I know about it. I just forgot. Sure. I've got it here." Keeping my head down I take care of her, shove her books in a bag, then slide them to the end of the counter, and start closing up the cash register.

She's standing there judging me. I can feel it in the little hairs on the nape of my neck. I just want to go home and forget this day. Except I'm coming right back for more tomorrow and the day after that and every day for the rest of my life because Bonnie is going to quit and Jackson is going to lose his job and—a sob slips out, but I don't look up.

"Are you okay?" Rachel asks. "Carolina? Um, I'm sorry. I didn't mean to, uh. I enjoyed talking about books with you."

I mutter, "Okay." Then I add, "I'm closing."

She waits another moment, then finally leaves. As soon as the door closes behind her, I dash to it, lock it, and turn over the open sign.

This day is officially closed.

Except I haven't given one blessed thought about what we're having for supper.

"I'm grilling tonight," Bryan announces as I walk in the front door. He's lying on the couch watching TV. "Dad and me. Pork chops."

"Okay. That sounds awesome." I pull off my coat and hang it on the coatrack beside the door. "Savannah home?"

"Don't think so. Was her car out there?"

"No, now that I think about it. Where's your dad?"

He shrugs in his prone position, eyes never leaving the screen. I yank down my fleece shirt, which rode up my back with my coat, as I walk into the kitchen. Sure enough there's a packet of boneless pork chops on the counter defrosting. Next to them is a box of rice pilaf. No, two boxes. Oh, and that's a big packet of pork chops. Wonder who else is coming for dinner?

I step to the basement door, and light spills out when I open it. Jackson yells up, "You're home! I was just coming up." I leave it open and go to see what vegetables are in the freezer.

Jackson runs up the stairs. This is the first time I've talked to him since he was in the store and I'm not happy about that, but the man who bounds up the final step, then across the kitchen to hug me is not the same man from the store this morning. It looks like he had a better day than I had.

He squeezes me. "Ooh, you're cold. I'll warm you up!" He pulls back to grin at me and then kiss me quickly. "How was your day?"

"Bad. How was yours?"

"Good! Bryan and I are grilling. He tell you?" He releases me and turns to the counter. "Pork chops on the grill! We've not had that for a while."

"Because it's winter," I growl, then stop myself. With a big smile I rush to say, "Not that we can't grill in the winter, we just haven't. Good idea!" He's picked up one of the rice pilaf box and is reading it. I ask, "So is it just us for dinner?"

Looking up at me, he grins. "Well, I invited Colt. And Phoenix. If I'm going to be home more, I want to see them more. They're family!"

"Okay. Another good idea." I open the freezer. "How did your and Colt's talk go this morning?"

"Really good. I think I talked him into staying here. We're going to start a business building decks and doing renovations for folks. Listen, I need to go finish up a couple things downstairs before dinner." He steps to me and kisses my forehead. "We can talk about all of it at dinner, right?"

"Right," I say to his back as he disappears down the stairwell. The door closes, and Phoenix comes walking down the hall toward me. She's wearing low-rise jeans and a comfy sweatshirt that leaves an inch of midriff visible. She's barefoot, and her hair is in that thick braid she wears so well. She looks about twenty.

I turn back to dig in the freezer.

"So what's this about Jackson and Colt going into business together?" she asks. "I didn't realize Jackson did construction type stuff."

With a bag of frozen lima beans in one hand and frozen corn in the other, I stand up. "He doesn't. However, for some reason, when he's with Colt or his father, he forgets all that. Forgets that he likes things on a blueprint. He likes writing things down in black and white for other people to figure out how to do." I toss the bags onto the counter, then dig out two pots. Sitting them on the stove, I turn and lean on the counter. She's leaning on the counter, too, at the end by the coffee pot.

"So how's this going to work, then?"

"I don't know." I cross my arms and look down. I have no idea if Jackson has told his brother about things at work, so I'm not saying anything.

She seems to realize I'm done talking and leans to stand straight. "Okay, then. Want me to set the table? I hear Colt and I are invited to dinner."

"Sure. Thanks."

She crosses behind me to the cabinet where the plates are while I'm at the sink running water in the pots. "You know I was telling you about me possibly doing a juice bar?"

"Yeah. How's that going?"

"Really, really good. I have an investor."

"That's great. Who?" I turn to her, but she ducks her head and heads for the dining room table.

"I can't talk about it yet, but soon I'll let you know." She sets the plates on the table, then returns to rummage through the silverware drawer. She counts out forks and knives, then with them in hand she shoves the drawer closed with her hip. "And, well, don't say anything to Colt yet, but I'm going to be moving out of here at the end of the week. Just felt I should let you know."

"Colt doesn't know you're coming home?" I abandon the vegetables and follow her into the dining room. I watch her set the table and wait for an answer. Once again, I'm a mom, so I can wait for an answer all day.

She lays cloth napkins from the basket in the middle of the table, puts down the plates and silverware, then pulls out a couple of hot mats from the drawer of the china closet and puts them in the center of the table. She looks up at me and sighs. "Colt…" She sighs again, but only shakes her head. "I don't know," she finally says as she walks out of the dining room and down the B&B hall to her room.

Well, I guess I can't go open her door and demand she talk, can I? Mom powers do have their limit, and I have lima beans to cook.

CHAPTER 37

"Half the fun of being at Ruby's is messing with her, but for today I guess I'll have to just mess with you." Laney drops her big pocketbook on the couch in the shop, then sets her travel cup on the coffee table. "Susan's on her way. I've got the muffins in here." She pulls out a basket, complete with checkered napkin and four muffins from her purse. Told you it was big.

"Didn't Ruby have a to-go bag?"

"Of course, but I wanted the whole experience. Until I can get Cayden in some daycare or find a nanny, I only have one morning a week when Mom can watch him and I can go out for coffee in peace." She runs her hands down her thighs, then eases onto the couch. "These stupid natural fabrics don't have any give, but apparently that's what young people want you to wear these days. Can't wait until I can go back to my synthetics. Now explain to me why I have to forego Ruby's again. Bonnie's working for Gertie now?"

I sit across from her, letting my stretch corduroy pants do what God made them for. "Laney, I don't think people care about the fabric of… never mind. Bonnie has always wanted to be a decorator apparently. Who knew?"

Laney nods and looks around. "Makes sense. She did all this. So you're on your own here all week. Tell me what you've heard from Shannon." She stretches to look out the front window. "Where is my sister? I don't want to have to hear things twice. I'm on limited time. Oh, there she is. Crossing the park."

We watch as Susan runs across the street and then through the front door. "Made it!" she says breathlessly. "You have coffee on, right? I didn't bring any from home." She's headed to the coffee pot when Laney whistles.

"Hey, come get my cup for a refill. My pants don't like getting up and down."

Susan swerves over and takes the outstretched cup. "I told you a little polyester or stretch would be okay."

Laney shakes her head. "Nope. All natural for me until Election Day. But you can imagine I'll be sporting some elastic at the victory party." She rolls her hand at me. "Okay, start talking. Bonnie, then Shannon." Susan sets the cups on the table and sits beside her sister.

"Bonnie is decorating Patty and Andy's house in time for the shower Thursday night. Matter of fact," I lean over and pick up thick envelopes with each of their names on them, "here are your invitations. Patty is distributing them today and she just dropped these off. I haven't opened mine yet."

The creamy blush envelope has a sheen to it, and the paper is thick. We pull out the beautiful invitations in the shape of a full-blown pink rose, and as we open them glitter showers our laps, the table, and the floor.

Laney tetches. "Are you kidding me? I wasn't planning on cleaning these stupid pants already. They'll cost an arm and leg, I'm sure." She wipes the glitter off and onto the floor. "Who does this stupid stuff? They better be right happy I didn't open this at my house. I would not be happy having to clean this glitter garbage up all over the place."

"Yeah, you mean like here in my store."

Susan jumped up after she opened hers and is brushing the sparkles off her long navy skirt. "Great. I have a meeting at Mountain Electric later." She smirks at me, covered in my own fairy dust. "You can just pretend its part of your Christmas decorations in the shop."

"That's true," I say, then bounce the sparkles off my light pink sweater as well as I can. "They sure got these printed up fast."

Susan sits back down. "Money greases wheels. So, Bonnie is coming back here to work, right?"

"I hope. I mean, there can't be that many decorating jobs for someone that's untrained and has no experience around here, right?"

The sisters make eye contact, and Susan winces. "Possibly. I mean, maybe."

"What? What have you heard? Is she quitting?"

"Oh, nothing like that. Just a lot of people were invited to the shower, and when money's no object it will probably look really good. Look what she did with this place."

Laney nods as she leans over to cut the muffins in half. "Besides, maybe it'll be good for you to have more responsibility around this place. Ruby is going old school this week, she said. Banana nut, blueberry crumble, and chocolate chip. She'd made something with bran and cranberries called Cran Bran muffins, but she said she was saving them to feed to the birds. I think she's about ready to call it quits on the healthy stuff."

"Speaking of healthy stuff," I say, picking up half of a banana nut muffin, "Phoenix has an investor and is putting in the juice bar. Not only that, she's thinking about eventually serving food. Healthy food, but she's a really good cook so we'd probably like hers."

"Investor? From here?" Susan asks.

I shrug. "She wouldn't say, but she's also pretty close-mouthed about Colt, so I'm wondering if it could be that judge she was involved with in Kentucky. I told y'all how he followed us around at the wedding things. He's pretty well off."

"What does she say about Colt? Nothing at all?" Laney asks as she eats her blueberry crumble muffin top first.

"Jackson invited them both to dinner last night. They acted like nothing was wrong. I mean, they didn't act like a couple, but they didn't act mad. It was weird. I think he just thinks she's taking a break and it means nothing. She's so hard to read. But she did say she's moving out at the end of this week."

"To where?" they ask at the same time, but all I can do is shrug.

"She wouldn't say, but she did ask Colt to put in a bid on doing the work for the juice bar."

"Colt is in the construction business now?" Laney asks. She lays the bottom of her muffin to the side of her napkin and takes half a banana nut one.

An extra-long sip of my coffee gives me a minute. I don't really want to say anything about Jackson's job or this new venture with his brother, so… I shrug again. "I guess so." I'll tell them more when I actually know something. So far I'm doing a pretty good job ignoring Jackson's job woes and our financial concerns. The less people know, the easier it is to ignore.

Susan sighs and holds her hand against her stomach. "Thanks for getting the muffin, but I'm not really hungry. Silas and I had a late dinner last night."

Laney stiffens, and it's not due to her all-natural pants. "Thought we weren't going to mention him."

"You thought that. I didn't agree to it. You were fine talking about him when I asked how to get rid of him."

I jump in. I've been waiting to get to this subject. "Yeah, so whatever happened to all that?"

Laney licks her finger and lifts crumbs as she mimics me. "Yeah, whatever happened to that?"

Susan clicks her teeth, then pauses. "Well, the reason we ate so late was that he moved out last night."

Laney's mouth flies open. "What? Where?"

"Where do you think?" I ask. "Heartbreak Hotel, or as you might know it, Crossings B&B."

"But you didn't say anything," Laney accuses first me, then Susan.

I lift my hands in surrender. "Not my story to tell. Besides, it all happened pretty quickly."

Susan nods. "I told him I needed some space. Everything between us happened too fast." She reaches over and lays her hand on her sister's knee. "You were right. I shouldn't have let him move into the house. It just happened, and so I told him he had to move out. I thought he'd go back to California or somewhere. It just never dawned on me he'd stay in town until Carolina texted me last night. We had dinner out at the interstate, we talked, and I came home. He went up to the B&B apparently."

I nod. "He showed up right before we went to bed saying he needed a room. I put him in the Southern Crescent room, and I didn't see him this morning."

Susan winces. "Did he say how long he's staying?"

"Nope. Nothing." Laney's furrowed brow focuses on her sister, then she turns to me, but I don't have anything else to say.

Apparently none of us can think of anything to say. We sit quietly for a few minutes before Laney speaks up. "Speaking of heartbreak, what's up with Shannon? You've still heard nothing?"

"Nope. Her dad is making a couple deliveries for her today, so I'm planning on quizzing him. He's easier to get stuff out of than her mom, I think. Her mom sounded outright giddy that she was out of town for a while. I don't get that at all. Have either of you talked to Peter or Missus?"

Susan laughs. "Us? You're the Bedwell whisperer. Still can't believe Peter told you Missus is moving into the guest wing. I'll believe that when I see it."

Laney screws up her face in thought. "Peter was kind of creepy yesterday at church, didn't y'all think?"

"Creepy?" I ask. "I don't know about that."

"Of course you don't," she says. "You were too busy becoming Delaney LaMotte's new best friend. Saw you over there with Anna, fawning all over her."

"She's doing a photo shoot of the baby for Anna and Will." I scoot forward in my seat. "Gotta admit after looking at her webpage, I'm kind of excited. She really *is* famous."

"But to already be engaged?" Susan stands and brushes her skirt some more. "I thought Silas and I were moving fast."

"But they dated in college. You have to remember that. They have a history." I also stand. "Guess I better turn over the open sign."

Laney reaches out a hand to her sister. "Help me get off this couch. Ya gotta admit, the two of them looked good together. Maybe it wasn't that he was creepy, maybe it just creeped me out them being so perfect." She rises and then lets out a breath of relief. "I'm not sitting down on anything that low the rest of the day. Matter of fact, I'm probably not sitting down on anything the rest of the day."

Susan, with both hands on her thin hips, says, "Why don't you just go home and change? You don't look comfortable at all."

"Well, duh, that's because I'm *not* comfortable at all. But I've only got a month before the election, and I don't plan on losing to that phony hometown stuff Missus is pulling. Now I'm going to go give Charles an interview for next week's *Vedette*." She pulls out several sheets of paper from her purse, then points them at Ruby's basket. "Can one of you return that to Ruby? I already had to talk to her once today."

Susan reaches over and yanks the papers out of her sister's hand. "You aren't kidding. You are *giving* him an interview.

This is all written out. You don't think he might want to ask his own questions?"

Laney grabs the papers back. "Then he can ask me. This just seemed like a lot easier." She turns her back on Susan. "Carolina, will you take the basket back?"

"Sure. When Susie Mae comes in or when someone trustworthy is here and I can leave for a bit. Why you don't drop it off on your way down the street is beyond me, but okay. Whatever."

Laney smiles her political smile. "Thank you, darling. Now I've got to go. The press awaits." She sails out the door, every square inch of natural fiber with her.

Susan and I look at each other, and Susan says, "You know she took that basket without asking Ruby."

"I figured as much. But listen, what are you going to do about Silas?"

Susan sighs and crosses her arms. "I don't know. I want to see how I feel with a little distance and, well…" She fades off and steps to the window to look out.

"Well what?"

"You can't tell anyone, but Griffin and I have been texting."

"What?"

She flips around to face me. "We just have so much history. We always liked each other, we just…" She shrugs. Then she grabs my arm. "But you can't tell anyone. Anyone, right?"

"Sure." I feel my forehead crease as I worry about my friend. "But don't let anything happen to confuse your life more than it already is. I mean, nothing about your lives has changed. He still wants the Laurel Cove life, and well, you don't, right?"

"Right. I mean, I think so." She pulls on the navy blue suit jacket she shrugged off on the couch, then slides her purse onto her shoulder. "It was all supposed to be so simple, but the kids and now the holidays and then Silas." She walks to the door and with her hand on the knob turns to me. "Honestly Carolina, I'm not good with all this change. I've tried to be, but..." She smiles at me, but it's weak. "I've got to go. Thanks for everything."

Life seems to fight simplicity with every fiber of its being, doesn't it?

CHAPTER 38

"Ma'am, I promise Shannon will take care of it when she gets back," I say—again. "Your wedding is quite a ways off, right?"

The young woman wails. "But I can't sleep at night for worrying about this! How can I use white roses when they were used to represent dead people at the depot? One of those dead people was my great-uncle, and I'll see his face in every white rose at my wedding!"

Her mother, standing stoically behind her, says, "Charity, you never even met him. He died over fifty years ago. *I* never even met him." She leans forward, placing a hand on each of her daughter's shoulders. "Thanks, Mrs. Jessup. Shannon will help us later, sweetie."

The pretty girl has reddish-blonde hair, wide brown eyes, and a stubborn mouth. Very stubborn, especially when she's not getting her way, and she's not happy about Shannon not being available at this crisis moment. However, her wedding isn't until March, so I'm trying to just smooth things over. I wonder if her mother's considered valium? If the girl won't take them, it couldn't hurt the mother.

"Listen, I'm sorry, but I do have to take care of these other customers." I smile and slip away from them. At the counter I say, "I'm sorry," again and ring up the books for the two women who've been shopping for a while and thoroughly enjoying themselves talking about books. I'm most angry at Charity because these are the people I would've preferred to be dealing with for the past half hour.

Yes, half hour. Charity has explained, complained, whined, and demanded for over thirty minutes. You understand, I would *never* prescribe valium on a whim, but *thirty* minutes? As I bag their purchases, the bell on the door rings, and I look up to see Shannon's father sailing in. I hold up my hand and try to stop him without saying his last name. "Hey. Yeah, come here!"

But he has a booming voice and he announces in it, "Just picking up the flowers on Shannon's orders. Doing my part to help my daughter!"

As Charity whirls toward him, her mother's eyes roll and she visibly deflates. My book customers leave, and I walk past the three of them—Mr. Chilton listening intently and sincerely to Charity's woes while her mother sags against the worktable. I get as far from them as possible, with as many shelves and books between us as possible, and I wait it out. Finally, Charity and her mother are leaving. I don't chance saying goodbye. As a matter of fact, I stay as still as possible waiting to hear that bell and the shutting of the door.

"Whew! You can come out now, Miss Carolina. They're gone."

"Hello," I say waltzing out of the shelving area. "I tell ya, I could never work with brides like Shannon does. That one especially!"

He pulls out a sheet of paper and lays it on the worktable, then goes to the cooler. "I've only got three to deliver today. One anniversary and two 'get well' ones."

"So how's Shannon?"

A frown crosses his face, then he brightens up. "Fine. Taking a little vacation, you know."

"I heard. Where?"

He looks around the cooler door. "Where? Where'd she go?"

"Yeah. On vacation?"

He concentrates on the flowers in front of him, pulling an arrangement of carnations and daisies out. "Oh, to the beach, I believe. She talks to her mother about things like that."

He reads his paper after setting the arrangement on the table, then as he goes back to the cooler, I say, "Good. Shannon enjoys the beach."

He nods, but is distracted as he examines the flowers in the case. "Would you say this is purple?"

I step over to look. "Yes." I move as he backs out again with the purple arrangement in hand.

"I'm not too good with pinks and purples. They look alike to me sometimes." He shrugs. "Wife says I'm a bit color-blind. So, how's Jackson these days? Hear he's working from home."

"Yeah, for a little while. When will Shannon be back?"

There's that frown again. It occurs to me that neither of us is telling the other the whole story. "Not sure. Like I said, she tells her mother stuff like that."

With his final arrangement in hand he heads to the door. "I'll come right back for those. I have a crate to sit them in in the car."

I pick up the two arrangements and his list and wait beside the big door to make it easier for him. The wind has picked up, so I don't want to take the flowers outside before he's ready to put them into his car.

"Why, thank you," he says as I hold open the door for him. "I'll take the bigger one first." He takes it, and I shift to hold the last arrangement in one hand. It's a small planter with a couple flowers stuck in with the plant and a sign that says, "Get Well Soon." I fold over the list so he can take it when he grabs the flowers, and I notice scribbling on the back in what looks like a woman's hand, but not Shannon's.

I was careful to not read it.

Not read it *out loud*, that's what I meant. Of course, I read it.

"Last one, and here's your list. Don't want to forget that. Tell Shannon I said hello if you talk to her!"

He agrees, then waves as he shields the plant from the wind.

So. Holiday Inn, Daytona Beach, Room 414. That's where Shannon is.

But who's Danny?

"She just walked right out that door with my basket, didn't she? Right out that door, plain as sin! Look here, Libby, the basket I accused you of throwing in the trash." Ruby is holding up the basket I had hoped to be able to slip in with, unnoticed.

Of course, my purse isn't big enough.

"I brought it back. No harm, no foul." I try to open the front door, but Ruby sticks out her skinny, strong arm and holds it shut.

"Where do you think you're going, missy? This here is a crime. I have exactly twelve of these baskets, and eleven just won't do. Here I was thinking I'd have to throw the whole set away." She drops her hand from the door and turns to the back. "Come with me."

I could leave now, but we all know Ruby wouldn't just drop this. I don't want The Great Basket Theft on my permanent record, so I follow her. "Any leftover muffins?" I ask. Might as well get fed while I'm here.

Libby has already sat one on a saucer next to a cup of coffee for me on the bar. "Here ya go. It's lunch time, enjoy." Libby goes back to the kitchen area, waving at my thanks. Ruby sits on one of the spinning bar stools and motions for me to take the one beside her. She leans over and pulls an order pad to her, then takes a pen from the pocket of her apron.

"Okay, Carolina, I want to take down your story. That way if I need to get the police involved I'll have it fresh from your recollection. Go."

"It was a dark and stormy night. There were twelve baskets when the lights went off. When they came back on… there were only eleven!" I take a big bite of the blueberry crumble muffin, then look to see if she's actually writing. She's not.

"Very funny. You read too many books. I can tell." She's leaning on her elbow staring at me.

I take a sip of coffee, then make a face. "You serving old coffee is the real crime. What's up with that?"

"We're closing. I'm tired. This basket fiasco has taken a lot out of me."

I laugh, but then look back to see Libby nodding at me. I soften my voice. "I'm sorry, Ruby. She just borrowed it for a bit. She should've told you she was borrowing it, but we know how Laney is." I smile at her and hope we can find common ground over Laney being Laney.

I pat her arm, but with the way her head swings around, I'm afraid she's going to take my own head right off. I jerk my hand back, but she only looks at me. Focuses, then stands. "Come here. I wanna tell you something."

She walks back to the front, locks the front door, and turns over the closed sign. She slides into the booth nearest the front window, then yells back at Libby. "Hon? You can go on home. I'll shut down the rest of it. Hurry now." She watches until Libby yells "Bye" at us, then leaves out the back door.

"She don't know nothing about what I'm fixin' to say." Ruby lays both arms on the table, then clasps her hands together. She's wearing another one of her Christmas sweatshirts. This one has cats in Santa hats forming a Christmas tree. I can't read the words at the bottom, but I'm sure it's something adorable. And stupid.

"I have a soft spot for you, Miss Carolina. I guess you know that, the way I treat you so nice. I don't mind playing favorites, that's just how the world is, but I can't help liking you and don't mind you knowing that. I can't talk about this with other folks from around here. They'll plum lose their minds."

"You're making me nervous. Are you okay?" I lay a hand on her clasped ones, but only for a second as she pulls her hands apart. Then she clasps them again. She does this a couple more times as she contorts her face, thinking through something. "Ruby, calm down," I say. "What's going on?"

She takes in a long breath, then lets it out. She sits completely still, staring at her hands, which are now lying palms down on the table between us. "You know my daughter? My Jewel?"

"Sure. She's really nice."

"She is. She is." She pauses and works her throat, clearing it, then swallowing, stretching her neck. Guess the words are stuck there.

"Is Jewel okay?"

She looks up at me, tears filling her eyes, and my heart jumps. "Righter than rain. She's moving to Florida."

"Oh. Moving?" I'm relieved, but I can see Ruby's not. "She's your only child, right?"

"Yep. Only one and we're real close, but it's her husband's job, you see. He got a promotion. A nice one, and they're moving the first of the year."

"Oh, Ruby. I'm sorry. I mean, I'm happy for them, but I know you spend a lot of time with her and your grandkids."

"I do. That I do." She sighs and leans back, her hands sliding to the edge of the table.

"It's so quiet," I say as we sit and listen to the silence. "So, you've not told Libby about Jewel?"

"Oh, of course. Libby's known Jewel since she was born. She likes to know what's going on with her."

"But… then why'd you ask her to leave? You said she didn't know."

Ruby looks up at me, her face calm, her hands still. "What she don't know is that I'm going with them. I'm moving to Florida. Shutting this place down."

Chapter 39

"Hey. What are you doing down here?"

With my nose buried in the neck of my coat, I almost ran right into my husband as I looked up to open my shop door.

"I came down to see Colt about some things." He motions with one hand behind him. "He's still in the bistro."

"What for?"

He pulls me toward him by hooking an arm around my shoulders. "Just another job. Come on, you look cold. What are *you* doing out here?"

Grabbing his coat sleeve, I spin around to face him and hiss, "Ruby is moving to Florida!"

"Ruby? Our Ruby?" He looks up the street. "Who told you that?"

"She did, but don't say anything. Her daughter is moving, so she's going with them. I'm still in shock."

"I guess so. That's really hard to imagine, but with all the changes here in town…" He shrugs and raises his eyebrows at me.

"What changes? Ruby can't go. Are you crazy?" I push away from him. "We have to stop her." I take one step toward the shop door, then stop and turn back to him. "What changes?"

"You know." He shrugs again. "Like Phoenix was talking about last night. Her juice bar and maybe serving food and stuff." He shivers. "Let's go inside. I'm cold." Walking around me, he opens the door and corrals me in that direction. I go, but I'm suspicious.

"There you are!" Susie Mae shouts in relief. "This lady needs some help."

Charity is back, and this time without the calming influence of her mother. She sees me, then dismisses me. "She can't help. I've already talked to her."

"No one can help you but Shannon!" I yell as I stomp back toward them. "And Shannon is in Daytona with some guy named Danny! So, that's it. That's all!" Yes, I know I'm shouting. Yes, I know I gave away Shannon's location and the name of her new friend, but come on. It's been a stressful day.

"Danny Kinnock?" Cathy Stone asks, coming out of the bookshelves behind me. What in the world is she doing in the shelves? Lord knows she's not looking for books.

"I don't know." I turn back to the front as I jerk my coat sleeve, trying to take it off without also taking my sweater off. I'm sweating to death, and everything is sticking to me. "I didn't say Danny."

"Yes, you did. I heard you," says a little voice from the same aisle as Cathy.

Cathy cocks one eyebrow at me. "See? Forrest heard you. He's very, very smart."

"Must've gotten it from his father," I mumble into my coat as I shove it onto the rack Bonnie put right near the door. Bonnie, who makes this place so nice and will probably never come back again. I turn to find Cathy behind me.

"Is it Danny Kinnock? I mean, they did date all through high school." She's grinning and hunched up at me.

"I honestly have no idea. And if she is with him, that's fine, right? We all want Shannon to be happy, right?" I walk away from her and realize Charity and Susie Mae are listening, and frowning as they do. Jackson is standing behind Cathy, and when I look at him he nods and says, "Right."

Cathy grins wider. "Oh, of course, but…" She licks her lips and widens her eyes. "Danny's married."

Great. "Then it's another Danny." I swish past her. "Forrest, are you finding some good books? Anything I can help you with?"

"So how did you find out where she went?" Cathy whispers from right behind me in the small aisle. "I thought no one knew where she was. And I know no one knows Danny is with her." She giggles. "Especially Alison." Then she taps me on the back. "You know Alison? That's his wife. We were all in school together."

I ignore her, but she doesn't realize it. She laughs and calls to her son, "Come on, Forrest. Time to go. Take what you want to the counter." She turns, and I turn to grab her arm.

"Cathy. Come on. It really could be a different Danny. It could be no one at all. I, uh, I just saw something written down that might not mean anything. Please don't say anything to this girl. This Alison. Or anyone. Please?"

Cathy listens, but even as it looks like she's listening, she's licking her lips and her pupils are dilated. I can see her list of texts and phone calls forming themselves in her mind. These are her classmates. These are people who talked about her when she got pregnant in high school. This is just simply too good to let lie, even if it turns out to be wrong.

Then, God help me, I had the thought that I could tell her Ruby's news. That would distract her with the news that her mother is out of a job, but it wouldn't distract her very long and, besides, I'd never do that. Right?

I release her arm. "Just think about how this could hurt people. I'm probably completely wrong."

She shrugs and walks over to join her son. Susie Mae is ringing up his books. She gives me a commiserating smile. She's well versed in letting secrets out of the bag. Jackson is sitting on the couch with a home carpentry magazine from the stack we keep for folks to buy for a quarter. Disgusted, I turn right into Charity.

"Oh! Sorry about that a minute ago, but you really do have to wait for Shannon."

She nods and lays her hand on my shoulder. "I understand, Mrs. Jessup. Just want you to know I'll be praying for you."

I manage a smile and a thank-you as she walks to the door. There she turns and says, "We're always looking for people to add to the list at church. Believe me, this situation will be *well* prayed over." She quickly leaves. Cathy gasps, then is rushing her son to follow the bride-to-be out the door.

"Shoot!" Cathy exclaims. "She goes to Shannon and Danny's church. She'll get all the good details. Come on, Forrest, move!" She's already got her phone to her ear by the time they pass the front window.

I slump onto the chair across from my civil engineer husband, who is reading about putting in a toilet. "Shoot me now."

He looks up, then around. "Why? What's going on?"

CHAPTER 40

Jackson left the store shortly after Cathy and Forrest, still blissfully ignorant of my faux pas. (See, I do take care of him.) Susie Mae avoids me, dusting every square inch of the store, leaving me to think. It's the last thing I probably need to do, but I feel like wallowing. There are no customers to distract me, just a constant checking of my phone to not miss when all of this hits the fan.

The afternoon light slides down the front window and brings a glow to the shop. Branches in the park cause the light to move and sway. Soft Christmas instrumentals, vanilla- and cinnamon-scented candles, little lights in swags of pine and magnolia around the shop. It's perfect, and I'm not enjoying it. Not at all.

"You keep sighing. Are you okay, Miss Caro?" Susie Mae asks. She's usually a talker, and I guess she's been quiet too long. She walks to the counter that I'm hunched over, my phone laying in front of me. She says sweetly, "There's really nothing you can do about it. I found that out, you know. What's gonna happen is gonna happen." She leans forward, making me look up at her. "Besides, people do what they do. If they don't want folks to find it out, then they shouldn't do it."

"That's true, but I would really hate it if I've hurt Shannon. She's been hurt enough."

"Oh, I know that. Everyone knows that about you. That's why folks like you." She flips around to lean against the counter. "Look out there. It's beautiful out there, with the sun and wind. And I love being in your shop. I'd work here for free! Wouldn't you?"

Straightening up, I sigh again, but this time it's a quieter, more contented sigh. She can't help being young and unaware of money problems, but then I realize she's had to face plenty of problems herself. So I smile at her. "You're right. Thanks."

Then she tenses. "Uh-oh." She dashes away from the counter, and I see what she saw. Missus is storming down the sidewalk. I brace for her to hit our door like a bulldozer, but then she walks right by.

Susie Mae and I look at each other, then race to the door to see where she went. She's not in sight, so I pull open the door. She's not on the sidewalk. The wind whips in, and we both fall back inside.

"She has to be in the bistro," I say. I can't help it, my eyes go to my coat. Someone needs to say, "Ignore it, stay away, don't be nosy," but the only other person here is Susie Mae Lyles, and she wouldn't say that if her young life depended on it.

Matter of fact, she looks at me with those big, dark eyes and asks, "You think something's wrong? Maybe you should check it out. Or I can step over there, if you're busy?"

My coat is in my hands, and I'm slipping it on even before the words come out of my mouth. "Yeah, no, I can go. I think I better make sure everything's okay."

"Good idea," she says as she opens the door for me. "I'll take care of things here."

Great. My partner in crime is a blog-writing, gossip-loving teenager.

The wind makes it hard to open the door to the bistro, but don't worry—I manage. "Hey, y'all. Everything okay?"

The shelving units are gone. The space is empty except for

Missus and Peter. Peter is again wearing a suit. It's brown this time with a vest. His tie is knotted neatly, and he looks completely at ease, like I just stepped into his presentation before the board of directors in some downtown Atlanta high-rise.

"Hello, Carolina. What can I do for you?" He glides past his mother and comes to shake my hand. Yes, I said shake my hand.

"What's going on with this place? Why's it empty?"

Peter looks around like he's seeing it for the first time. Then he laughs. "Oh, all the questions." He looks at his watch. "I'm going to need to leave. Can't let my fiancée wait too long." He holds his arm out toward the door for me.

I ignore him, step to the side, and look at his mother. "Are you okay? You sure looked mad racing down the sidewalk."

Missus' eyes narrow. "Tell me what you think of my son moving me out of the bedroom I shared with his father for over fifty years without telling me."

I shake my head at her. "But you were there when he said Sunday that he and Delaney were moving into that part of the house, and you were—"

"Yes, yes, I know all that. I was there, as you said, but it was never to happen immediately. They aren't even married!"

"Mother. What does it matter when it happens? Things need to change now. That was one change I could make quickly; others take more time. Now, I really do need to be going." This time he not only holds out his arm, he opens the door. "Carolina? Mother?"

Missus rushes past me, her nose in the air and laser beams shooting from her eyes as she passes her son. I watch them, then follow her. At the closest point to him, I stop. "What's going on, Peter?"

He smiles. "Nothing. I just don't want to be late for dinner with Delaney. You must remember what it was like when you were newly in love and always wanted to be together?" His smile looked more like a sneer suddenly, and I push on by him.

The door shuts behind me, and I scurry to catch up to Missus. "Hey, what's going on?" I say when I reach her.

She stops and looks at me. "It's true apparently. That old saying, 'Be careful what you wish for.'" She shakes her head. "Never mind. It's fine. Have a good night."

She walks on, buffeted by the wind, and as she passes Ruby's dark windows, a wave of sadness washes over and through me. I turn and look inside the front window of Blooming Books. Light spills out and promises warmth; the smells, the sounds reach out to me. This all wasn't even here this time last year. There's that song based on Ecclesiastes, I think. About everything turning? A time to build up, a time to break down. A season for everything under heaven. I sigh again.

That may all be true, but it doesn't really help.

CHAPTER 41

"This is really going to be weird, isn't it? Everyone's going to be staring at me." Anna repeats her lament, which has increased in frequency since we finished dinner. She and Will came to the house to have dinner with us before the shower. Now she, Savannah, and I are driving to Patty's new house for the big event. Jackson wasn't home from the office by the time we had to leave, so I haven't heard anything about his job yet.

"Can you turn on some music?" Savannah asks from the seat behind me. She and I have quit trying to calm Anna or even to answer her questions.

"Sure," I say as I press the radio button, then look at my daughter-in-law. "Have you talked to Patty? How does their house look? I can't get anything out of Bonnie. She only stopped in the store to say hi for a minute today." It was quiet at work and home yesterday and last night with everything—Ruby, Jackson, Shannon—all hanging in midair.

Anna shakes her head, staring straight ahead, her hand clutching the door handle like she's deciding whether or not to jump out.

"Honey, you have to relax. Sit back and breathe." As I roll up to the stop sign at the bottom of the hill, I gently push her back against the seat. "Breathe. Look at me and breathe."

She turns her gray eyes at me. They are stretched in terror, then she sucks in a deep breath.

"Okay, blow it out." She never looks away from me as she lets the air escape. "Take another breath," I instruct and watch as her eyes lose their alarm and her shoulders soften. "Give me your hands." I massage them a bit, then we both jump when the car behind me beeps.

"Oops!" We drop hands, and I pull forward. "Probably someone excited about going to the shower." I chuckle. "I hate that this is so close to your due date, but with your classes and then our trip to Kentucky, it just kept getting pushed back. You'll be fine. Before you know it this van will be crammed full of baby things and we'll be on our way home."

Her voice is small and squeaky. "You really think people will come and bring gifts?"

Savannah meets my eyes in the rearview mirror and rolls hers. She laughs and reaches up to pat Anna's shoulder. "They better! That's the whole idea. I can't wait to see how my little niece Francie is going to be all decked out. You know she's going to have the cutest clothes ever!"

"But where will we put all that? The cabin is tiny, I don't…"

"Stop," I tell her. "Not a thing for you to worry about. We have plenty of storage at our house. Plenty." As we turn onto the correct street, I study the small, closely spaced houses we're passing. "Okay, there's Susan's house, and—oh, wow." There are cars everywhere along both sides of the street. I can feel Anna's tension level soaring, then Savannah says, "Patty just texted me that they left a space in the driveway for the guest of honor."

Anna squeaks, "That's me, right?"

Women are walking along the street. I wait for a couple I recognize from church to cross the driveway before pulling in. "If this house isn't any bigger than Susan's, I don't know where all these people are going to fit." I park and shut off the van.

"Come on. The sooner we get it started, the sooner it'll be done, and you'll be back in the cabin with Will."

Savannah gets out on the passenger side and holds Anna's arm in the driveway. I'm proud of how she's taking care of Anna as they come around the front of the van, and then we all three walk up the front sidewalk. Voices fill the night air with ladies calling out to Anna or me or Savannah. One of the part-time workers at the Dollar Store comes up behind us, and when Anna sees her, she actually smiles. She's worked this up in her mind and has forgotten she'll know so many people here and that people genuinely like her. She'll be fine once we get things started.

Pulling open the door for Anna and Savannah to go on through I get my first peek at Bonnie's handiwork. And it's stunning.

I guess that's good. Good for Bonnie. Not good for me.

We're all pulled in by the tangerine wall in the distance across lush green rugs. The dark brown couches disappear underneath artfully placed pillows in the same tangerine and green, with splashes of sunny yellow. Once inside, the colors envelop us in warmth, which I would've never imagined would be the case with such bright colors. Small framed mirrors line the hallway to our left and make it alluring and bright. Metal sconces beneath the mirrors each hold a tulip, which bends out, calling you to walk that way. We turn to the right and find a dining room with a modern table of highly polished wood, more tulips, and chair cushions in an assortment of patterns that should look like they were picked up at a garage sale, but instead look absolutely perfect. I've left Anna talking to people in the living room and am ignoring anyone who calls my name. The kitchen has to be on the right, behind the dining room, and I want to see it. Have to see it.

Green glass greets me, several shades of green glass—on the cabinet doors, the light fixtures, and on the counter as canisters holding votive candles and more white tulips. The orange in here is on the floor, on the carpet runners on each side of the island. The countertops are a dark stone. It's all so young, so warm, and looks effortless.

Just like our store.

"How ya like it?" Gertie asks as she comes in through the door at the other end of the kitchen. "I knew that Bonnie was missing her calling. She has a gift."

"You're right. This is simply amazing. I bet Patty loves it."

Gertie rolls her eyes, crosses her arms, and lets out a pshaw. "She's saying she could never be comfortable somewhere like this. She'll get used to it, though."

Savannah creeps inside the kitchen door, her mouth hanging open. "I know I sure could get used to it. Bonnie did this?"

Gertie nods, then claps her hands. "Let's get this shindig on the road. Y'all brought the guest of honor, right?"

Savannah waves toward the living room. "Patty showed Anna where to sit. She said the food is set up in the bedrooms?"

"Yep, we wanted folks to see the house without food and gifts clogging it all up, and since there's nothing in them rooms yet, we've got the food in one and presents in the other." She's shooed us ahead of her as she talks. The main rooms are crowded, and Gertie whistles to get everyone's attention. "There's food and punch in the first room to right down the hall. All the presents are in the last room, and we'll bring them out a couple at a time for Anna to open. Your coats and pocketbooks are in the last room on the left down that same hall, of course. Other room on the left is the powder room. Have something to eat and visit. You'll be sore disappointed I know, but we just don't have room to play no games. Go on now, eat!"

Guests begin moving around the room, and I sneak back through the kitchen and around through the door on the other end that comes out behind the dining room table. I forgot and left our gift in the car. I'm glad we got to park in the driveway.

I make it out the front door, and the cold air feels good. It's hot in the house. I haven't seen Susan or Laney or Missus, but Phoenix is coming up the driveway. I'd offered for her to ride with us, but she'd had to leave earlier.

"Looks like a madhouse in there," she says. "You leaving already? Aren't you with the guest of honor?"

"Forgot the gift in the van." In a couple steps we meet and I ask, "So, are you still moving out of the B&B?"

"I am." She smiles and swings her dark red hair over the shoulder of her white wool coat. "That's why I had to leave early tonight. To come downtown and finalize things." Her smile grows, but she just looks at me.

"What are you smiling at? Is it about Colt?"

She shrugs. "A bit. Not really, though. More about another male you're close to."

"Jackson?" I say without thinking, but she only laughs.

"No, of course not. I better go inside. Don't worry, you'll find out soon enough." She steps into the grass to go around me, and I turn to watch her.

"Don't forget to get your gift," she calls from the sidewalk.

I'd already started following her, so I stop and turn around. "That's right. The gift." I press my key fob, and the back door of the van lifts. Whatever Phoenix is doing, it has nothing to do with me. Or Jackson. My phone is on vibrate, but I pull it out of my pocket to see if he's texted or called. Nope. Nothing.

Lifting out the big bag with the huge pink bow on it, I close the van door and start inside. It does look like a madhouse inside the small building, every window spilling out light with figures moving back and forth. Out here in the quiet dark, it feels like the house is pulsating. I'm not going to think about Phoenix or Ruby or Shannon or Jackson. I'm going to go enjoy this shower.

Unless I get a chance to talk to Phoenix some more. Or maybe I can corner Ruby and start operation Florida-No-Go.

Wonder if Shannon's mother was invited tonight? I definitely need to see if she's here. Maybe I should put my phone's ringer back on. I can always step out and talk to Jackson if he calls.

But other than those things, I'm going to concentrate on the shower.

Wait, what did I come out here for? I stop and look around me. In the light from the lantern beside the sidewalk, something pink at the end of my arm catches my eye, and I actually lift my hand to look at it.

Oh, that's right. The gift.

Chapter 42

"You're being awfully quiet," I say to Savannah. It's late and dark as we drive down the country road from Anna and Will's cabin. There's only our headlights outside the car and inside only the dim lights from the dash.

"Just thinking about Anna and how nervous she was earlier. It was interesting watching her being the center of attention. That really isn't something she's ever had, is it?"

"No. It was fun to see her get into it when she started opening the gifts."

"So many gifts. Francie is already so loved, isn't she?"

"She is. Seeing all those tiny outfits just made me even more excited to hold her."

After a pause, Savannah says, "Yeah. Me too." There's another pause, but I can tell by the way she's moved to sit up straighter and the glimpse of her furrowed brow that she has more to say. "Do you ever think about what would have happened if we hadn't moved here? What if we'd stayed in Marietta?"

"Sometimes. Do you?"

"Sometimes, yeah. Like Francie would never have happened. You owning the shop, us meeting all the people from the B&B, to not know my friends here or…"

"Or Ricky?"

She looks at me and grins. "Yeah, I guess. It's kind of weird.

I'm really excited about our date tomorrow. He seems different. Grown-up, maybe?"

"Maybe. Maybe you're different, too. You've learned a lot this year with the acting, chasing Alex this summer..."

She moans. "He was different, older. I couldn't help myself."

"Exactly," I say. "You couldn't help yourself and that taught you about yourself. Then that whole awful thing with Isaac." The car grows quiet again.

She sighs. "I'm still kind of surprised I stood up for myself with him and his parents."

"I'm not."

"Really?"

"Nope. Now, I'm very, very proud of you, but you've never let people push you around." I laugh. "And believe me, I've tried!"

She laughs, too. "Are you saying I'm stubborn?"

"I'm saying you know who you are. That will serve you well. It already has."

"Thanks," she says and then leans forward, but she stops. "Is it okay if I turn on some music? And not Christmas music?"

"Sure, and hey, you were so sweet to Anna tonight. She's lucky to have you for a sister-in-law."

She smiles at me, then turns on the radio, quickly finding her station. We drive on through the dark, not much farther to home where Jackson is. Where Jackson is asleep. All I got from him was a text telling me we'd talk in the morning, but that he was exhausted and was going to bed. It's been hard with him around so much, and yet him being gone so much was one of my biggest concerns when we moved here. He's got to be anxious about his job, and I need to be more of a support than a pain. Okay. Good talk, Carolina. Just remember it in the morning.

I never thought we'd be out this late, but first there was getting everyone else to leave the shower, then loading up all the gifts in the van. Then we had to drive to the cabin and unload everything, which Will helped with but he also slowed us down wanting to see everything. First we were dividing things to leave there and to take back to our house, but then Savannah finally said we should unload everything. This weekend they can bring what they wanted us to keep for them.

Missus was very subdued at the shower, and I think she was avoiding me. It was hard to tell with that crowd, but it felt that way. She sat to the side of Anna on a folding chair and kept her comments to the gifts or the food.

Oh, the food was glorious. The caterer specializes in Southern elegant food and it was both Southern and elegant in a way I had never imagined. Lemon bars with fresh mint, snickerdoodles on a base of chocolate, pecan pie bars that were better than any pecan pie I've ever had. And if that didn't blow up the Southern party ratings system, get this – there was a cheese straw bar! That's right. Those tangy, cheesy snack crackers that have graced Southern parties since before there were college football games to tailgate at.

First there was an assortment of cheese straws with more red pepper, or herbs such as basil or thyme, or with a bit of sweetness, or made of white cheese. Then there were dips. Rich tomato sauce, mustards, hot sauces, sweet dips like a brown sugar glaze you'd put on a ham. It was a huge hit and so much fun.

So much fun I almost forgot everything else and just enjoyed myself.

Almost.

Our cups sit across from each other on the kitchen table. Jackson's cup is steaming with its first fill of the day. I poured it when I heard our bedroom door open upstairs. My cup is on its third refill. Yep, I've been up a while.

Sleep came fast when I got to bed last night, but then I woke up and couldn't go back to sleep. Finally I came downstairs, thinking maybe reading would help me nod off, and it did. Then I woke up again and gave up trying.

Do you have any idea how many people are on Facebook at the crack of dawn?

"Hey there," Jackson says, coming into the kitchen. He bends over to kiss me and then sits down across from me. "Oh, that's good," he says, taking a sip of the coffee. "You weren't in bed when the alarm went off. Couldn't sleep?"

"Not really." I pause, thinking maybe I'll just patiently wait and let him tell me what happened with work yesterday in his own good time—but the caffeine is kicking in so… "Okay, what happened yesterday?"

"Well, it was pretty tense. A couple of the younger guys were laid off. We took them out to dinner and for a drink. That's why I didn't get home until late."

"But no one else?"

He shakes his head, but he's staring at the cup between his hands. "No. Not now."

"So that's good, right?"

Shrugging, he takes a deep breath. "I guess so. I mean, I guess."

"Honey, don't make me drag it out of you. What is going on?" Keeping my voice low, I try to smile, but I think it may look more like I'm baring my teeth at him because when he looks up alarm crosses his face. So I take a deep breath, lean back, and smile.

"Oh, yeah, sorry. It's just I, well, I did talk to Tom, he's my boss that came in from Chicago for the meeting, and there's really not many other projects for me to work on right now and not really any in the pipeline, so well… I'm going to go part-time."

It all came out in a rush, but I think I heard the important part. "You're going to do what?"

"It's not that big a deal. It means more time here. I'll get three quarters of my pay, and we'll keep our full benefits." He stops explaining.

That's good because I've stopped breathing.

Then he sits up straight and excitedly explains, "See, Colt and I have some ideas and even some contracts, but I can't do it the way I've been working out of town. This way I'm no longer actually in charge of the project in South Georgia. I'll be co-manager of it. Tom thinks it'll work better this way, too. That project is coming to a point where it no longer needs someone like me full time."

"Okay, um, you really think this is a good idea?"

"Sure. Plus, I can help you more with the B&B and even with Blooming Books, and I'll be here for the kids. Especially Will and Anna with the baby coming."

"Yeah, that sounds nice, but you don't think it'll hurt you with your company? What about your résumé? I mean, how will it look to have been part time? Is there even such a thing as a part-time engineer?"

"I understand what you're thinking, and Tom and I talked about all that." He shrugs. "Honestly, I think this helps my position in the company. Tom seemed relieved when I approached him about it."

Swallowing, I choke, "You approached him? You *asked* to go part-time?"

"Oh, yeah. I did." He nods and then sits still.

Frozen in my seat, I manage to whisper, "Okay." Then a little stronger I say, "If you think it's a good idea, then I'm good. We'll figure it out."

His phone rings, and he takes it out of his pocket. With a

big grin he says, "It's Colt." He jumps up to walk into the dining room, and I hear him say, "Yeah, I told her. It's all good."

How early is too early to start happy hour?

Chapter 43

"Ruby never does it like this," Laney says holding the newspaper in one hand and Cayden in the other in the back area of Blooming Books.

"What do you want me to say?" I turn away from her again, but she keeps circling around to be in front of me. It's like she knows I know something more about why Ruby is hosting a pie and coffee night tonight at her restaurant and advertising it in the paper.

"Ruby likes that power of us all guessing if she'll be open after a game or event. You know how she is. Why would she be announcing it this time? And like this, in the newspaper? You know how she feels about the newspaper. No, something is going on." She slams the paper down on Shannon's worktable. "What on earth is so interesting that you have your head stuck down there? Cayden, honey, it's all right. Momma won't do that again." She walks off jiggling her crying baby as I peek out.

"Just looking for a pen I dropped." I pick up the newspaper she has folded to a small rectangle. There's a picture of a cup of coffee and a piece of pie. "Ruby invites Chancey to come try her delicious pies made especially for this one-time event."

I've not told anyone what Ruby told me. Well, except Jackson, and he's so excited about his new part-time gig, he's completely forgotten about it. I was hoping I imagined it. No Ruby's on Chancey's Main Street? I sigh, and Laney flips to look at me.

"You *do* know something. I had a feeling, but now I know it. What's going on?" She strides toward me, and the new direction catches Cayden off guard. He suddenly stops crying and scowls at me. I reach out my arms to him, and he leans to me.

"Give him to me. I don't know anything about Ruby, but, well, there is something on my mind." Having Cayden in my arms, I can look at him while I decide who and what to distract his mother with. Shannon? Phoenix? Jackson?

"Did Phoenix move out?" she asks.

Okay, that was easy. "She says she is this afternoon. She came to town yesterday to, and I quote, to 'finalize' things. What could she mean?"

Laney shakes her head as she walks back to the counter where she dumped her fancy leather diaper bag. Cayden's head whips around to follow her, so I go there, too. "Must be something to do with the studio. Didn't you say she's doing a juice bar?"

"Yep. And thinking about doing some kind of healthy food."

"Thank goodness. Ruby can stop those disgusting experiments." When she says Ruby, she quickly looks up at me, and I just as quickly look down. She rolls her eyes. "You *are* keeping a secret. You're the worst liar, but I don't feel like messing with you anymore. Listen, have you talked to Susan?"

Oh, about Susan and Griffin texting. Oh no. "No," I blurt and walk away bouncing Cayden and murmuring gibberish to him.

She sighs, and I look around Cayden to see her thinking and staring out the window. She clicks her tongue then says, "You're not going to believe this."

"What?" I can't help grinning. I wonder how she found out about them texting.

"Silas called Shaw and is meeting him for lunch today."

Well, that throws me for a loop. "Silas? Why?"

She shrugs and sighs. "I don't know. I just want him to go away, but he's not. He's up there in your B&B—what do you think? Could he actually love my sister?" She looks pained, and Cayden reaches for her. She takes him and nuzzles him to her chest.

"I really haven't talked to him much. It's been kind of busy with the shower and me running the shop by myself. I don't know, but I get the feeling he's really attracted to the whole hometown thing here and for him Susan is the key. But, I don't know. Surely he'll get tired of this place. Besides, aren't he and Susan kind of taking a break?" I walk around a bit then exasperated say, "She and Griffin haven't been apart that long! They all need to just take their time, I think. I mean, who knows what could happen?"

"What? What are you talking about now?" She's grabbed my upper arm and is trying to make me turn towards her.

"Nothing. You're paranoid today." I playfully smack her hand and walk behind the counter. "I need to get back to work, but real quick, what did you think of Patty and Andy's house last night?"

"I hate to say it, but you might've lost Bonnie to decorating. How she did that in just a couple of days is beyond me. And in such a tacky little house! I mean, compare that to how tired Susan's house looks after all this time and all she's done to it."

"Yeah, it's a reminder of what you can do with a lot of money in hand. But shoot, I couldn't do that with all the money and all the time in the world." I watch as she sits on one of the straight-backed chairs and picks up a children's book from the basket beside it. She opens it and absentmindedly points to the pictures for her grabbing son. Then I add with a sigh in my voice, "But I guess I need to work more here now anyway."

She's staring at me with one cocked eyebrow. "Why is that? You going to finally tell me what's going on with Jackson?"

Here it is—the moment of truth. "He's going part time at his engineering job and going to work with Colt."

I can tell Laney's trying to be polite. She doesn't say any of the things I know she wants to say. "Doing what?"

"Renovating, construction, who knows. Colt apparently already has contracts, but Jackson isn't actually good at that kind of thing. Like I said, who knows?"

"Well, sugar, if *you* don't know, who do you think does?" She turns the page for Cayden. "Are y'all going to be okay financially?"

"I think so. He keeps all the benefits and most of his salary with the railroad. Plus, he has great hopes for this venture with Colt. Then there's this place and the B&B. He'll be able to help with both of those."

She closes the book, causing a squawk from her son, but she ignores him and stands up. "Okay, well, let me know if I can help in any way. For now, I've got a full day, and I need to go on and get it started." She puts on a big shawl cape that covers both her and the baby. "This is easier than dealing with two coats as long as it's not too cold." At the door she stops and they turn to me, looking like a two-headed being covered in olive wool. "Has Savannah said anything about Angie?"

"No, why?"

She shakes her head. "Something's going on, and Jenna is silent as the grave, which we both know is a sure sign something's up. Angie's not been talking, but there's nothing new about that. She's barely said two words to me since we forbid her from seeing Alex."

"So, that's still on? I mean, off? They're not supposed to be going out anymore?"

"Not if she wants to live in our house. We made it extremely clear where we stand." Laney lifts her chin and shrugs. "Must've not been that serious anyway since she gave him up that easy, right?" She opens the door. "It sure is a beautiful day out here. See you at Ruby's tonight."

"Right." I close the door and watch her stride across the street. I've heard quite a bit about Laney's rambunctious teenage years, how if her parents said the sky was blue she'd fight to the death screaming it was green.

So Angie gave up Alex just like that? Well, isn't that special? And delusional.

Forbidding a teenager to date someone is a sure way to make sure you aren't told they are *most definitely* dating.

Chapter 44

"Why is Ruby crying?" Andy asks me from across the booth. "Is this normal?" He shakes the shock of red hair atop his round face. "I've not lived here long, but this doesn't seem normal."

Patty comes back to the table with another piece of pie for them to share. She sits it down, mashes herself into the booth, then whispers, "Ruby's crying. Why is Ruby crying?"

Andy's eyes go wide. "That's what I was just asking!" But then the pie absorbs his attention. He lifts his fork. "What kind is this?"

"Bourbon pecan." At the look of alarm on her husband's face, she says, "I asked, and it bakes out in the cooking. It's more for flavoring."

He pats her stomach. "Gotta look out for our little one. So, how'd you like our house, Carolina? Isn't it something?"

"It is beautiful. I'm in awe of Bonnie." They've both put forkfuls in their mouths and are taking a moment to glory in the pie. Ruby's event started at seven, and it's been full ever since. I'm assuming she's making her big announcement tonight, so I was here when she unlocked the door. She wouldn't talk to me, and when I tried to gently query Libby, she just shrugged and said they'd been baking pies all day, but that Ruby was paying her double so she was good with it all. Then she rushed off with her decaf coffee pot to another table. I claimed this back booth, closest to the kitchen; Jackson should be getting here soon. Like I thought, he'd completely forgotten what I'd told him about Ruby moving to Florida. He wasn't planning on actually coming because he and Colt were getting together about business.

"Carolina, you have to have a bite of this," Patty says as she pushes the small plate toward me.

"Okay, just one bite." I'm trying to not go crazy. I already had a small sliver of the chocolate cream and another of her peanut butter pie, which is my favorite. I slice off a bite with my fork. It's thick like the middle of a pecan pie, but darker and the flavor doesn't make me think of bourbon as much as smoke and fire and, oh gracious, it's good.

"So, seriously, what's up with Ruby?" Patty asks, holding on to the edge of her plate so I don't keep eating her piece of pie. Actually a good idea on her part.

"I don't know. Where's your mother?"

"In the cave. Friday nights are busy over there. I'm going to take her some pie in a minute. How's Anna feeling?" Patty's concern for Anna is laced with concern for herself as her hand drops to cover her stomach.

"She's doing okay. Just ready for it all to be over. How's your morning sickness? Still bad?"

"It's better, I guess. I tried that trick you suggested of staying in bed and eating a couple crackers. That does help."

Andy is scraping the plate with his fork, then licking the tines clean between each scraping. "You should see some of the ideas Bonnie has for the nursery." He looks up at me. "Except Patty doesn't want to find out the baby's sex. How crazy is that?"

"Crazy?" Patty turns in the booth to stare at him. Tears leap to her eyes. "I'm not crazy. Tell him, Carolina!"

Andy and I both are taken aback. Guess Patty has found a

bit of her inner mother bear. It's a tad scary how much she just sounded like Gertie.

"I'm joking, sweetheart. Just joking. I think it's a good idea." He looks back to me, but manages to not roll his eyes—so their marriage might make it after all.

I move to slide out of the booth. "Y'all want to help me eat another piece of pie? There's some fruit pie that folks are going by with that's still hot." I don't wait for an answer because I know what it is. We'd already discussed that this is dinner. Ruby is still telling everyone upon arrival that she has more pies made than can possibly be eaten, and it's all on her. I mean, what else can we do?

At the counter, I line up for the hot, wine-red and dark purple pie. Ruby is back near the oven. She wipes her face with her hands, then when she looks up, we catch eyes. She nods, then looks back to her ovens. Her daughter, Jewel, is helping along with Ruby's older grandkids—bussing tables, cutting and serving pie, refilling coffee cups. Poor Chancey, but I can see how she wants to be with them. I got to know some of her grandkids this summer, and they're good kids. But still, poor us.

"Hey, there you are," Laney says. She walks up to stand next to me at the counter. "So, anything happen yet? Cayden had a blowout in his diaper that made us late." She leans toward me. "I don't think I'll be eating any chocolate pie tonight, if you get my drift."

"Oh, gross. I'm glad I had mine before you got here."

She grins, but then grows serious as she leans even closer. "Shaw says he really enjoyed having lunch with Silas, but that's all he'll say. Maybe it was a goodbye lunch, and you'll lose both guests today from the B&B. Phoenix just came in, but she's not with Colt."

I turn to see her and wave as she sees me. She moves through people like she's coming to me. I turn when my name is called, and I'm handed a piece of the steaming pie. "Thanks," I say and move away while Laney takes my spot.

"Hey Carolina," Phoenix says. "Is Bonnie coming tonight?"

"Hey to you, too. I don't know if she is. Why?"

"I have a job for her. My new house." She's wearing a black, skin-tight jumpsuit with her hair up in a messy bun that threatens to tumble over her forehead. She looks very young, very hip, and very, well, *very*.

"You bought a house?"

"Leasing to buy." She looks me straight in the eye with that tipped-up chin, and I try to not ask what she knows I'm going to ask. It seems like it would be fun to be mysterious, not do what everyone expects occasionally, but that just doesn't ever work for me. "In town?"

"Very much so. I'm buying Peter's house, right across the street from the studio." She smiles, even reaching out to steal a pinch of crust from my pie. "I'm truly a part of Chancey now!"

I blurt out, "What about Colt?" Then with a tip of my eyes and a nod, I let her know he just came in. She looks in that direction. Jackson is behind him, and they both smile when they see us.

She turns her back on them and shakes her head at me. "That's over. I'm involved with someone else." Then she catches herself. "No, I don't mean involved, I, uh…" Then she presses her lips together and shakes her head at me, her eyes telling me to forget what I heard.

Oh. If only I could.

Half of Ruby's is in a sugar coma. The other half is eating, and there's a sudden lull as I dart to our booth, waving Jackson in that direction, which is the direct opposite of the way Colt is heading toward Phoenix.

The lull continues a bit longer, and with the smell of coffee and pie, the background of light chatter, and a full stomach, I'm feeling especially cozy next to Jackson in our booth. Patty and

Laney are seated across from us while Andy and Shaw perch on chairs at the end of the table. Cayden is making the rounds of the restaurant, lap to lap, and is currently with his Aunt Susan at a table near the front.

My eyes have been glued to Ruby as she keeps coming to the counter and looking out like she's waiting for just the right moment. I'm glad I quit eating after just one bite of the hot berry pie, because my stomach is in knots, especially now that Ruby has come to the counter and is standing there like this is it. Then Laney, facing the front of the restaurant, curses, which gets my attention.

"What is she doing with that boy?" she spits. She starts to come out of her seat, and I look over my shoulder. Coming in the front door are Alex and Angie, followed by Peter, Delaney, and Missus. They talk their way toward the back where the pies are. Angie is staying on the other side of the restaurant and not looking in her parents' direction.

Laney pushes again to stand up, but Shaw puts a hand on his wife's shoulder. "Not here, honey. We'll talk to her when we all get home."

Laney cuts her eyes at him, but does settle back down.

At the counter, Peter holds a hand up, clears his throat, then reaches his other hand out to Ruby. "Ruby, we just want to say how much we appreciate this evening. My dear fiancée, Delaney, has heard so much about the generosity and neighborliness of our town, but for her to be able to see it like this is just so very special."

Patty whispers, but not very quietly, "Is this all for them? No one told me."

I direct my attention at her for a moment and shake my head. Then I look back at Peter. I mean, that is what it sounds like he's saying, but where would he get that idea? He's not wearing a suit exactly tonight, I mean his coat and pants don't match, but he's dressed more formally than anyone other than his mother. She has on another blue suit with a skirt, hose, and low heels. Even Delaney feels more dressed down in her long dress and boots.

Peter holds both hands up in front of him. "Let's all give Ruby a round of applause!"

Missus rolls her eyes, and I notice her hands don't actually touch each other. When she gives Ruby anything but a piece of her mind, that'll be the day. Several of us smile, though, and Laney seems to relax.

Then Peter holds his hands up again. "As everyone has been wondering what is to become of the building where I opened the bistro, and promptly failed—" He pauses for the smattering of laughter that follows. He even laughs at himself, but it feels a little rehearsed and very un-Peter.

"Oh, why I ever thought I could run a store!" His exaggerated shrug causes more laughter, but only increases my suspicion, which I see mirrored on a few other faces. But he continues, "I'm honored to announce a new business will be taking over the bistro spot here on Main Street." He reaches over and pulls Alex toward him. Alex has his arm looped in Angie's, so she's pulled closer, too. Laney and Shaw both tense as their daughter's eyes flit to them, but only for a second.

Peter shakes both of their hands. "I'm announcing the coming of AC's, the first full-service restaurant on Main Street in Chancey. With my full backing, they'll be opening after the first of the year! Everyone congratulate this young, up-and-coming couple making their homes, both business *and* residential, in Chancey!"

"Over my dead body!" Laney shouts. She struggles against her husband. "Let me outta here, Shaw!"

"Laney," I try, but she's determined. By the time she's almost out, Angie is standing at the end of our booth. Laney falls back onto the end of the seat as her daughter looms over her.

"Mom. Stop. You're embarrassing yourself. We'll talk about all this later."

She flips back around, but when Laney snaps, "Angie!" the young woman spins to face us.

"Mom, seriously? Everyone in this town knows what you did when *you* turned eighteen. I'm eighteen as of next week. We'll talk later." She stalks back to Alex's side, her chin held high.

Laney turns around and faces the front again, her jaw set in stone. Susan comes over to slide in beside her in the booth.

Before they can talk, Peter loudly continues his blowhard speech. Too bad he couldn't have done so before Laney and Angie aired their dirty laundry in public.

"Along with AC's, I'm also proud to announce that I've invested in the other end of the Main Street. Phoenix, come here." He holds his arm out in front of Delaney so that she has to step back as Phoenix struts toward his outstretched arm. "Everyone knows our beautiful Phoenix, right? She has a vision of not only her magnificent dance studio but also of a juice bar serving healthy food in Chancey. Something not everyone is apparently versed in. Right, Ruby?"

Ruby was already frowning at this takeover of her special night, but now she's scowling, lips buried in a vise of wrinkles. She says nothing, just glares at him, hands on her hips, intently listening.

Phoenix waves like a beauty queen, tall and statuesque in her all-black ensemble. Peter leaves his hand on her back, and then the way she looks at him is a little too, okay, I'm not going to even think that. Peter winks at her. Wait, did Peter always wink? "Should I tell them?" he asks her, but then he ignores the dimming of her eyes as she shakes her head at him.

"Along with being partners in her vision of the juice bar, Phoenix and I signed another contract yesterday. She's now leasing the house I spent so much time *playing* with this last year." He raises his eyebrows and laughs again. "Most of you in this room could've told me I'm no carpenter!" He turns then to Colt who's standing next to the wall, the space where Phoenix had been standing next to him, empty. "Right, coach? Leave the handiwork to those who enjoy working with their hands."

Colt, realizing he's in the spotlight, tries to hide his hurt behind a smile, but it's obvious he had no idea Phoenix had a new home. Jackson curses under his breath, then adds to me. "Colt signed the contract to finish the rehab on that house just this afternoon. Looks like we'll be working for Phoenix."

"Again, I apologize for monopolizing the conversation, Ruby," Peter says as he turns to her, "but I wanted to share all this good news *for* the town, *with* the town. And what better place to do it than the spot we all have come to gather for so many years." His voice takes on a sad note. "Although…"

He pauses, and I catch my breath. He wouldn't. Please, Peter, don't ruin this for Ruby. Of course he knows she's leaving. Somehow he knows. This is *not* Peter Bedwell. Or maybe… maybe it is. Maybe I'm finally seeing the real version of the man I thought was our friend.

He steps up to Ruby and reaches out a hand. "I hear you have some news to share?"

She blinks at him, then her face falls. She turns away and darts back to the ovens where her daughter wraps her arms around her.

Murmurs grow around the room. I close my eyes. I can't watch this. Peter's voice deepens. "It's such fortuitous timing that just as these two new ventures are starting, one old venture has reached its end. It is truly the end of an era."

I open my eyes to see Laney and Patty's eyes grow wide with horror. Gasps around us make my stomach flip and tears come to my eyes. This isn't right. This isn't how it should have been announced. I don't want Ruby's to close at all, but I'm even sicker about this display by Peter. I look to Missus, but she has her head down. I'd like to think she's embarrassed, but that's too much to hope for.

Peter is also looking down, shaking his head. Then he moves his gaze around the room, commiserating with the rest of us peons. He sighs loudly. "Everyone, let's give Ruby one *final* round of applause."

"Final?" I hear someone whisper. The folks who are not too stunned leap to their feet to applaud.

Ruby finally comes back towards the counter, her daughter's arm around her shoulders. Ruby doesn't hide the tears in her eyes. Instead she wipes them with her apron, then holds up a hand. Everyone immediately quiets down. We all turn to her at the rear of the café. I take a shuddering breath and grip Jackson's hand, but there's a pause. Ruby's eyes have been pulled to the front of the store. There's a commotion up there, and before I know it, Will comes pushing his way through the crowd, seemingly oblivious to all the feet he's stepping on.

"Mom! Dad!" He can't find us, so he yells into our general direction. "We're headed to the hospital. Anna's water broke. We figured we'd come straight here and tell you since it's on the way." He's grinning, then frowning, confused, as he'll be for at least the next eighteen years.

I pop up like a prairie dog, and then I'm breathlessly digging my way out of the booth. "Anna's in the car?"

"Yes. We'll see you at the hospital!" he says as he turns to dash back out. As I grab Jackson's arm to steady myself at the end of the booth, I remember Ruby. She was just getting ready to tell everyone her news. Looking at her, my mouth falls open. I don't want her to say it, but I really need to go. Across the room, I see Peter wink at me as he and his mother turn their backs on Ruby and motion for folks to let them through. I guess they already know her news and don't care to stick around—oh, that's right; they'll be headed to the hospital, too.

Jackson is pulling on my arm, urging me to go, but I resist. Is Ruby really leaving Chancey? I can't *not* hear this, right? Laney looks from me to Ruby, and Susan shakes her head at me. "Carolina? What are you doing?! Go!"

Ruby holds her hands up. "Yes, go, Carolina, but first just one word. As Carolina already knows, the announcement I called y'all here for is that it *is* the end of an era." She pauses as folks gasp and beg her to say it isn't so. She nods her head. "Yes, it is." Her voice drifts off as she bows her head for a moment in the shocked silence.

Then she speaks up, head still tilted toward the floor. "Thank you, Peter. As you said, this *is* how your father would've wanted it. Everyone gathered together and his namesake preparing to come into the world." She looks up to the side, where Peter and his mother have turned back around to face her. For the first time tonight Peter doesn't look so certain, and Missus has that mean look back in her eye.

Ruby looks around the room. When she gets back to me, her eyebrow twitches, and then she smiles as she places both hands on the counter. "I brought you all here tonight because… because this here counter is no longer just any plain ol' counter. It's the F.M. Bedwell Counter, and there will be a plaque with F.M.'s name on it right here, front and center!" She's staring down F.M.'s wife and son as she shouts, "I ain't goin' nowhere if'n it means leaving Chancey to scoundrels like you! Now, Carolina and Jackson, go get that baby born!" She whoops to everyone else, "Y'all got room for more pie?"

There's laughter by this point, albeit confused laughter, but the round of applause is thunderous and sure. Laney points at me and mouths, "We need to talk, but go!"

Ruby isn't leaving, and our granddaughter is on her way! Jackson has his car keys in hand. I look around to make sure I have my phone and purse and coat, and then…

Missus pops up in front of Jackson. "We'll meet you at the hospital. We have to go back to the house to get the car since we walked, but tell Anna we'll be there soon." She turns to look over her shoulder and snaps, "Hurry along, Peter. Our family needs us."

Jackson and I stumble into each other as Missus pushes past us, then half turns to scold us. "Aren't you coming, Carolina? I can assure you that you do *not* need another piece of pie."

I must have tensed up because my husband wraps an arm around my shoulder. "Don't let her get to you," he whispers. "You don't want to spend the day of our first grandchild's birth in jail."

Chapter 45

"She's perfect." Laying in Jackson's arms on the couch, staring at the lights of our Christmas tree, I don't need to look again at the pictures on my phone to make that statement. I have them memorized.

Frances Marion Jessup arrived just before midnight. Anna's delivery was textbook, and when we saw her afterwards she truly was glowing. Will, however, looked like a wrung-out dishcloth. He'd already fallen asleep in the chair beside Anna's bed by the time we left to come home. The hospital halls were quiet and dark, with nurses seated at their stations offering us sweet smiles and whispered congratulations. Missus, Peter, and Delaney left a bit before us along with Savannah, Ricky, and Bryan.

"I almost didn't recognize Savannah and Ricky when they got there," Jackson says. It's after two o'clock in the morning, but we were too wound up to sleep. We turned on the Christmas tree lights, poured glasses of wine, and collapsed on the couch.

"They looked so grown up."

Jackson kisses my forehead. "And acted so grown up."

They'd come straight from their date, Savannah in a red dress wearing strappy black heels. Her dark hair hung down in soft waves, and her blue eyes stood out as she'd lightened up on the eyeliner, but done something darker with her eye shadow. Ricky had on a sports coat and white dress shirt. No longer sporting the scruffy, shaggy haircut of his high school days, he was trim and polished. Grown up. Especially the way he was with Bryan. It was a glimpse of the future that kept my vision as blurry as knowing our granddaughter would be arriving any minute.

"Also admirable the way he handled Peter," Jackson says, then shrugs. "Or maybe he's truly that interested in all of Peter's grand plans for Chancey."

I jerk to sit up. "And Ruby's staying! You don't think she'll change her mind, do you? I mean, she can go see her daughter and grandkids, right? She doesn't have to *move* there."

He pulls me back against him. "Right. And honestly, I think she'd chew off her own arm before she'd let Peter jerk her around like that."

I settle into him and get comfortable, but only for a minute I promise myself. "I want to go to bed, but I don't want to have to get up."

"Then don't. Another minute," my husband breathes in my hair.

Pink, yellow, blue, and green lights are hazy as my eyelids grow heavy. A foil snowflake, a felt drum, a painted kitten catch my eyes and thoughts. I don't have to see them clearly to remember the small hands that presented them as offerings for the tree years ago. The small hands that were larger each year as they clamored to put on their own handmade ornaments. The china bell my grandmother sent for Jackson's and my first tree. The crystal icicle the kids bought me by pooling their money one year. Each precious ornament takes its moment to reflect and glory in the glow of the lights. Time goes so fast. All the warnings of it speeding up each year, although heeded, can't truly capture the way life races along. And now, we have a grandchild.

There are moments I think I want the world to stop. I want things to stay just like this. But then what all would I miss? So, I'll close my eyes and today will be gone. Left to live in memory, pictures…

…and a Baby's First Christmas ornament.

Chapter 46

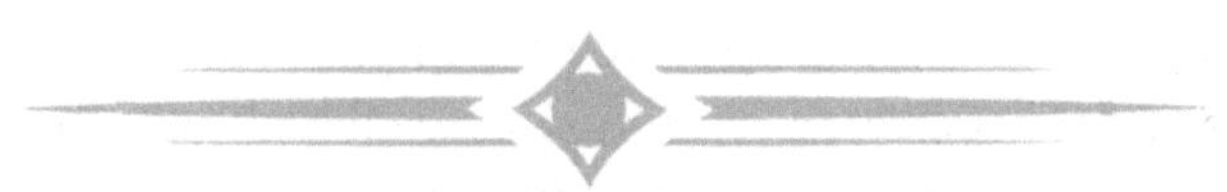

"Congratulations!"

"Shannon! You're back!" Coming in the back door of the shop, I'm greeted by my partner at her usual place beside her worktable. She's working on what looks like a big church arrangement.

"Yes. Can't stay at the beach forever, despite how heavenly it was." She's studying the flowers, so I can study her. She looks fine. Not depressed. Not unhappy. Just fine.

"So, it was heavenly?"

"Absolutely. Things here went fine, it looks like. But tell me about that baby!" She chuckles. "I might have to press you into delivery service, since I already have three orders headed to that particular room."

"Oh, I didn't even think of flowers. Should I—"

"No, you'll be doing more than your share in the coming days. However, don't ever tell *anyone* I said you didn't have to send flowers."

As I walk past her, I hug her with one arm. She doesn't really yield, but she doesn't stiffen either, so I'm thinking we're good? "It's been a busy week here." I hang up my coat, stuff my purse under the counter, then walk to the coffee pot. "Can I refill you?"

"No, thanks. I'm good. What's this about Bonnie not working this week? I was really upset when I heard you were having to hold everything down yourself. She's not usually that inconsiderate."

"Gertie hired her to decorate Patty and Andy's house last minute. I'm afraid she'll be doing more of that and less working here. It was amazing, though; we saw it at the baby shower. She's coming in later today, as I'm figuring we'll be busy since it's the last Saturday before Christmas. Plus, she knows the baby came and that I'll want to go to the hospital."

"Go ahead and turn over the open sign, why don't you? Might as well get things started."

I walk to the front, talking over my shoulder. "So, how are you doing? Your folks sounded like you were having the time of your life on your vacation."

"Yep." Then there's a clunk as she lays down her florist shears rather hard. "Look, I know you know about Danny. I also know you spilled the beans. I trust you enough to know it wasn't done maliciously, and you tend to let things slip out like that. At least I'm assuming that's what happened."

With the open sign facing out, I walk to the table to face her and I nod. "That *is* what happened. I'm so sorry. I had no idea about anyone named Danny."

"Forget him for now." She jerks a new oasis, the green stuff flowers and greenery are stuck into, over to her. "This one is from your parents. They called me a couple weeks back to order it. Pink carnations. So, this Delaney woman?"

"Yeah, Delaney LaMotte. She's a photographer, and apparently they knew each other in college."

"Really?" That got her attention. "So she's not, uh," she smiles at me she finishes, "young?"

"No, she's not as young as you. She's my age. Peter's age."

She goes back to greening the arrangement, but she has that smile. That smile of women throughout history, the one that says, 'She's not as young as I am. She's *old*.' "Well, that's interesting." She moves to the cooler and bends into it to pull out a container of pink carnations from the bottom shelf.

"Hello," I say to two women coming in the front door. They look around, then head toward the bookshelves. "I'll be right there, but let me know if there's anything I can help you with."

Shannon stands up and looks toward the customers, then she immediately squats down again. "Oh, no. Oh, no way!" She sways on her bent legs, with her head scrunched down, too. She reaches out to hold onto the leg of the table so she won't fall over. She's on the shorter, rounder side, and squatting isn't in her top ten moves.

"What is it? Do you know them?" I whisper.

Nodding, she tries to duck-walk around the table, but that's not even in her top twenty moves.

"Hi, uh, is Shannon Chilton here?" The two women have turned and are now advancing on us. Shannon is running out of places to hide. She's only out of their view because there are empty flower buckets and some boxes on the floor at the front side of the table.

I perk up for my part. "Who?" Okay, we've established before I'm not the swiftest thinker when under pressure. "Oh, Shannon! Well, I don't think so," I lie as she's grabbing my leg to steady herself. "Why don't you ladies have a seat up there, and I'll, uh, look for her."

They turn to each other and I realize they are mother and daughter. The mother is heavier, but has the same curly hair and long nose. Same flushed face, too. The daughter smiles at me and waves a hand. "Okay."

Shannon says, "Whew," and rolls onto her behind at my feet. "Get rid of them!" she mouths, complete with hand gestures involving my slashing their throats. As I walk around the table, I see my partner literally crawling, on her hands and knees, across the wide open space at the rear of our shop, headed for the bathroom.

Any bets that when I meet these women, one of them is married to a guy named Danny?

"They're waiting to talk to Shannon," I announce loudly as Bonnie comes sailing in the front door. She stops to hug and congratulate me, then waits for me to introduce her to our two customers. "This is Wilma and her daughter, Allison."

"Nice to meet you." Bonnie shakes their hands, then starts unbuttoning her coat. "I'd have gotten here earlier if I'd known Shannon wasn't going to be here first thing this morning. Her text last night said—"

Laughing, loudly, I lay my hand on Bonnie's arm and give her a little push, "Oh, don't worry about it. As you can see, everything's fine here." I push her a little harder to go away, then turn to the women. "As I said, you can wait here or down at Ruby's. I'll tell Shannon you stopped by."

The daughter shrugs. "I didn't eat anything. Maybe a muffin…"

"No," her mother decrees as she sits back down. "We'll wait here." She gives me a look that tells me she knows I'm lying. Her daughter shrugs again and sits down beside her mother.

I scurry back to Bonnie, who is standing next to the completed flower arrangement and the piece of oasis, soaked in water, waiting to be used. She questions me with her eyes, pointing to Shannon's tools and even the carnations laying on the table next to the trimmers. I grab the carnations and dump them back into the bucket of water, then point to the closed bathroom door. Bonnie shoos me in that direction and goes to the front, offering to get the women a cup of coffee.

"Let me in," I whisper.

Shannon opens the door, and I rush inside the very small

room. "They aren't leaving. You have to come out and talk to them."

"I can't. I hate her. Hate her mother, too."

"Seems to me they might should be the ones with reason to harbor ill will." Her head snaps up, and she glares at me. I hold up a hand. "That's just what I've heard. Tell me your side."

She huffs and then sits down on the closed toilet seat. "They're separated."

"Oh, Shannon."

"I know! But they really are. He's living back at home with his mother. Besides, she stole him from me first."

"So y'all did date back in high school?" I lean against the door since the only seat is taken.

"Yes. Even in junior high. Then he got on the varsity football team and started traveling to the games. Of course, she was a cheerleader, and she stole him!"

"Shhh! I do not want them back here demanding this door be broken down. So if they're separated, why is she here?"

"She hates me."

"Or she loves Danny?"

That gets me another glare. "She doesn't know how to love him."

"Did he really go to Florida with you?"

"I swear we had separate rooms. We haven't done anything physical." Then she looks down. "Well, we kissed some." She sighs, then looks around the little room that we honestly need to paint or do something to. "I really learned my lesson with Peter. Danny said he agreed. Said if he and Alison hadn't start- ed having sex, they probably wouldn't have gotten married. So we just wanted to see if we got along. We were both so tired and so used up that we mostly just hung out. Ate seafood. Went to some movies." She raises her face and looks straight at me. "Honest. And as I said earlier, it was heaven."

We both sigh, and she stands up. "Guess I better go out there and talk to them."

"Okay, let me go distract them so that you can sneak over to the back door. Open and close it like you just came back in. I'll tell them you had to go out back for something."

She grabs my forearm. "Thanks. I appreciate it."

I open the door and sail up toward the front. I loudly lament, "Oh, we've not turned on the Christmas music. Bonnie, what should we play today? Mannheim Steamroller? Or maybe an oldie but a goodie like Wayne Newton or I know— The Carpenters!"

Bonnie rolls her eyes at me and grins, but she joins right in. "Oh, my goodness. I knew something was missing. I did get the candles lit and turned on the little lights, though. Are you ladies ready for Christmas?"

Alison frowns, and her mother stands up. "Did you find her?"

"Find who?" Bonnie asks.

"She was supposed to be looking for Shannon!" Wilma strides toward me as I reach the counter.

"Oh, yes. I'm sorry. She, uh, had to go out back to look for something. She should be coming in any minute." I smile at her as I look for some music on my phone. Scrolling and scrolling, I wait for Shannon to do her part by opening and closing the back door. I sneak a peek up and see the bathroom door is standing open. I drop the pretense and openly look around the back. It's darker than up here by the windows, but there's nowhere to really hide. Plus, she was wearing a light green sweater I should be able to see. "Bonnie, can you do the music," I mumble as I hand her my phone and walk to the back. I open the door and look out just in time to see Shannon's car leaving.

I sigh and turn to Wilma with a simpering apology grin. I'm going to blame being up so late on me not seeing that coming.

My arrival in Anna's room at the hospital is first announced by the balloons I push ahead of me, then by the arrangement of pink carnations, then by the teddy bear planter with an assortment of plants, all of it draped in yards of pink ribbon. "Sorry I'm late. I had to wait until Shannon finished all this."

When I see the clear plastic bassinet next to the bed, I can't free up my arms fast enough. "Here, Mom, let me help," Will says and before another full minute has passed I'm standing over the crib and staring at my beautiful granddaughter.

Anna sighs such a contented sigh. "You want to hold her? She just ate and has been changed."

Will untangles himself from the balloon ribbons and comes to my side. "Here, I can show you how to hold her. You have to be careful of her head."

I chuckle and look at him, but he's completely sincere. "Sure, son. Although your head seems to have survived my handling just fine."

He stares at me for a moment, then shakes his head. "Yeah, I guess."

I sit down and listen carefully to Will's instructions and concerns so I can win the prize. That bundle in my arms. Then she's in place, and I can relax.

Anna is bubbling over. "Oh, these are from your grandparents, Will. I love carnations. The planter is from the Dollar Store! How awesome is that? Who sent the balloons? Are they tied to the vase with the rose bud?"

Will slowly backs away from me. "You okay, Mom?"

"Yes. I'm fine," I reassure him, with a wink at my grinning daughter-in-law.

He maneuvers through the balloons again to find the tag. "They're from our Sunday School class. That's really cool."

He waits for my nod of assurance that Francie and I are fine before he finally sits down.

Feeling her tiny body nestle into me melts my heart which was already a puddle. "Your daddy said he came by earlier. Have you had too many visitors?"

"It's not been too bad," Anna says. "Grandmissus came while Jackson was here, and she said she's coming back later to bring me an *appropriate* bed jacket. She was appalled that I was wearing my gown to receive callers."

Will laughs. "You should've seen Missus' face when Anna explained it was a nursing gown, so it made nursing easier."

I try not to shake or make a loud sound as I laugh. Francie stirred when her daddy laughed, puckering up her sweet little mouth that looked so much like she wanted a kiss that I gave her one.

We chatted quietly while she slept. When they brought Anna's lunch tray, the baby started really stretching and twisting around, so I stood up. "I'll walk with her so that you can eat. I think she's getting hungry. Will, your daddy said he's going to bring you a sandwich, right?"

He pulls out his phone. "Yeah, he texted he'll be here after while. He and I went down and had a big breakfast in the cafeteria this morning, so I'm not really hungry." He gets up to stretch and then come see his daughter. "What's this he and Uncle Colt are working on? I hear they've already got several jobs lined up. Does Dad even do stuff like that?"

"Not that I know of, but he seems pretty sure of it. I can't believe they're signing all these contracts. Next thing you know they'll drag you into it."

I'm busy walking and bouncing an increasingly disturbed baby when Anna says, "You didn't tell your mom?"

"Tell me what?"

Will has both hands shoved in the back pockets of his jeans as he looks from his wife to me. "I am going to work with them some. You know, work around school."

"Don't you already have a job to work around school?" I'm trying to keep the bouncing calm, but all of a sudden it's not easy. I'm not feeling all that calm.

"The dealership, you mean?"

"Yes. The dealership."

He folds his arms and shrugs. "I'm thinking of handing in my resignation. I mean, I need to in order to help Dad and Colt."

"Will, not only is your dad not handy with construction stuff, you aren't either! What are you guys thinking?" I can talk louder because Francie has started full-on crying. It's still that sweet newborn cry, which is only loud to new parents, but there's no need to pretend she's not awake.

Things get a bit hectic with us getting rid of the lunch tray, getting the baby situated in Anna's arms, dealing with the covers, her gown, and then Francie's tears, but just in time the door opens and a nurse bustles in. "I told y'all to holler when it was time to feed her. There's no need in things being more difficult than need be. Lord in heaven, get these balloons out of my face."

I fade back toward the door, just as it cracks open again. "Hey there, Grandma," Susan says from the doorframe. She gestures with a gift basket. "I'm just dropping this off, not staying. Last thing y'all need is more company." She steps in beside me and peeks over the nurse's shoulder. "Oh, she's beautiful. Anna looks great."

She sits the cellophane-wrapped basket down in my chair, and I catch Will's eye.

"I'm going to leave. You good here?"

He tries to smile that he's good, but seriously, we all know he's not good. He's scared to death. As he should be. Susan and I catch eyes, then step out into the hallway.

"Whew, remember those first days? How terrifying," she says with a laugh. "As they were wheeling me out with Leslie, I kept thinking, 'Someone should stop this. They should not be letting me take this baby home!'"

We chuckle as we walk to the elevator. When I reach for the button, she swats my hand away. "No, I'll do it!"

"Okay." That was weird, but I wait beside her quietly. Then inside the elevator she again jumps to press the button for the lobby. She smiles at me like something's up. Okay…

We walk through the lobby, saying hello to a couple people, then at the big doors to the outside she leaps ahead of me and grabs the big silver bar to open it. But she doesn't push it, she just stands there, her hand resting on it. She smiles and then motions with her head and eyes for me to look. To look at what? The door? The handl—

"Oh, Susan! Is that an engagement ring?"

"Finally, you noticed! Yes, isn't it beautiful?"

"It is." I grab her hand and hold it to see the ring better. A square-cut diamond sparkles from its white-gold setting. "It is most definitely a beautiful engagement ring, but, well…" I close my eyes for a second, then open them and ask, "Who gave it to you?"

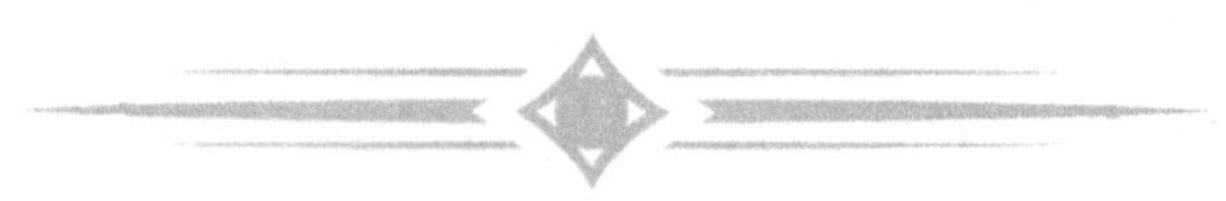

Chapter 48

"What? Who gave it to me?" Susan shoves open the door. "Why would you ask that?"

"Yeah," asks another voice in a less demanding but more suspicious tone. "Why would you ask that?" Laney strolls up to us looking at me, but then turns to face her sister. "Why would she ask that?"

"Can't y'all just be happy for me? For me and *Silas*!"

Laney's frown deepens. "You thought she might be back with Griffin, didn't you? You mentioned Griffin the other day."

"No, I didn't."

"Carolina! You weren't supposed to say anything!" Susan catches herself, but it's too late. Now the sisters stare at each other with their mouths hanging open.

"Girls, I have to get back to the shop, but I need some background on Shannon and this Danny Kinnock fellow."

They blink as they change lanes of thinking. Laney shivers and points. "Let's go sit in my car. It's right there."

"You parked in the fire lane?" I ask, walking to her car.

"I left my blinkers on. Besides, like the hospital is going to catch on fire the ten minutes I'm here. I always park here. That way you don't have to visit anyone very long 'cause you can legitimately say you have to move your car. Oh, how's our baby?"

"She's great." I reach for the heater knob as I claim the front passenger seat. Susan's skinny; she can sit in the back. Plus, if I let them sit next to each other they'll get back onto the engagement ring, and I don't have time for all that right now. Lord knows we'll talk about it enough—eventually. "So Shannon and Danny Kinnock."

Laney takes a deep breath. "They're younger than us and older than our kids, so I don't know a lot, but they dated in high school. Then I think he got popular, and well, Shannon didn't. No surprise there."

Susan pipes in. "Wilma Green, wait, that's her maiden name—"

"Like the Greens that own the tree farm and crafts place?"

Both nod, and Susan continues. "Yeah, Wilma Green married one of the Bunch boys, and they had four daughters. Can you imagine? Alison is the youngest, and from what I remember Wilma just wanted those girls married and done with. So Alison and Danny married right after high school graduation. They never did seem real happy. 'Course having all them kids right off the bat probably didn't help."

"Oh. They have kids?"

Laney nods. "Several, but again, not around my kids' age, so I don't know their names or nothing. So did he and Shannon really go to the beach together last week?"

Shaking my head, I stop her. "I can't talk about all that. I've got to hurry. So have he and Shannon gotten together in the recent past?"

"Oh no," they both say.

"Shannon wouldn't even speak to him, and they're all in the same church." Susan reaches through the seats to turn the heater down. "That's why I didn't believe it when people said they'd run off last week."

I open my door. "Okay, that helps. I'll fill y'all in, but I've got to go now. The shop was getting crazy when I left."

Susan opens her back door, but she yelps and I look back

inside. Laney has her hand clamped on her sister's arm. "Not you," she says. "You're getting back in here and telling me what's going on with you and Griffin."

I ignore Susan's plea for help and slam the big car door. This is between them. Besides, I've got my own Peyton Place waiting for me back downtown. I jog across the street and jump into my van. Pulling out of the parking lot I can't help grinning. It's a beautiful day, I've held my granddaughter and it's one week until Christmas. Turn those carols up louder!

"Where's Jackson?" I ask when Peter opens my passenger door and gets in the van.

"He and Colt were in the middle of something when you called." He shrugs, his wool dress coat exaggerating the movement. Or maybe I noticed the coat because I'm freezing. On the way from the hospital the van stopped. Simply stopped running. I managed to pull off to the side of the road, and after failing to get it started again, I called Jackson who said he'd be right here.

I shiver, and Peter frowns. "Aren't you cold? Where's your coat?"

"At the shop. I'm fine. When is Jackson coming?"

"Not sure. He said he'd deal with it later. Like I said he and his brother were in the middle of something, so I told him I could pick you up. Get what you need from in here. My car is nice and warm."

Shivering, I press Jackson's name on my phone. I can't believe he did this to me. The last, absolutely last person I want to be with right now is Peter Bedwell. The phone rings and rings, though, and I hang up when it goes to Jackson's voicemail.

Peter shrugs again and smiles at me. "My car really will be

much warmer. You'll be back at your shop in no time." His smile grows, and he leans toward me. "I promise I won't bite." He laughs and gets out of my dead van, slams the door, and walks to his large black SUV.

Shoot. Where's a Christmas miracle when you need one?

Chapter 49

Grabbing my purse, phone, and keys, I get out and follow him along the shoulder of the two-lane road. He has his car started, and the heat blowing full blast as I jump in. Trying to get the shivering under control so he doesn't feel so very noble, I calmly say, "Nice car. It's new, isn't it?"

"Yes. It is." He stares in his rearview mirror like he's waiting for a car to pass, but he still hasn't taken the car out of park.

"Aren't we leaving?" I watch his eyes in the mirror. I realize he's not actually staring at anything. "What are you looking at?"

He turns to look at me. "I want to talk to you for a minute. I'm glad you and Delaney have hit it off so well. I'd like for you to be friends."

I can't help but pull a face. "That's just weird." When he looks at me all defensive, all 'How am I being weird?', I can't help the words that tumble out of my mouth. "In fact, why are you acting so weird lately? First you didn't know if you even wanted to stay in Chancey, now you're buying it up like a kid in a candy store?" Warming up, I relax a little. "This car is new? And these investments around town? Wait, why do you all of a sudden have money?" I flounce a bit to face him. "A *lot* of money."

"Carolina, polite people don't talk about money. They definitely don't ask such invasive questions of their friends."

"Oh, quit being so condescending. Besides, I'm beginning to doubt we were ever actually friends."

He takes a breath, but still looks like he thinks he's smarter than everyone else. "Really? Why, I thought we were rather good friends." He lifts his gloved hands. "Of course, I'll admit I don't have a lot of experience at having friends." I think he surprised himself with his admission. He looks away, out the window to his left.

"Whose fault is that?" I shake my head. "Can we go now? I really need to get back to the shop."

"Of course," he answers and jerks from park into drive. He pulls a rough U-turn, and we bounce onto the opposite shoulder then back onto the road. His brow is furrowed and his voice moody. "I tried to be like everyone else in town. Tried to start a business, have friends, fall in love, but that didn't work out, did it?"

"It doesn't always work out at first. You have to take time, be willing to fail and try again."

"I've had a whole life of failing and trying again because I didn't want my mother to be right. But she *is* right."

"Right about what?"

He clinches his jaw several times, but doesn't say anything. We pull up in front of the shop in no time, and he jerks the car into park. I try again. "What is Missus right about?"

After a moment he turns to me. "Who I am. I'm Peter Bedwell, and it's time I acted like it. You want to know where all the money is coming from? From me. It's been mine all along." He unlocks my door and motions with his hand for me to go.

"Thanks for the ride, uh..." But I can't think of anything else to say.

He nods. "You're welcome." He pulls away before I even get the door closed.

"Hey, there you are. And you *didn't* wear a coat, did you?"

I whirl around at my husband's voice as he pushes out of the door to what used to be the bistro.

"Why did you send Peter to pick me up? I called *you*!"

"We were mixing up plaster. I couldn't go right that minute, and since I figured you didn't have a coat, which I was obviously right about, I was worried. Luckily Peter was there and offered to go get you." We stare at each other for a moment, then he throws up his hands. "Go inside and get warm. I've got to get back to work."

With a growl I move to the door of the store and plow inside. Stupid coat!

There are a couple of people checking out at the counter. I see that Susie Mae was able to come in. I tell her "hi" but move on past her. Shannon sees me and puts her head down, focusing on the flowers in front of her.

"Now! We are talking now," I hiss at her. "No more putting me off. I'm really ticked you left this morning instead of talking to Alison and her mother. You really put me on the spot."

"I know," she says with a sigh. "Did Anna like her flowers, at least?"

"Yes. Look, I understand you wanted to get those orders done and I waited like you asked, but come on, what's going on? I just found out Danny and Alison have kids!"

"Yeah, so what?" She looks around, then whispers, "He's filing for divorce. Talked to a lawyer this morning. It happens all the time."

"Do your parents know about this? They seemed so happy for you."

She concentrates on the ferns she's placing around the edge of an arrangement. "They might think he's already divorced."

"Oh, really? Wonder how they got that idea." She won't look at me or say anything and I grow tired of waiting. Plus a group of shoppers have come in, and I need to help Susie Mae and Bonnie. "Okay, then. This is what you're doing. It'll be a mess, but you're my friend and I want to be here for you. But no more running away. You're going to have to face Alison at some point."

"I know. Matter of fact she's going to meet me here when we close." Now she looks up at me. "Please say you'll stay here when she comes. Please. I need a friend."

Everything in me says to tell her no. She tricked me earlier. I don't know these people. This is definitely going to be a mess. But… what I do know is that she really doesn't have any other friends. "Okay. I'll stay for a little while, but then I have a new grandbaby to see."

She reaches out, and I'm suddenly in the middle of the most awkward hug ever.

You know, there are some things Southerners should just be *born* knowing how to do.

Or maybe that should be my New Year's resolution—teach Shannon how to hug.

Chapter 50

"Did you see my mom's ring?" Susie Mae asks me as we straighten the bookshelves before closing. I'd wondered if she knew about the engagement.

"Yes. She brought a basket for Anna and Will to the hospital."

She nods and fidgets with getting the row of books perfect. She's fidgety when she's not anxious, so she's almost vibrating now. "Do you think they'll do it? Get married?"

"Huh." I stop and look at her. "Funny, because I know they're engaged, but I hadn't even thought about them actually getting married. Maybe I've just been too busy. What do you think?"

"I think I'm glad Leslie is coming home this weekend. She can talk to Mom."

"I'm sure your mom would like to hear what you think."

She does a one shoulder shrug and moves around to the next aisle of books. She says louder, "Did you know Dad's getting me a car for Christmas?"

"No, I didn't." I move to the aisle she's on, but she steps toward the front of the store.

"I'm going to leave if that's okay."

"Sure. Any plans tonight?"

"Just hanging out with friends up at Dad's house." She pulls on her coat, puts her purse strap over her head so that it hangs across her chest, then pulls on the door. "See y'all later."

Bonnie left a little early for a Christmas party at the Laurel Cove clubhouse. The clock hits five, and Shannon has taken a seat on the front couch. She turned over the closed sign on her way there, but left the front door unlocked.

"I feel like I'm going to throw up," she says as I sit in one of the chairs across from her. "Alison hates me and I hate her, yet here I am, waiting for her to show up."

"Is Danny worth it?"

I notice that her legs don't completely reach the floor. She's back to wearing her colored tights, flared skirts, and tight sweaters. It would be a hard look for a tall, thin person to pull off, but that's Shannon. When the bell rings she jumps and closes her eyes. I stand up.

"Hello. Come in." Shannon is right to be nervous. Alison and her mother walk in like they are hunting prey. They march to the chairs across from Shannon and perch on the edges.

Wilma Bunch is dressed in holiday wear—black dress slacks and a short, red wool jacket with a peppermint-striped silk scarf tied into a bow on the side of her neck. She's wearing a bracelet of jeweled peppermints and smells of a spicy perfume. Her makeup is party makeup, and now I want to go to a dress-up Christmas party. She looks at me. "Mrs. Jessup, sorry for intruding during shopping hours as we did earlier."

"No worries, and please, call me Carolina. Shannon asked me to stay. I hope that's okay?" I move to the end of the couch near the front windows and slowly sit down. I figure once I'm sitting, it'll be harder for two polite Southern ladies to tell me no.

"Oh, of course." She looks at Alison, who is looking down at the coffee table. "Alison?"

The younger woman pushes her hair out of her face and levels her eyes on Shannon. "So you actually went to the beach with Danny." It's not a question, it's a statement, but then she catches her breath. "I mean, really, he did go with you, right?"

Shannon and I exchange a quick glance, and then she nods. "Yeah. Sorry, I shouldn't've, I know that. I—"

Alison holds up both hands. "Oh no. No need to apologize. Danny is free to do whatever he wants. I've been trying to divorce him forever! I heard he actually went to see a lawyer this morning? Is that true?"

She and her mother lean forward. When Shannon nods, then adds, "Yeah, I think so," they both let out a sigh and visibly relax.

Mrs. Bunch is all smiles as she stands up. "The sooner we get Danny Kinnock out of our lives the better. Everything's been drawn up for—what do you think, dear? Has it been about eighteen months? We've got it so the divorce can be final in only a month!"

Alison nods, shrugs, then tilts her head as she looks at Shannon. "Maybe he'll be happy with you. I hope so, for the kids' sake." She braces her hands on her knees and joins her mother in standing. "Mom has to get to her party, so we'll let you go. Sorry this afternoon got so confusing. I just wanted you to know, despite all those gossipy people around talking, that it's all good."

They walk to the door. After a moment of gaping at each other, Shannon and I jump up and follow them.

Shannon stammers, "Okay. I'm glad, I guess. You know I hadn't talked to Danny in years, then we ran into each other last weekend and I was pretty upset. But we didn't plan any of this."

Mrs. Bunch shushes her. "Of course we don't think that. Danny couldn't plan his way out of brown paper sack! Good luck to you both, and to you and yours, Carolina. I'll have to come back to your store sometime when I don't have so much on my mind." She leaves with her daughter close behind.

The door closes behind Wilma and Alison. The bell jingles, then fades into silence. Shannon and I still haven't moved a muscle. I breathe out and slowly shake my head. What in the world has Shannon gotten herself in to? Who is this Danny Kinnock?

"You okay?" I ask.

She's still staring out the door, then she turns to me and frowns. "That was a little concerning, don't you think?"

"Yes, I do. But no hurry on your part, right? Just take your time." I step behind the counter and pull out my purse. "You and Danny can get to know each other again."

She still hasn't moved.

"Shannon?"

She turns and looks around the store. "Yeah, well, we'll see." She bustles past me. "I have a little work to finish. You getting a ride home with Jackson? I heard your van had to be towed."

"Yep. We're going to the hospital and then out to dinner. Don't work too late, and lock the door behind me, okay?"

She nods, but doesn't look up.

What was it Missus said earlier this week? Oh, I remember—be careful what you wish for.

Yeah, that fits.

"It almost doesn't seem fair, does it?"

On Sunday morning, Jackson is squatted down beside the fireplace in Will and Anna's cabin. We skipped church to get things ready for the new family. Besides, we'll be going to church later this week for the Christmas Eve service, so that counts.

"What's not fair?" I'm watching for the topping on Ruby's blueberry crumble muffins to brown in the small oven, so I only take a quick look his direction. "They should be here any minute. Is the fire taking?"

"Yep. I've got a nice stack of wood here and another right outside the front door." He walks over to the center of the cabin. We got here a couple hours ago and went through all the shower gifts, which were still piled everywhere. We're taking everything they don't need right away back to our house, so the truck bed is full and covered with a tied-down tarp. There are clean sheets on the bed, and Francie's cradle is ready for her. The refrigerator is stocked, there's a breakfast casserole in the oven with the muffins, and dinner for tonight just needs to be heated. I pull the muffins out of the oven and turn it off. The casserole can stay warm in there. Ruby brought the muffins to welcome Francie, but also to say that she knew I didn't tell Peter she was moving. One of her grandkids had told his teacher, who happens to be in Athena's group. Don't you love when you get exonerated from something you didn't even know you had to be worried about?

On the counter, I place a Christmas towel into the muffin basket. "So what's not fair then?"

He puts his hands in his jeans pockets. "Just so many people all confused about what they're doing. Colt is just flat-out ignoring that Phoenix says they're through. He thinks she just needs some space. At least with our new business already having so many jobs I know he's staying in town."

We're going to have to talk about this new business at some point, but with the baby coming, Christmas this week, and now my van possibly done for, I just can't do it. It's easier to talk about other people's troubles. "And Susan can't be as thrilled as she's making out about being engaged." I shake my head and mumble. "She just can't be." I pick up a crumb and eat it. "And there's Shannon. Last thing I said to her last night was that there's no hurry, but what does she text this morning? She and Danny are a couple. It's official."

He comes to help me eat the warm crumbs on the counter. "That is strange isn't it? Them getting together after dating a long time ago, and then same thing with Peter and Delaney? You said they're having some big engagement party on New Year's Eve that we have to go to?"

"Yeah, earlier I wanted to go to a nice party, but now I'm not so sure." We'd received the invite in the mail when we got home last night. Two real paper invitations in one week—we're climbing that social ladder like it's on fire and we're barefoot. "Why is everyone in such a huge hurry?" Down to the tiny crumbs, I'm having to lick my thumb for them to stick to. Between pickups, I glance across the island, and my husband is staring at me with that sappy grin of his.

"Maybe they all just want so badly to find what we have." He walks to the end of the counter, and I meet him there for a hug. Then we spring apart when we hear the car. "They're here!"

We hurry outside. I help Anna out and up the stone path, and Jackson tries to help Will get the carrier out of the car seat. Anna draws in a quick breath as we enter the cabin.

"It's so beautiful. And it smells so good!"

"Breakfast is ready. The muffins are warm, and the casserole is just sitting in the oven for whenever you're ready." I seat her in the padded glider Missus bought them. "And we're leaving as soon as we get you three settled. You have everything you need."

"Oh, stay and have breakfast with us. Will, look at everything they've done!" she says, but he's being so careful with the carrier that he can't look.

"Should I put her in the cradle?" he asks.

At the same time Jackson and I say, "No!" We laugh, and I explain. "She's sleeping. Let her stay right there. You don't mess with sleeping babies."

Will sets the seat beside Anna, then he squats down to straighten the blanket I bought for them at the Greens. Anna cried when I took it to them at the hospital last night.

Jackson picks up our coats, and they frown at us. "Stay. You've worked so hard…" But we'd already promised ourselves we wouldn't change our minds.

"No," I say. "Call us if you need us, but enjoy this first day home. Remember, Grandma and Grandpa get here in a couple days. Then next weekend is Christmas, so everyone will be wanting to see you. Not only us, but Missus, too. But don't worry about all that. Relax today. You need a little time to yourselves."

Anna frowns. "Grandmissus has already said she expects us there for Christmas brunch."

Jackson shakes his head. "You do whatever is best for you. Just let us know."

Will laughs and says, "Oh, we wouldn't dream of missing Christmas dinner. Turkey and dressing. Grandma's making dumplings, right?"

Anna's frown deepens, and Jackson puts an arm around his son. "We will make sure y'all get fed everything we eat. Don't think about all that today." He winks at Anna, and I'm so proud of him as he leans over and places his hand on her shoulder. "You're the mom now. You do what you think is best, and the rest of us will fall in line. And if this boy doesn't," he tips his head in Will's direction and winks at her again, "you just let me know."

Anna visibly relaxes. Will nods as he bends down to rock Francie's carrier, as she's begun to stir.

Jackson and I take one final look at the new family as we pull the door shut and walk into the cold sunshine, his arm now around me. Jackson squeezes me, and I stop beside the car to look back with him.

"You know, all the people we were talking about who seem to have such confused lives?" I take his arm and pull him to look back at the cabin, too. "Who's had a more confusing year than those two in there? And yet…"

Jackson pulls me into a hug and then a kiss. Holding me tight he says, "Guess that's why they play the game."

We push away from each other and walk to the door of the truck. "What? What game?"

He steps onto the running board and looks over the roof at me. "That's what they say when a football game doesn't go as expected: 'That's why they play the game.' I guess you can say the same about life. If Will's life had gone as expected…" He shrugs and gets in the truck.

I shiver even though I am actually wearing a coat for once. What if I'd gotten my way with my son's life? What if I'd gotten my way with *my* life? I open the door and climb up, but before getting in the cab, I take one more look at the little house with the curls of smoke drifting above the chimney, twinkling Christmas tree lights in the window, and the huge pink bow on the front door.

I slide inside and scoot to the middle to sit next to my husband. "I think I finally understand what that saying, 'Be careful what you wish for' means."

"Because you might get your wish?" he says as he begins to back up.

"Of course that, but I also think it's because we're not very good at knowing what it is that we *need* to wish for to actually *be happy*." I lay my head on his shoulder and close my eyes. Carols play on the radio, and we wind down the country road.

Seriously. How could I wish for more?

**Sign up for my newsletter at
www.kaydewshostak.com**

**Chancey Books has its own Facebook page and
I love having readers for Facebook friends
on my personal page!
Twitter - @kaydewshostak**

I so appreciate your review at Amazon.com